Rookery Villa

and other strange tales

Edwin Hird

To Janice, Edward and
Emily. Hope this
doesn't scare the
pants off you!

Best wishes,

Edwin

(scary Emily first appears on p159,
Janice on p10 but not scary)

<u>Acknowledgements</u>

Thanks to Alex for editing, proof reading and other technical help and support.

Thanks to my dear wife, Joyce, for putting up with me while I wrote this book.

Some of these stories have been going round in my head for years – thanks to Alex and Zak for giving me the inspiration to finally put finger to keyboard on an 'if they can do it, I can do it' basis.

Rookery Villa

and other strange tales

Contents

Rookery Villa

Chapter 1

Heather and Graham sat at the kitchen table eating their breakfast. It was Saturday morning, and they both had a mountain of homework to do, as it was getting scarily close to end of term exams. Their teachers were all singing from the same hymn sheet.

"Do this homework and you will cover everything you need for the exam," they had all said. Fiona, their mother, was making coffee, and dad Ian popped his head round the door.

"When you've finished breakfast, come into the living room before you do anything else. We've something important to talk about." As soon as she had left the room Heather whispered to Graham.

"What have you done now? He didn't look pleased."

"What have I done? Nothing! What have you done?"

"I've done nothing. What do you think? Is there trouble?"

"What d'you mean? What sort of trouble?"

"You know, divorce or something."

"No, can't be. I don't know anybody more in love than those two."

"I know what you mean, but what if they're at each other's throats when we aren't around?"

"Can't see it, but you could be right. We'll find out soon, anyway. Hush, Mum's coming back." Fiona took the coffee pot and a plate of biscuits into the living room and came back for mugs and milk. Heather and Graham put the breakfast pots into the dishwasher and went through and sat down together on the sofa. Ian was in his usual chair, looking a bit grim. Fiona poured the coffees.

"Now, then," said Ian. He always started with those two words when it was something serious. "Your mum and I need to talk to you to let you know what's happening. We haven't mentioned it before now, because we weren't sure ourselves." Fiona nodded. Heather and Graham glanced at each other, then looked back at Ian. "We've got some bad news. Don't panic – it isn't dreadful, but it's bad. Do you remember about this time last year, old Mr Carruthers died?" They nodded. "Well, young Mr Carruthers has decided to close the business down and sell the premises to a property developer, who wants to turn it into four luxury flats. This means Mum is out of a job."

"Good," said Graham.

"Excellent," said Heather, and she grabbed his hand and they smiled big smiles. Fiona and Ian looked shocked.

"Well, thank you very much," said Fiona, nearly in tears. "I thought you might have been a bit more supportive." Ian was looking very cross. Heather realised how this must have sounded, and explained.

"No, Mum, we are sorry for you, but we knew we hadn't done anything, so we were expecting something much worse. Don't think we don't care, it's just, well, we were expecting really bad 'bad news'." Fiona and Ian's expressions changed to puzzlement.

"Much worse? What do you mean?" Fiona asked.

"Something really bad," answered Graham, "like divorce or something." Fiona and Ian looked at each other, momentarily shocked, then burst out laughing. Graham jumped up and hugged Fiona, and Heather jumped up and hugged Ian. "I take it divorce isn't on the cards, then," she said with a grin. Fiona and Ian shook their heads, big smiles on their faces.

"No," said Fiona, "but go and sit down and have a biscuit. It isn't as simple as it might sound." They returned to their seats, collecting biscuits and coffee on the way.

"No," said Ian. "It's a bit more than just losing her job. This flat is part of her salary, so when she loses her job, we lose our home at the same time." Their faces dropped.

"So where are we going to live?" asked Heather.

"Are we going to have one of the new flats?" asked Graham. Ian shook his head.

"We don't know yet," he replied. "I've seen the plans, and they look very nice – better than this one – but we don't know the price. And we'll have less money coming in. What I earn is more than enough to cover the bills as they stand at the moment, but we will have the added cost of accommodation – rent or mortgage, or whatever. And, it will take them at least six months to build them; I think more like a year."

"So where will we live until then?" asked Heather.

"Well, we've got a plan. That's the main thing to talk about," said Fiona. "How would you like to live with Gran until we can get our own place?" The children's faces lit up.

"That would be amazing," said Graham. "She's totally mad."

"What you mean is she gives you sweets," said Ian.

"That too, but she's a laugh."

"Don't joke about Gran being mad," said Fiona, sternly. "She's getting on a bit and I'm wondering if she's in the early stages of dementia. Last week when I went round there was a cup of cold coffee in the fridge. She thought she'd put it in the microwave." Graham tried to suppress a giggle. "Don't laugh. It's not funny."

"But Dad does that all the time," said Graham. Ian looked away.

"Anyway," said Fiona, "if she gets worse we might need to stay there permanently."

"Yes," said Ian. "We'll see how she gets on. We might be moving at the end of next month – we're waiting to hear when we have to leave this place, and if there is any financial compensation if we go early. You two will have the bedrooms you used to stay in when you were little, and you can have Grandad's old piano room for doing music and your homework, and when your friends come round. But there'll be no fighting over it. You need to agree which one will have it on which days, and if you can't agree amicably Mum and I will decide. Understand?" They nodded. "And if you behave, we might put a TV in so you don't have to watch old folks' programmes." They giggled.

"Yes, that would be brill. Thanks," said Heather.

"Thanks, Dad," echoed Graham. "And when the rugby's on you can come in to watch it in peace, Dad, without the women."

"Do you mind?" said Heather, indignantly. "I enjoy the rugby, and I understand the offside rule."

"Isn't that football? The offside rule I mean," said Fiona.

"No, Mum," said Heather, rolling her eyes. "There's offside in rugby too."

"Oh. Never mind. Anyway, we've promised Gran we'll go round tomorrow to see what needs moving so we don't have to do everything at the last minute. Some of the spare furniture will go in the garage round the back. She's expecting us about three thirty, and she might have home-made cake and biscuits."

"Yum!"

Chapter 2

On Sunday, the family had a light lunch, then went round to visit Gran. Rookery Villa was a double-fronted house in a nice part of town. It had two sitting rooms at the front, one big and one small, and a big kitchen diner and toilet at the back, with access to the garage. Upstairs there were two double bedrooms at one side and two small bedrooms at the other, with a bathroom in the middle directly opposite the stairs. When it was first built it was in the country, but the town had gradually spread out. In the front garden was a big tree, which gave it its name. It was tall; much taller than the house, and the tallest thing for quite a distance. It hadn't borne leaves for well over twenty years, and everyone believed it was dead, but it was solid and showed no sign of decay. The rooks roosted there every night, and apart from droppings on the lawn, they weren't a problem, but sometimes a bit noisy. Heather and Graham always enjoyed visiting Gran, and when they got there they rushed in and greeted her with lots of hugs.

"Oh, hello," she said. "What brings you round here today?" The children glanced at each other.

"We're coming to stay in a few weeks, Gran, and we came to have a look at our rooms. We haven't stayed here for about four years," replied Heather.

"Oh, that will be exciting. Well, you know where they are. Go and have a look. I expect you'll all want tea." By this time Fiona and Ian had come in.

"Yes, please, Janice, that'll be just what we need," said Ian.

"The children tell me they're coming to stay." Fiona rolled her eyes.

"Yes, Mum," she said. "We talked about that just the other day. Don't you remember?" Gran thought for a moment then smiled.

"Oh, yes, of course. I remember now. You're coming to stay too. I'll just make a pot of tea then we can sit down and talk about it." She disappeared into the kitchen just as the children came downstairs.

"I don't remember my room being that small," said Graham. "But it's much bigger than the one I've got at the moment."

"Me too," said Heather. "But at least you've got a bit of a view of the big tree and the front garden. All I can see is the top of the shed and the backs of houses in the other streets."

"Yes, but your room is bigger than mine."

"Stop arguing or I'll make you both sleep in the garage round the back," said Ian. "Dear me, we haven't moved in yet and you're at each other's throats already." The children looked at each other and laughed.

"We're just doing it to wind you up, Dad," said Heather.

"Yes, said Graham. "Don't take it so seriously. I'm going to have a look at our homework and music room." He dashed out. "Dad!" he called. "Come and look at this!" Ian followed him to the room but stopped at the doorway.

"Janice!" he called. "What's all this junk in here?"

"I can't hear what you're saying," she replied from the other room. "I'm pouring the tea. Come and sit down and have a biscuit." Graham and Ian followed her into the sitting room and sat down.

"What is it, Ian?" asked Fiona.

"Looks like all manner of electronic junk. How long has that been there, Janice? What is it?"

"Oh, don't fuss," she replied. "It belongs to Mr Watson."

"Who's Mr Watson, Mum?"

"He's a nice man. He's helping me out with the noises." She carried on eating her biscuit.

"Noises? What noises?" said Ian.

"The noises in the night. He says they're psychic phenomena. His special measuring machines detect noise and electro-things. He was very pleased when he found out." Fiona and Ian looked at each other horrified. The children were trying not to laugh.

"Why didn't you tell us about this?" said Fiona. "He could be trying to steal your valuables or money or anything. You shouldn't let strangers into your home. Anything could happen. You could have been sexually assaulted."

"Oh, no, dear, I don't go in for that sort of thing. Not at my age."

"Mum, you don't understand." She was getting exasperated. Ian butted in.

"Look, Janice, what you did wasn't wise. Fortunately, no harm has come of it, and in a few weeks' time we'll be here to keep an eye on you, but until then, don't let any strangers in when you're alone."

"But he isn't a stranger. He's a nice man," Gran objected.

"Who is he, then?" asked Fiona.

"Well, you know Valerie who used to work in the Post Office, he's a friend of her sister, Mary."

"Who's Valerie? I don't know any Valerie."

12

"Yes, you do. Valerie Green. Her son was in your class at school." Fiona sat and thought for a moment.

"No, there wasn't anyone called 'Green' in my class."

"Don't be silly," said Gran. "Of course there was. I think his name might have been Paul."

"Paul Brown?"

"Yes, that's probably him. I told you her son was in your class."

"But his name wasn't Green. How was I supposed to know that?"

"You just don't listen properly." By this point the children were almost wetting themselves with suppressed laughter. They went out into the hall, followed by Ian, and all three had a good laugh. They came back in and sat down and picked up more biscuits. "What's going on out there?" asked Gran, which set them off laughing again, and Graham almost choked on his biscuit.

"Nothing, Janice," said Ian with a smile. "But what's all this about noises? And why didn't you come to us?"

"I didn't want to bother you when Valerie said Mary's friend could help. He does it all the time. He's a bit of a local expert."

"Expert in what? You still haven't told us what it's all about."

"Yes, I have. It's the noises." She picked up another biscuit.

"Mum, what noises? Tell us about the noises."

"Oh, all right. Shortly after your dad died I started hearing noises in the night. I thought it might be Derek coming back. Valerie popped in for a cup of coffee one day and I mentioned it, and she gave me Mr Watson's phone number, so I phoned him and he came round the next day. He was very excited and said he would investigate for me."

"After Derek died?" said Ian exasperatedly. "That was more than three years ago. You mean to tell me this Watson bloke has had his kit in that room all that time and you haven't mentioned it?"

"Is it really three years? Yes, I suppose it must be. And it's *Mr* Watson. There's no need to be rude to the man when you haven't actually met him yet."

"Mum, give me his phone number please. I'll phone him up and ask him to take it away. We need that room. And don't worry, I'll be polite." Gran fished the number out of her purse and passed it over. Fiona took it and went into the piano room so that she knew what she was talking about. "For goodness' sake, Mum!" she said when she saw it. "There's enough stuff here to control a flight to the moon!"

"Well, dear, Valerie said he was very thorough." Fiona phoned Mr Watson.

"Hello? Hello, is that Mr Watson? I'm Fiona Oliver, Mrs Henderson's daughter. You have some electronic equipment in her house. Yes. Well, we'd like you to take it away. Tomorrow. Today would be better. Yes. No. We need to use the room for other things. Yes. Yes, six thirty would be fine. Thankyou." She returned to the sitting room.

"Is the deed done?" asked Ian.

"Yes, he's coming today at six thirty. He asked that we don't touch anything because it's delicate."

"So let me get this right, Gran," said Graham. "Is this Mr Watson some sort of ghost hunter or something?" Gran thought for a moment.

14

"Yes, I suppose he is," she said slowly. "Yes."
Graham's face lit up.

"So as well as being a complete stranger he's also a complete nutter," said Ian.

"Now calm down, dear," said Fiona with her hand on his arm. "He might not be a nutter. Let's not jump to conclusions."

"He might not be a *complete* nutter," said Heather, giggling, "but he obviously isn't normal."

"Give the bloke a chance," said Graham. "There's all sorts of stuff we don't understand but that doesn't mean it doesn't exist."

"We'll see if he's a nutter or not at six thirty," said Ian. "I'm not taking any crap from him. He clears the stuff away and that should be the last we see of him."

Mr Watson arrived at six thirty on the dot. He was polite and apologetic, and assured Ian that he was a *bona fide* researcher who was trying to help. He went into the piano room and Graham followed him.

"How does this all work? What are you trying to detect?" Graham asked, much to Fiona's annoyance. Mr Watson explained the cameras and microphones with motion sensors and the electromagnetic detectors and recording equipment and internet links and everything. Graham was entranced, and by seven o'clock Mr Watson hadn't dismantled anything. Ian was starting to get cross.

"Come on, Graham," he said. "Let Mr Watson get on with it or we'll be here all night."

"Yes, sorry," said Mr Watson. "It's so refreshing to find someone with an interest in the technical side of things. I'll be sorry to take this away, but I understand your

15

need to have use of the room. I wonder if I could put a small detector in the corner up by the ceiling. It wouldn't be in the way and I've had some good results from here."

"No!" said Ian. "We want it all out. When you say 'good results', what do you mean?"

"I've had some electromagnetic disturbances in the middle of the night. Very interesting."

"And are these disturbances still going on?" Ian was curious now. Mr Watson took a small notebook from his jacket pocket and flicked through the pages.

"Well," he said slowly, "The last one was about two years ago." Ian and Graham looked at each other, Graham trying hard not to laugh.

"That's it," said Ian. "You've had nothing for two years so just stop talking and get this stuff out now. I appreciate you were trying to help, but if nothing's happened for two years, well, I think help is no longer needed."

"Sorry," said Mr Watson, and he dismantled the equipment and loaded it into the back of his car. It was approaching nine o'clock when he finally drove away. Ian got the vacuum cleaner out and ran over the carpet which was quite dusty and had bits of wire all over it. When he was finished he went back into the sitting room and Gran made another pot of tea.

"My bedroom's directly above the piano room," said Graham with a broad grin. "Does that mean I might get electromagnetic disturbances?" No-one found his remark amusing.

"I hope I don't get any," said Heather.

Fiona glanced at the clock. "Look at the time!" she said. "School and work tomorrow, so I think we should be

16

going. We have packed lunches to put up." They bade Gran 'goodnight' and got into the car. Fiona was cross.

"I wish she'd told us about the noises. Do you think they're anything to do with Granddad?"

"No," replied Ian. "Probably birds on the roof. You know what that tree is like when the rooks get into it. The house isn't called 'Rookery Villa' for nothing."

"I'll be glad when we're in there to keep an eye on her."

Chapter 3

Three months later the family moved into Rookery Villa. The paperwork for the sale of the building had taken longer than expected, and young Mr Carruthers had asked them to stay until the property was formally passed over to the new owner. He said it was so that vandals or squatters wouldn't move in, but Ian thought it was just so that he could avoid paying a lot of financial compensation. Fiona had been the caretaker there for over twenty years, and the flat was part of her salary. It was the only home the children had known, and despite always complaining about their bedrooms being too small, they were sad to leave. Fiona was now unemployed, but that didn't worry her. Over the last few years moving furniture and equipment and other things had become a bit of a strain. Ian did much of the heavy lifting when he was in, but his work sometimes meant he didn't get home until after ten, and things needed to be moved, so she was glad of the opportunity to rest a bit. She would do much of the housework in the new home, as Gran was starting to struggle with some of it, and the flexibility would help when it came to ferrying the children about to their after school activities – music, drama, sports, you name it, they were doing it. The money part of Fiona's salary wasn't much, but it would still be missed, especially if they were saving up to find their own place, which would have to be paid for, be it rent or mortgage, but it was increasingly looking like they would be staying put to keep an eye on Gran.

One Saturday morning, shortly after moving in, there was a call on Heather's mobile; she was in the piano room doing homework.

"Graham," she called, "can you give me a hand please?" Graham came in to see what was needed. "It's my friend, Kelly. She needs help to get up the front steps." Graham looked puzzled but went to the front door. There was a girl the same age as Heather, in a wheelchair.

"Oh, hello," he said. "I'm Heather's brother, Graham." She smiled.

"Yes, I know," she answered. "I'm Kelly. Heather and I are going to do some homework together."

"I've seen you at school, but I didn't know your name. You've never been to visit us before."

"No," she tapped the wheelchair armrest. "It was a bit difficult to get up the stairs into your flat." Graham looked embarrassed.

"Yes, of course. How should I get you up the steps? Would backwards be best?" She nodded, and he turned the chair round and hauled her up the three steps into the hall.

"Thanks," she said. "That's excellent. I can manage now." Heather was in the hall and guided her into the piano room.

"Thanks, Graham," she said. "We might need you later when it's time for Kelly to go."

"No probs," he answered, and went back into the sitting room where he was watching motor sport on TV.

Back in the piano room Heather told Kelly about Mr Watson and his 'ghost hunting' equipment. Kelly's eyes widened and her mouth hung open.

"Did this man have a scruffy dark beard and thick eyebrows?" she asked.

Heather nodded in disbelief. "You know this man?"

Kelly shook her head. "No, I've seen him though. His daughter, Theresa, was in my brother's year. She left last

19

year. The head gave a big sigh of relief when she went." She giggled. "She was known as 'Nutter Watson' because she was a bit, well, not exactly mad, but certainly not normal." Heather looked curious.

"Not normal? In what way?"

"Well, she was a scientific genius. I think she got a place at Cambridge to do Chemistry or something. She was very clever but had no idea about where genius turned into lunacy."

"Lunacy?"

"Yes, that's probably the wrong word, but she had very little grip on where the real world ended and her fantasy world began. One day she set fire to the chemistry lab and when the fire brigade turned up she was still in there taking measurements. She complained when they tried to rescue her, saying they were ruining her experiment. Another day she blew the physics lab electrics apart trying to make artificial lightning indoors. That's why all the benches in there have big scorch marks. Yes, the head and the caretaker were pleased to see the back of her."

"I remember the fire in the chemistry lab, but I never found out what it was all about. And I remember physics lessons being in the music room for about three weeks. Wow. A real life genius nutter in our own school! So is her dad clever too?"

"Yes, apparently. But David, my brother, says he's the same when it comes to reality. He went over to borrow a text book or something one day, and Mr Watson was working on fixing some broken equipment on the dining table and he spent the whole afternoon explaining how it worked and what it was for. He says Mrs Watson looked fed up because she was trying to get the house ready for a dinner party or something. But he's a really nice bloke, despite being a bit strange."

"Well, when he came round here to take his kit away, dad almost had to throw him out because Graham was asking questions and he'd been here well over half an hour before he actually did anything. But yes, he struck me as a really nice bloke too."

"Theresa's really nice too, so they say, but none of her friends will let her into their houses in case she wrecks the place. Did he find anything while his kit was here?"

"He says he had a few 'readings', whatever that means, but not many, and a long time ago."

"David says he set his machines up in a friend's house and got loads of readings, but that's because the friend was in the room above doing things with electromagnets. Deliberately messing up the readings." They both giggled, then got on with their homework. When it was time to go Heather got Graham to help get Kelly down the steps. He pushed her home – she only lived about two hundred yards away - and came back with a broad grin on his face.

"What's up with you?" asked Heather. "Are you in love or something?"

"Don't be silly," Graham replied. "But she is very nice, and very pretty too. Will she be coming round again?"

"Probably."

"Ok. Let me know if she needs help with the steps."

Kelly became a regular visitor on Saturday mornings, and Graham made a point of being available to help her up and down the steps. They were madly in love with each other, but neither would admit it to the other, or to anyone else for that matter. During school holidays she still came round, and they played Scrabble or Monopoly or other games, or sometimes just sat and talked. The lives of Kelly and the Oliver family were going to be intertwined in ways they didn't imagine.

Chapter 4

A few months passed without event. The family settled into their new home with Gran; it was a return to her childhood home for Fiona, and it brought back happy memories. Gran was happy to have the family around her, and Fiona was happy that her mother was rarely on her own, and there was always someone in to take deliveries of mail order items. Despite losing Fiona's salary they managed, and were able to put some savings aside, although it looked increasingly unlikely they would move out and leave Gran alone. She didn't have what could be described as full-on dementia, but she was getting increasingly forgetful about simple things. Nothing to worry about at the moment, but they would need to take steps if she got much worse. Kelly continued being a regular visitor, but she and Graham still didn't admit to being in love.

One Tuesday in late September the weather had been rather unremarkable all day, then in late afternoon the white clouds turned grey and blotted out the sun and the patches of blue sky. It became darker than one might expect at that time of day for a mild September afternoon, then suddenly it became very dark. The cars had to put their lights on, and people looked up at the sky anticipating rain, which didn't happen. Suddenly there was a flash of lightning with an instantaneous crack of thunder. The lightning hit the big tree in the front garden and some of the smaller branches smouldered at the ends. The lights in the house went out; it was so dark it was almost like night. Ian was just arriving home from work. He had been out visiting a supplier, and decided it wasn't worth going back to the office, so he was about half an hour earlier than usual. He was putting his key in the lock just as the power failed, so he grabbed the torch from the cupboard under the stairs as he passed. In the sitting room Gran was asleep in the chair and Fiona was out taking the children to orchestra practice. Ian looked out the front window and noticed that there were no houses with lights on; even the street lights, which had come on when the sky turned dark, were out. He found a few candles in the kitchen cupboard and some little candlesticks, a bit like saucers with handles, and lit two and took them into the sitting room. Gran was just stirring.

"Oh, what's happened?" she said sleepily. "I think I've missed Countdown again." Ian smiled at her through the gloom.

"Sorry, Janice, you're missing everything at the moment. The power's off. And not just us – the entire street. I don't know what Fiona had planned for tea tonight, but it might have to be a takeaway if the power doesn't come back on soon."

"Never mind," she replied. "We haven't had fish and chips for ages."

"Friday night, actually."

"Really? I don't remember that. Anyway, they say fish is good for the brain." At that Fiona arrived home and asked what was going on. They sat around the candles and chatted about the day's events until it was time to collect the children.

"I'll get them, if you want," said Ian. "Shall I get fish and chips on the way back?"

"Oh, fish and chips again!" said Fiona. "We just had that on Friday."

"That's what Ian said," piped up Gran. "But I don't remember that."

"Yes, Mum, we did have them on Friday. Anyway, they're quite close so they might not have power either."

"Don't worry," said Ian. "I'll get something of some sort."

Ian arrived home with two children complete with instruments and music stands, and two big bags of foil cartons.

"You were right," he said to Fiona. "The chippy had no power, so I went to the Chinese instead." He carried the bags into the kitchen and put the cartons onto the kitchen table. Fiona followed, and dished out the food.

"Are you having chopsticks, Gran?" asked Graham.

"Get away with you," Gran answered with a smile. "You know I can't manage those things. I don't know why they can't just make do with a knife and fork like normal folk."

"Chopsticks were around long before forks were invented, actually, Gran," Heather chimed in. "But some things are easier with forks, I admit." They all tucked in and enjoyed their candle-lit meal. By ten o'clock the power still hadn't come back on, so they decided to have an early night.

Graham lay in bed, unable to sleep. He couldn't read because the lights weren't working, so he just lay there thinking about tomorrow's lessons, hoping to drop off. Then he heard footsteps. What's Heather doing up at this time of night? Going to the toilet, perhaps, or getting a drink. He glanced at the bottom of his bedroom door. It wasn't like her to leave her room without putting the light on. Then he realised she couldn't put the light on. He laughed at himself for being so stupid and lay there waiting for her to return. He didn't know how long he lay there in the dark, but he never heard her coming back. Eventually he dropped off but woke up the next morning feeling decidedly unrefreshed. As they sat down to breakfast he asked Heather about it.

"What time did you go back to bed?"

"What are you talking about?"

"Last night. Don't know what time, because the clock was off, you got up to go to the toilet or something, and I never heard you come back."

"No, you must be hearing things. I didn't get up at all last night."

"Are you sure?"

"Of course I'm sure. I know when I go to the toilet. It's a bit basic. I wouldn't go there without realising."

"Well, noone else would come to our end of the house. There's just you and me and it wasn't me."

"Well it wasn't me either." Heather was starting to get cross.

"What's all this about?" asked Fiona.

"He's accusing me of going to the toilet." Heather growled, pointing accusingly at Graham. Fiona laughed.

"It isn't a crime, you know. Now grow up and settle down and finish your breakfast or you'll be late for school." They put their heads down and carried on eating.

"She always says that when she wants us to shut up," Graham muttered under his breath. "There's plenty of time. I was just asking because I heard you walk past my room."

"Well shut up then and stop accusing me of doing things I haven't done. It wasn't me."

When they got home from school Graham and Heather still weren't on good terms. Graham didn't have much homework, so he finished it quickly and went to his room to read, because he wasn't interested in the programmes on TV. He was laying on his bed with a book when he heard footsteps. Thinking it was Heather winding him up, he angrily got off the bed and opened the door. There was noone there. He left the door ajar and went back to his reading. After a while he heard the footsteps again, and this time he was ready. He dashed out onto the landing, but again there was noone there. He wasn't entirely sure, but he thought he saw someone out of the corner of his eye, but no, it couldn't be, because that was a dead end. Fed up with the interruptions he put the book down and went downstairs. Heather was still doing homework, Fiona was doing something in the kitchen, and Ian hadn't got home from work. He sat in the sitting room next to Gran, who was half asleep.

"Gran," he asked gently. "When you heard the noises, you know, when Mr Watson came, what sort of noises were they?"

"Well, that was a long time ago," she answered. "Let me see if I can remember. I think they were footsteps in the middle of the night at first, then thumping noises, like when you drop a big book onto the floor. After Mr Watson came they carried on happening for a few weeks more, then they stopped."

"Do you remember when they started?"

"Come on, Graham, I can't remember what happened this morning and you're expecting me to remember all that way back?"

"But Gran, you can remember what happened in the war."

"Blooming cheek! You know I wasn't born then! But yes, I know what you mean. I think it was about two or three weeks after Granddad died. I thought he was trying to come back, or speak to me, or something. But when the noises stopped, well, I thought that was that."

Graham could see she was getting upset, so he didn't press her any further. He held her hand for a minute, then he went back to his room and picked up his book. He couldn't concentrate so he put it down and lay there thinking. He owed Heather an apology, but that could wait. More importantly, had he heard the same footsteps Gran had? What would happen next? Would he hear the thuds? What had triggered it? Why had it suddenly started happening again? If, indeed, it was the same thing. All these thoughts, and others, went round and round inside his head. He thought about Granddad. A really nice old man, always willing to help anyone, good at fixing broken toys, always had a bag of sweets in his pocket, always had a funny story to tell about when he was young. Was it him trying to contact them? It would be good if he could, but some people would find that a bit spooky. He went downstairs and apologised to Heather, but he didn't tell her anything about his chat with Gran. She wouldn't understand; she was the sensible one, too sensible, sensible to the point of being boring sometimes. He went back to the sitting room and slumped in the armchair and watched Gran's programmes until tea was ready.

That night he went to bed as usual, then at about one o'clock, when everyone else had been in bed long enough to be asleep, he put his slippers on and sat on his pillow at the end of the corridor. He struggled to stay awake, and at about half two he heard the footsteps again. It wasn't totally dark, as the street light shone in through the landing window, but he couldn't see anything, other than the doors and the wooden floor and the stairs. He could tell that the footsteps were just a yard or two away, but there was nothing to be seen. They stopped. Silence. He waited another half an hour; the silence continued, so he went back to bed. The next day Graham was tense. He spent much of the day wondering if he should speak to Gran again, or tell dad about the footsteps. He didn't see any point in telling mum, because she would just say he had been watching too much junk on TV or playing too many rubbish computer games. What would Dad say? Would he take it seriously or dismiss it as wild dreams? He decided, for the time being, not to tell anyone. If there were more noises he would think again, but for now, if he stopped thinking about it, it might go away and that would be the end of the problem.

Saturday morning was very non-descript, weather-wise. Light grey clouds covering the sky, but not looking like rain; a gentle breeze which was neither warm nor cold. Shortly after breakfast Heather's mobile rang. Graham didn't wait to be asked. He went to the front door and there was Kelly. He greeted her with a big smile, which she returned, then he hauled her wheelchair up the three steps and into the house. Heather appeared from the kitchen with three mugs of coffee which she carried into the piano room, and Graham followed pushing Kelly. As soon as Graham let go of the handles Kelly started shouting.

"Graham! Graham, get me out of here!" Graham and Heather glanced at each other, then Graham grabbed the wheelchair handles. "Hurry up! You've got to get me out of here! Now!" She started screaming and crying. Graham unceremoniously bumped her down the steps to the front garden. She was crying and looked scared. Graham knelt on one side and took her hand; Heather knelt on the other and put her arm round Kelly's shoulders. Graham dragged a slightly grubby handkerchief out of his pocket to wipe her tears, then Fiona came out to see what was going on. She knelt on one knee in front of the sobbing girl.

"Kelly, dear," she said, taking the other hand. "Whatever is wrong? I've never seen you like this before. Graham, go and get her a glass of water, and bring some tissues or a towel or something to wipe her face." Graham ran into the house and returned with the water and a hand towel from the kitchen. Fiona gently wiped Kelly's face and pushed her hair out of her eyes.

"I'm sorry, Mrs Oliver," said Kelly between sobs. "I felt there was something wrong in that room."

"Do you want to come back into the house to talk about it, or would you rather stay out here?"

"I might be okay in the house, but not in that room. It's evil. There's something bad in there."

"Okay, we'll go back in, but into the sitting room. Gran's in there but she's probably asleep. Graham, get her up the steps, please." Graham did as instructed and they went to the sitting room, where Gran was sitting knitting.

"Oh, hello, Kelly, dear," began Gran, until she noticed the anxious looks on everyone's faces. "Is there something wrong?"

"Don't worry, Mum, Kelly's been upset by something. She's just come in to calm down and tell us what the problem is. Heather, do you want to make some coffee?"

"Just made it, Mum. It's in the piano room. I'll go and get it and make some for you and Gran." She disappeared, and returned with the three mugs, then brought two more from the kitchen. Fiona hadn't left Kelly's side, and was down on one knee again, holding her hand.

"Sorry, Kelly," she said with a grimace. "I'll have to get up. My knees are complaining." This brought a smile to Kelly's face. Fiona sat in an armchair and Graham replaced her on the floor, holding Kelly's hand. "Now then, tell me all about this. We don't like our friends to be upset, especially regular visitors like you. What happened?"

"I'm sorry, Mrs Oliver," she began.

"No need to apologise, dear."

"I know, but I feel such a fool and I've upset your morning. As soon as I got into the piano room I felt, well, I'm not sure how to describe it. I felt as though there was something evil in the room trying to harm me. I know it sounds silly but that's the best I can do to describe it. Evil. I know Heather and Graham were there, but I felt, well, sort of threatened by whatever it was."

"Do you feel ok in here?" asked Fiona.

"Yes, fine. The evil thing isn't here."

"Do you want to try going back into the piano room, to see if it's still in there?" Kelly looked anxiously at Heather and Graham. "You don't have to if you don't want, but it might help us find out what it is. The three of us will be with you all the time."

"Yes, all right, I'll give it a go." Fiona went in first, followed by Heather, then Graham slowly pushed Kelly

31

through the door. As soon as she was in she started crying again.

"No! No! Get me out!" Graham quickly pulled her out and they all went back into the sitting room. Just then Ian arrived. He'd been to the garden centre to get some bags of compost for the back garden.

"What's the matter?" he asked when he saw Kelly's tear-stained face. Fiona took him aside and explained what had gone on. He came into the sitting room and sat down. "I'm sorry, Kelly, I don't know what to say."

"Don't worry, Mr Oliver," she said. "It's not your fault – it's mine." Everyone disagreed with her on this point. Gran, who had remained silent during all this, had disappeared and returned with a plate of biscuits, which she put on a little table in the middle of the room. They talked to Kelly, assuring her that they wouldn't let any harm come to her, and she tried to explain how she felt, but with little success. "I've never felt like that before. I don't know how to describe it. I can't find the words. It was horrible, but that's about as far as I can get."

"I'll have a look at the room later," he said. "Are you staying for lunch? You're welcome to if you want. It's just sandwiches, but you can stay." Kelly glanced at her wristwatch. She shook her head.

"Thanks, but no. Mum will have something ready by the time I get back. Can you take me home now, Graham, please?" Graham and Heather took her the short distance to her house, and Heather tried to explain to Kelly's mum what had happened. She looked concerned but said nothing like that had happened before. Heather and Graham slowly walked back in silence. When they got home Ian was in the piano room looking round under the furniture, into corners, but didn't find anything. Graham went in and shut the door.

"Dad, I need a word with you."

"What is it, son?"

"Well, this is my fault. Something strange happened and I didn't tell anyone." He explained about the footsteps in the middle of the night, and about his conversation with Gran.

"It's not your fault, son. You didn't do anything wrong. What happened would have happened anyway, and if you'd told me I couldn't have done anything to prevent it. If I'd believed you, that is. No, don't blame yourself." They both had another look round, then went into the kitchen for lunch.

Chapter 5

Kelly didn't come into Rookery Villa for a while. She still came round on Saturday mornings, but they stayed by the front step. Graham brought a couple of garden chairs from the garage, and they sat and chatted, with coffee and biscuits on a little table. Then the weather started to turn a bit cooler and staying outside wasn't quite as attractive. Heather and Graham went to Kelly's house, but that didn't really work. The house wasn't very big, and as well as Kelly and her parents there were her two sisters and a brother, so there often weren't enough chairs, and absolutely no privacy whatsoever, and nowhere to do homework. One day Graham suggested Kelly give Rookery Villa another go, and after a great deal of thought and discussion, Kelly agreed. She came round the following Saturday morning; Graham hauled her up the steps as usual and turned her round to face the piano room door. Heather opened it and went in, and after a quick look around (not that she was expecting to see anything, but just in case) she beckoned them in. Graham pushed the wheelchair very slowly. Kelly shut her eyes.

"You're in," said Heather, with a smile. "Open your eyes." Kelly opened her eyes one at a time and breathed a sigh of relief. "Well?"

"It's okay. It isn't like it used to be, but the feeling of evil isn't here." The three friends cheered and hugged each other. Fiona came to see what the noise was and beamed at Kelly when they told her.

"Welcome back, Kelly," she said.

"Thankyou, Mrs Oliver. You don't know how important this is to me, to be able to visit my closest friends without worrying about it." When Ian came in from the garden at lunchtime they told him, and he was pleased too.

"I'd been thinking about getting this Watson bloke back, but after hearing about his mad daughter, well, I decided that wasn't going to be a good idea." While Fiona was preparing lunch he took Graham to one side. "Whose idea was this anyway? Was it yours?" Graham nodded with a grin. "And the footsteps, have they stopped?"

"Yes, Dad, just over a week ago. That's what made me think it might be okay." Ian patted him on the shoulder.

"Well done, son. Good thinking. Let me know if they come back."

The footsteps didn't come back, but something else happened. One Sunday Graham was in the piano room doing his homework when he heard a dull thud from upstairs. He knew Heather was out, and Fiona and Dad were watching TV with Gran. He crept along and looked through the crack in the door. Yes, they were there, all three, watching some rubbish TV programme. He crept upstairs and went into his room, which was directly above the piano room. Everything was normal. Did it happen, or did he imagine it? He went back down and carried on with the homework. About an hour later he heard it again. He finished off his homework and went up to his room. He lay on the bed reading a book and heard the noise again. It was a dull thud, just like he had heard downstairs, but this time it seemed to come from the piano room. Then he remembered his conversation with Gran. She had said it was like the sound of a big book being dropped onto the floor, and that was exactly what this was like. What should he do? Should he tell Dad? Should he tell Kelly? The last

35

thing he wanted was for her to stop visiting again. He didn't hear the noise any more than day, but on Monday he heard it when he was in the piano room doing his homework, at about five o'clock. Heather was in the room too, but she showed no signs of hearing it. Perhaps it was in his imagination. That evening after tea there came a knock at the door. Graham went to see who it was. It was a middle-aged man in a suit.

"Sorry to bother you," the man said. "I'm DCI Morris, CID. Can I come in please?"

"Oh, yes, s'ppose."

"Who is it?" shouted Ian from the other room.

"It's the police," Graham shouted back. Mr Morris wiped his feet and Graham showed him into the sitting room. Ian turned the sound down on the TV and offered him a seat.

"How can we help you?" he said.

"It's about Miss Heather Oliver," he said. He looked at Heather who was shocked. "Would that be you?" She nodded.

"What's she done?" asked Fiona.

"I haven't done anything," Heather was quick to reply.

"Well," Morris began slowly, "I'm here in connection with a disturbance at Honeysuckle Cottage on Thursday of last week. You were seen there hammering on the door, shouting, and making threats."

"But I don't know where Honeysuckle Cottage is. And I haven't been out, apart from going to school," Heather protested.

"What sort of shouting and threats?" asked Ian. "And where is Honeysuckle Cottage? I haven't heard of it either." Morris took a notebook from his pocket and opened it.

"Er, 'You'll get what you deserve, you're in for it, you're a dead man,' were the exact words. The occupant, Mr Shaw, who is an elderly gentleman and not in the best of health, was very upset by this."

"I'm sure he would be," said Ian. "But our Heather wouldn't do anything like that. Where is this place, and exactly when is she supposed to have done this?"

"I know where it is," interrupted Gran. "We used to play near there when I was a girl. It's behind those trees over the road." Everyone looked at her in astonishment.

"That's correct, madam. The incident took place on Thursday, at seven thirty in the evening. Where were you at that time, miss?" Heather was flustered.

"Well, I was, er, yes, I was at choir practice at school. Dad picked me up and brought me home at about half eight."

"Yes, that's right, I did," said Ian, nodding.

"And was there anyone who could confirm that?"

"I've just said, I picked her up and brought her home."

"You picked her up at half eight, I believe. What about at half seven?"

"Well, there were two teachers and about twenty children. I was there from half six to half eight. I never left the hall other than to go to the toilet."

"And at what time did you go to the toilet, miss?" She turned pale.

"We have a break halfway through, at about half seven. But I didn't leave the school."

"Can I have the names of the teachers, please? I assume it's the local high school?"

"Yes, Mr Williams and Mrs Macfarlane." She was starting to cry. Fiona put her arm round her shoulders.

"Thankyou. That's all for now. I may need to come back to ask more questions." He stood up and left the room followed by Ian.

"Look, Mr Morris, Heather isn't the type of girl to get up to mischief. I hope you realise that," said Ian sternly.

"Thankyou, Mr Oliver. I'll be in touch." He left.

The next morning Mr Morris came back. Obviously Heather was at school, but he had come to see Gran.

"Are you Mrs Janice Henderson?" he asked.

"Yes, I am," she replied.

"Where were you at seven thirty in the evening last Thursday?"

"I was here, watching TV."

"And is anyone able to confirm that?"

"Yes," Fiona jumped in. "I can."

"Were you here at seven thirty, Mrs Oliver?" Fiona began to look a bit vague.

"Well, not at exactly seven thirty, but I was here just before and just after. I had popped out to the corner shop for milk, but I was gone less than ten minutes, twenty at the most."

"So you weren't here at the actual time of the incident."

"When you put it like that, no, I wasn't. But my mother, Mrs Henderson that is, hasn't been out of the house since her husband's funeral, and that's almost four years ago." Mr Morris groped in his inside pocket and produced a plastic bag, from which he took a small rectangular object. He took it out of the bag and passed it to Gran.

"Is this yours, madam?" She took it from him and lifted her glasses to look at it.

"Yes, it is. It's my bus pass." Fiona grabbed it from her and examined it. A look of horror spread across her face.

"Where did you get this?" she demanded.

"It was found at the scene of the disturbance, next to Mr Shaw's body."

"Next to his body?" said Fiona. "You didn't tell us he was dead!"

"That's because we hadn't determined if he was unlawfully killed or if he took his own life. That is still undecided, but we are pursuing both possibilities."

"But my mum hasn't been out for almost four years! She can't possibly have killed him!"

"I'm sorry, madam, but you seem to be missing the point. We have evidence that she was on the scene, and noone can vouch for her whereabouts at the exact time in question. I'll go now, but I will probably have to come back to ask more questions. Thankyou, ladies." He showed himself out leaving the two women staring at each other open mouthed.

The children arrived home at about half four and had only been in about fifteen minutes when there was a knock at the door. It was DCI Morris again. Fiona invited him in and showed him into the sitting room.

"I don't know why you've come back so soon. My mother and I have told you everything we can."

"No, madam," he said. "I'm here to speak to Miss Oliver." Fiona called Heather, who came into the room looking glum. Graham followed and they sat down together on the sofa. "Miss Oliver, I would like to ask you about the words you shouted at Mr Shaw."

Fiona butted in. "You mean the words you allege she shouted, don't you?"

"Sorry, madam, that's correct. The words you allegedly shouted." He took his notebook out of his pocket and found the page. "The words 'you'll get what you deserve, you're in for it, you're a dead man' were shouted at him. We have a reliable witness who claims to have heard you say this. Have you ever said those words?" Heather turned pale. She nodded slowly. Fiona and Graham looked horrified.

"Not at Honeysuckle Cottage, because I don't know where it is, but I have said those exact words. It was about two weeks ago in the drama group. I am an East End gangster." Tears ran down her face.

DCI Morris was writing in his notebook, speaking slowly as he wrote. "I am an East End gangster."

Fiona butted in again. "You can't write that. She wasn't saying she was a gangster. She is playing the part of a gangster. Don't you know the difference between real life and acting?" By now she was shouting. Graham reached across and grabbed her arm.

"Mum! Calm down! Losing your temper isn't going to help."

"Yes, you're right, Graham. I'm sorry, Mr Morris, but you can't write that as a direct quote. She was telling you what part she was playing in the school play."

"Be that as it may, Mrs Oliver, she did say that. And furthermore, I have a reliable witness who saw her running away from the scene." Fiona and Graham began to laugh – Heather began to cry again.

"Roll up your trouser leg, darling," Fiona said while Graham put his arm around her. She rolled up her left trouser leg to reveal a withered leg, not much thicker than a baby's arm.

"You see?" said Fiona. "She can't run. She never has been able to. Explain that." She sat back in the chair with her arms folded. DCI Morris seemed nonplussed.

"Be that as it may, I have a very reliable witness, and how do you explain this?" He took another plastic bag from his pocket and took a mobile phone from it and passed it across to Heather. "Is this yours, miss? It was found at the scene." She took it from him and they all fell silent while she examined it. She turned it on. After pressing a few buttons she nodded gravely.

"Yes," she said. "It's mine but how did you get it?"

"I've told you. It was found at the scene."

"But I used it ... I used it on ... actually I can't remember when I last used it. Last week probably." Graham shifted uncomfortably in his seat. He knew she didn't have a call from Kelly because Kelly didn't come round, and Heather didn't go anywhere at the weekend because she had an absolute mountain of homework in the run up to mock A-levels.

"You can keep that now," said DCI Morris. "We've got all the evidence we need from it, including fingerprints which match yours."

"Well of course they match mine. It's my phone."

"Just a minute," said Fiona. "How come you have Heather's fingerprints on file? She's never been in trouble with the police."

"I can't say. Perhaps to eliminate her from a crime. Eh?"

"Mum, when some stuff was stolen at school last year they took the fingerprints of all the girls in my class. That must be how they've got them."

"Are they allowed to do that?" asked Graham. DCI Morris ignored Graham's question.

"Anyway, I've done for today. I will probably need to come back as the case progresses." So saying, he left. The family sat in silence staring at each other. Graham put his arm round Heather's shoulders.

"I know you didn't do it, sis," he said as she began to cry again.

"Dad will be furious when he gets home. He'll go to the station and raise a right stink about this. We are being accused of someone else's crime, on very dodgy evidence," said Fiona, starting to get angry again.

"Look, mum," said Graham. "We know Heather and Gran weren't there, but he does have tangible evidence. But yes, dad will know what to do."

Ian was away visiting customers in a distant part of the country, so he didn't get back until Friday evening. Fiona was right; he *was* furious and decided to go to the police station on the Saturday morning.

Chapter 6

At eight thirty on Saturday morning Ian entered the police station. He was greeted by a young constable in uniform.

"How can I help you, sir?"

"I would like to speak to DCI Morris," he said. The young officer looked puzzled.

"DCI Morris, sir?"

"Yes, DCI Morris, CID. He's been to my house three times this week, accusing members of my family of crimes they didn't commit." The constable looked down a list, then took a laminated sheet from the desk drawer and looked through that as well. He shook his head.

"I'm sorry, sir, we don't have anyone of that name at this station, not in CID, and not in any other department either. Whereabouts do you live, sir?" Ian gave him their address and postcode. The constable shook his head again. "Well, that's definitely in our area. You shouldn't get a visit from any other station. Just a minute and I'll check." He sat down and tapped a few words into the computer. "No, sir, there isn't anyone of that name in the neighbouring areas either."

"Well I want to register a complaint. Who is the senior officer here? I want to see him or her now, please."

"Just a moment, sir, I'll see if I can find someone more senior to help." He went into an adjoining room and spoke to another officer. Ian could see them through the glass but couldn't hear what he said; the other officer made a phone call, then came to the front desk.

"I'm sorry about this, sir, we can't find anyone of that name, but the superintendent is happy to have a word with you. Come this way, please." Ian followed the officer along a corridor and into a room at the end. There was an older officer sitting at a desk, and he rose to his feet as Ian went in, and offered Ian his hand, which Ian took.

"I'm Superintendent Wilkinson, sir. Would you like to take a seat?"

"Thankyou. I was angry when I came here this morning. Now I'm still angry, but I'm confused as well." Ian related the visits of DCI Morris, adding the details of Heather's leg, and Gran's not leaving the house. The superintendent stroked his chin for a moment and gazed out of the window. He had been making notes while Ian was speaking and glanced at the sheet then looked up at Ian.

"I think I know the man you're talking about," he said gravely. "Can you describe him?" Ian breathed a sigh of relief.

"Good. I thought I was going mad. Yes, I can describe him."

"Don't be too hasty, sir. Tell me what he looked like, please." Ian nodded, and described the man. The superintendent nodded. "Yes, that sounds very much like him. What about his eyes?"

"Oh, yes. His left eye wasn't open properly, looked as though he'd been in a fight."

"Yes, that's Morris. It wasn't a fight. He was in a road traffic accident as a young officer. His sight wasn't affected, just his appearance."

"So you know who I'm talking about. Can you call him off?" The superintendent shook his head.

"No need for that, sir. DCI Morris is dead." Ian was shocked.

"Oh, I'm sorry to hear that. Please pass my condolences on to his family. How did he die?"

"He was investigating an incident at Honeysuckle Cottage when a tree came down in a thunderstorm and crushed him. He died instantly, and the cottage was more or less demolished."

"When did this happen? My wife saw him a few days ago." The superintendent shook his head. He looked Ian in the eye and wiped a tear away.

"Thirty years ago. I knew him when I joined the force. I was in his team. I was a detective constable, just transferred to CID. That's why noone knows about him. I'm the only one in the station who was here thirty years ago." Ian sat in silence for a moment, struggling to take it in. "I realise this doesn't answer your question, sir, but I can't help you any further. I can't tell a dead officer to stop visiting you. I don't know what to suggest."

"Quite. I don't know what to do now." They stood and shook hands, and the superintendent escorted Ian back to the front desk. "Sorry to have bothered you." He left and slowly walked home.

"What was that all about, sir?" asked the young constable. "Who is DCI Morris?"

"Sorry, Jim, I can't answer that question. I'm going out for a while."

The morning was cloudy, but it wasn't cold. Kelly was making her way along the street with her school bag to do some homework with Heather. She got as far as the big tree, and she stopped. She began to cry and took her mobile out of her bag. She pulled herself together and dried her tears before phoning Graham.

"Hello, Kelly. Are you here yet?" said Graham.

"No, Graham, I can't come to your house this morning."

"Oh, I was looking forward to seeing you again. What's up?" She started crying again. "Kelly, what's wrong?"

"Oh, Graham, I can't come to your house. There's something evil about it. It wants to destroy me. I'm on the way, but I can't come any further. I'm by the tree, but I'm turning round to go home."

"Oh Kelly, is this like before?"

"Yes, but much worse. It's the house, not just the one room. It's the whole house. It hates me, and it's going to destroy me." By now she was crying uncontrollably and was struggling to speak. "Graham?"

"Yes?"

"Graham, I love you, Graham."

Graham was silent for a moment. "I love you too, Kelly. I love you too."

Suddenly there was a huge flash of lightning, blindingly bright, with an instantaneous crack of thunder which was deafening. The lightning struck the big tree, which burst into flames. It started to fall. Graham had come to the front door, and as the tree fell he ran forward to Kelly.

"Look out!" he shouted, grabbing her wheelchair and pushing it away with all his might. The tree came crashing to the ground, with bits of burning wood flying off in all directions. Fifteen minutes later the fire service arrived and quickly extinguished the flames. When the smoke cleared they found Kelly, still in her wheelchair which was now well and truly mangled, and Graham, with his arm around her, both crushed to death and partly burned. They were holding hands.

Holiday Breakdown

Chapter 1

"Well! I am surprised! Who'd have thought it?" Ellen muttered through clenched teeth, her arms firmly folded as she glared straight ahead. Dave's mouth opened to reply, but he thought better of it. Sarah giggled from the back seat. "It's not funny, Sarah," Ellen snapped. "I told him to do something about this car three weeks ago but he couldn't be bothered. He'll have to do something now and he won't get any help from me."

"Come on, Dave, let's have a look at it – without the help of the great mechanic," said Sarah, getting out. Dave grinned as he released the bonnet catch then followed Sarah to the front of the car. It began to rain.

"Marvellous!" grunted Paul. "We'll probably have to walk miles in the pouring rain and catch pneumonia or something."

"I'm not walking anywhere," replied Ellen. She checked her mobile, but there was no signal; Paul's was the same. "If they can't fix it Dave can find a phone and call out the RAC while we sit here in comfort."

"I don't remember seeing any phone boxes since the last village which must be quite a few miles back."

"He's going to have a long walk."

They were somewhere in the North Yorkshire moors in early September at the end of a three-week holiday. They had driven from their North London homes up to Berwick, then slowly made their way south staying in hotels, caravans, bed and breakfasts, anywhere they could find accommodation. They had visited Holy Island, Hadrian's Wall, Beamish Museum, Durham Cathedral, and many other less famous places of great natural beauty or historic interest. Sarah had been something of a nuisance, enacting extracts from Hamlet and Macbeth every time she stood on wind-swept battlements. They had taken a guided tour of the nuclear power station at Hartlepool, where Sarah again got carried away. She and Dave both knew how these things worked, and they corrected the guide on more than one occasion, much to the annoyance of Paul and Ellen, neither of whom had wanted to go there in the first place. From there they went down the coast to Whitby, then cut across the moors, intending to spend a couple of days in Harrogate, to see if it was really as boring as all their friends back home had insisted, before making the long journey south. It was Friday, and they were not due back to work until Tuesday, although they intended on being home on Sunday to have a day to recover. They had left the main road at Sarah's suggestion, because the winding side road looked "romantic, the very embodiment of rural tranquillity." She insisted that they couldn't possibly ignore a place so obviously full of "soul, character, and unearthly magnetism enhanced by desolation". They hadn't even been sure which road they were on, until they came to a small village which helped Ellen locate their position on the map. The car lurched along the bumpy road at twenty miles per hour giving them all a good shaking. Dave thought this was fun, but Paul and Ellen failed to find any enjoyment in the uncomfortable and tedious ride. Sarah wanted tranquillity, and she certainly got it.

Just over the trees they saw a column of smoke rising. Ellen had spotted it just as it was starting to get dark and decided it might be a sign of civilisation. Paul went to investigate while Dave and Sarah were still working under the bonnet. They hadn't seen a soul for over an hour, so this was a sign of hope. Ellen watched him as he jogged away looking perfectly at home, even though he had been a city boy all his life. He was back in five minutes and stood puffing and wheezing, his hands on his thighs.

"The coach wouldn't be impressed!" laughed Dave.
"You should try it," gasped Paul. "It's hard work. We should bring the team up here for training. What's the score with the car, mate?"

"I think the alternator's knackered. I would imagine some garage round here will have one," answered Dave.

"Never mind that!" Ellen cut him off. "What about the smoke?"

"There's an old farmhouse with a light on downstairs. Perhaps we could stay the night."

"Right. Come on. Let's find out." When Ellen took command the others knew the best thing to do was to follow. She had been Head Girl at school, and had displayed great leadership potential, which caused her problems at work. She was a creative designer for a top advertising company specialising in luxury goods. She had some wonderful ideas, but felt she had to interfere with the filming and photography and special effects and make-up - she had something to say about everything, and justified herself by reminding people that she was the creator and thus had a right to be involved in her advert. She was in her element taking charge in this crisis, and it cheered her up immensely. She calmed down a lot, and decided to forgive Dave, and to apologise to him, once Sarah and Paul were out of earshot. She had met Dave at university, and they immediately fell in love, even though their friends thought them very much a mismatch. Ellen was artistic and flamboyant, expressing herself very well, and at every

53

opportunity, an expert at the use of the English language, but she was completely out of her depth with anything technical. Dave, on the other hand, was very much a technical wizard. He took up electronics at the age of seven and spent a lot of his spare time taking things apart and putting them back together. He was a man of few words, unable to see the point of talking when he could be doing something instead. He had no interest whatsoever in the artistic side of life, with one exception. He liked music, and played classical guitar.

Ellen set off across the heather with Dave and Sarah following close behind. Ellen was quite an Amazon; almost six feet tall, strong, well built and attractive, with a mane of curly brown hair. Dave strode after her, both occasionally stumbling. Sarah trotted after them, almost childlike compared to her two big friends.

"Wait for me!" Paul called, still tired from his earlier run.

"Hurry up - it's almost dark," Ellen called back to him. "We can't expect them to open the door to any random stranger much later than this."

"This isn't London," Sarah reminded her. "They don't expect to be mugged around here." They reached the grass where the ground began to rise and waited for Paul. He was short and stocky, very muscular, with short dark hair; he played rugby with Dave. Paul and Sarah had met at Dave and Ellen's engagement party and married six months later. He was the cleverest of the four and excelled at what could be best described as 'mathematical gymnastics', which made him very good at his job. He was an investment advisor for a large insurance company in the city, and often had to do complicated mental arithmetic whilst carrying on several telephone conversations. He was quite a serious person, and often got fed up with Sarah and Dave's humour, but rarely complained, as he had the ability to 'switch off' and think about more important things. His hobby, apart from rugby, was painting, and he had often been urged to follow it as a career, but he was too good at finance to give it up. He also used art to relax, and felt he wouldn't be able to do this if he were being paid for it. As soon as he reached them, Ellen and Dave set off at a merciless pace up the hill while Sarah and Paul followed at a distance. By the time they were in sight of the farmhouse the darkness and mist made it difficult to see where they were walking, and Ellen trod in something wet more than once. There was light from two downstairs windows which helped them avoid a substantial vegetable garden. The rest of the house was in total darkness. As they got to the door Dave looked up. The top of the house disappeared into the starless sky.

"I hope inside's friendlier than outside," he whispered to Ellen.

"Don't worry," she whispered back. "It must be better than sleeping in the car." Ellen knocked at the door. It sounded very old and heavy. The handle turned and the door swung open silently. A figure stood before them holding an old oil lamp. Temporarily dazzled by the sudden bright light they could at first only see the lamp and its reflection in a pair of eyes which darted from one face to the next.

"Er, we were wondering if, er," Ellen stammered, for once not her fluent self, "if we could stay the night. We, er, well, we'll, er ..." her voiced tailed off as the eyes met hers.

Chapter 2

The lamp was drawn back into the house illuminating a round, homely woman with grey hair and rosy cheeks. She wore a large cotton apron over a woollen skirt and cardigan. A shawl covered her shoulders. Her eyes twinkled as she smiled. Ellen explained their predicament.

"Come in, dearies, come in. It's getting chilly with this door open. Of course you're welcome to stay. I expect you'll be needing a mug of tea. I'll put kettle on. Take your wet things off and sit by the fire." She ushered them into a huge kitchen and slammed the door. Before them stood a large rectangular table with five wooden chairs around it. She turned the lamp up and put it in the middle of the table. It lit the whole room. Shelves and cupboards surrounded this half of the room bearing pots, pans, plates, and an assortment of cooking equipment that wouldn't have been out of place in a museum. At the other end of the room was a black-lead fireplace topped by a wooden mantlepiece bearing little brass and china ornaments. A sofa and two armchairs were arranged around it. She put a log on the fire and sparks flew up the huge stone chimney.

"Actually, while we've our coats on Dave and I should get some things from the car," said Paul. "That is, if we're staying." He glanced enquiringly at Sarah who turned to Ellen for an answer. Ellen's mouth opened, but she didn't get the chance to speak.

"Of course you are, dearies. There's nowhere else to go round here," the old woman announced. "Now, you men run and get what you need while your wives help me get some supper ready. Be sharp, now." Ellen nodded at Paul.

57

He and Dave left. "Now then, how long is it since you had your tea?" the woman asked Ellen.

"Well, actually we haven't eaten since about four thirty," replied Ellen, "but we don't want to inconvenience you at all. Something quick and simple will be more than adequate, and we must talk about payment. We're willing to pay you the going rate for bed & breakfast."

"Half past four? Disgraceful! It's a miracle that you and your man have grown so well if that's the way you treat your bodies. You'll need to get some decent food down you before you go to bed. And as for payment, I'll take nothing and hear no more about it. If an old woman can't do a good turn without expecting something in return, well, the world's becoming a tragic place."

"Right. That's it. Come on, Sarah, we can't take charity from the poor. Get your coat back on. We're going." Ellen picked up her coat and started to put it on.

"Now don't be hasty, deary. Look at your little friend - she's wet through. And besides, I'm glad of the company. Your money's of no use to me, love, but I'm getting on a bit, so you and your men folk could do a couple of little jobs as payment, if that suits. That way your silly pride won't be hurt. My, you're a stubborn one! If I didn't know better I'd swear you were a Yorkshire lass, I would!" Ellen and Sarah glanced at each other then turned to the old woman and smiled. Ellen took her coat off.

"Fine," Ellen held out her hand. "I'm Ellen Roberts. This is Sarah Chambers. My husband is Dave. Sarah's husband is Paul. Dave is the big one." They shook hands warmly. "Now, what can we do to help?"

"Sarah can stay by the fire. She's soaked. You come with me."

Dave and Paul trudged back to the car. The rain had started again, and they were both weary.

"She seems a decent old stick," said Paul.

"I don't know, Paul, there's something not right about all this. I don't feel comfortable in that room." Dave shook his head. "Still, I suppose I shouldn't complain. We'll have a warmer drier night than we would in the car, but I want to be away ASAP tomorrow."

"Why not think of it as just another stop on the holiday? This place might be delightful in the morning. If it stops raining, that is. I saw the farmhouse before it got properly dark, and it would make a wonderful painting. It looked really homely. Anyway, I think you've upset Ellen enough for one day already."

"Don't remind me, mate. Don't remind me." They reached the car and opened the boot.

"I don't know about you, but I'm taking the lot. If I leave anything here she's bound to want it. Why do women need so many different things?" Dave shook his head as he unloaded the boot.

"Sarah's less fashion conscious. We've all we need in one case. Let me give you a hand with your stuff." They headed back to the farmhouse.

Ellen followed the old woman into a walk-in pantry.

"Take this bread and butter it. Here's the butter, you'll find knives in the kitchen. I'll bring the rest once I've sorted what's what."

"Do you have margarine? We prefer it."

"Margarine? Nay, lass. Never heard of it. If you don't want my best butter there's some good beef dripping. It's on the shelf behind you."

"Er, no. Butter will be fine." Ellen returned to the kitchen and found a big bread knife in the drawer of the kitchen table. She set about sawing the home-made loaf into slices. The old woman came back carrying a joint of ham, a wedge of cheese, and a metal cooking vessel.

"I've some good broth in here. I'll warm it up. The men will need it when they get back, and Sarah needs some as well. Cut some slices of ham when you've ... bless my soul! What do you think you're doing to that bread? Give it here, lass, I'll do that. Go and fetch some pickle and mustard from the pantry. Now then, young Sarah, you feeling better?" Ellen set off for the pantry with a candle. Sarah had been staring into the burning logs. She looked up.

"Yes thanks, much better."

"Good. Look after yourself." The old woman had finished with the bread so she went across to the fire and hauled the metal pot onto a hook over the fire. "There's not much left but it'll be plenty. Should be warmed by the time the men are back. Where's young Ellen got to? Could've been half way to Whitby and back by now." They returned from the pantry together.

"Sorry - I was interested in some of the things there - things my Gran used to talk about - 'When I were a lass you had real ...' - if you know what I mean."

"Ee! So you've Yorkshire blood in them veins!"

"But how did you know I wasn't from Yorkshire?"

"What made you think I was poor?"

"Well, all your things are so old, and, I don't want to appear rude, but there are no signs of luxury."

"I've all I need. Is there food on the table? Is there fire in the grate? Am I poor?"

"If you put it that way, I suppose not."

"No, but you're not from Yorkshire!"

"I'm not, but how did you know?"

"I just knows." During this exchange Sarah had moved across to the table and was buttering the bread. She smiled broadly. It wasn't every day someone got the better of Ellen.

"I knows all sorts of things without being told, deary." She winked knowingly at Sarah whose smile disappeared with a shudder. She suddenly felt uncomfortable. "I'm right and you're wrong, but don't fret over it. I've many more years' experience than you two put together. Them as lives longest sees most." The old woman sighed with an air of resigned superiority. Be a good lass and stir the broth. There's a big spoon in the table drawer." Sarah carried on buttering, her mind obviously on other things. "Look sharp, Sarah, the men will be back any minute!"

"By the way, what's your name?" asked Ellen from the fireside.

"You can call me 'Ma' - everyone else does."

Paul and Dave staggered in drenched. It had taken them over half an hour because of the weather and the weight of the cases. It was now fully dark, and their footsteps had been hampered by unseen clumps of heather and rabbit-holes. The meal was ready now, and the three women were sitting round the fire chatting over mugs of hot tea.

"Look at these drowned rats! Get your coats and boots off and come and sit by the fire. Ellen, get some bowls off that dresser and dish out the broth. Sarah, pour these lads some hot tea. I'll see to your cases." Ma picked up two cases and disappeared through a door in the other end of the room.

"Let me help," said Ellen, getting up. "Sarah, see to the broth." She picked up the other things and followed Ma through the door and up some steep uneven stairs, stumbling in the dark. Ma went through a door on her left and put the cases down. She lit a candle which cast strange shadows round the small room. Ellen followed.

"This is your room, deary. There's fresh water in the jug for washing and matches by the bed if you need. Bring Sarah's things." She left quickly with the candle. Ellen followed the flickering light into the room opposite. It was identical but for a door in the far corner. Ellen put the case and bag in the corner of the room and looked around. In one corner was a wooden bed covered by a patchwork quilt. In the opposite corner was a wash-stand with a bowl, pitcher, and two towels. Thick dark curtains hung already closed at the small window. The third corner had the small door. Before she had a chance to take in anymore, Ma had gone, plunging the room into darkness. Ellen turned quickly and hit her shoulder on the edge of the half-open door. Out on the landing there was no light. She felt her way along the walls and down the uneven stairs then found the door handle. She breathed a sigh of relief when she heard the others chatting as she opened the big heavy door.

"Come along, deary, your broth's waiting." Paul and Dave were much drier now, had finished their broth, and were tucking in to ham and cheese sandwiches.

"Ma, this is delicious." declared Paul. "I've never tasted pickle or mustard like this before. Are they homemade?"

"Of course, and the bread, cheese, and butter. I slaughtered the pig and cured the ham myself too." They froze. "Don't be daft. The pig's got to die, or we can't eat it. You townsfolk have some queer notions. How do you think we can have meat without killing?"

"She's right," said Sarah as she carried on chewing. "Every time we eat meat it's because some innocent beast has had its life brutally snatched away." She held the slice of ham out at arm's length and addressed her audience tragically. "Alas, poor piglet. I knew him, Horatio."

"Now how did you know his name was Horatio?" Sarah went pale. Ma laughed. "Only joking, deary." Sarah smiled and carried on eating. "He was really called George." She winked and got up to put the kettle on the fire. They finished their meal and moved over to the fire. They sat round it with big mugs of tea. Dave got up.

"Where's the toilet, please?"

"Through there," Ma replied, pointing to a small door behind the front door. "There's a netty through one door, and the pump and a bucket behind t'other, but mind your head." Dave lit a candle and left the room. Ellen silently mouthed to Sarah, "Pump and bucket? Netty?" Sarah shrugged her shoulders and drank her tea. Dave returned. As he sat down Ma got up and took his candle.

"I'm off to bed now. Put the lamp out before you come up. Good night!" They all thanked her and bade her goodnight, then she left. They waited until her footsteps couldn't be heard, then Ellen spoke.

"What, pray tell, is a netty?"

"Well, it's a sort of toilet," said Dave. "Come and see." They followed Dave through the door. He held the candle aloft and pointed down to a wooden bench with a hole in it.

"This is it. You use it like a toilet, but it can't be flushed, so you get a bucket of water from the next room to pour down. By the way, the paper's a bit rough. It's old newspaper cut into squares. Follow me." He led the way to the adjacent room and demonstrated the use of the pump. "This, I believe, is where our water for washing and drinking comes from." Sarah and Ellen grimaced at each other in disgust. "Don't worry, it tastes alright, in fact, it's probably cleaner than what we drink at home." They returned to the kitchen and sat round the fire and one by one visited the netty.

"All in all I think we've been pretty lucky, despite the primitive equipment," said Ellen. "I must admit I was more than just a little scared when we were confronted by the lamp and the spooky eyes when she answered the door."

"'Is there anybody there?' said the traveller, knocking at the moonlit door," quoted Sarah, complete with dramatic representation.

"No, but seriously," Ellen went on, "this place isn't bad, and the old girl is quite a character. I wouldn't mind staying another day."

"Well, I didn't feel comfortable at first. There's something ... I can't quite put my finger on it, but there's something not right about all this," said Dave, "but I'm happier now. We've eaten plenty and we're all still alive."

"Yes, but I know what you mean, Dave," said Sarah. "She's spooky, but she's kind. I think she's quite harmless."

"How much are we paying her? We've eaten a few quid's worth already, and there's breakfast to come yet."

"Paul never stops thinking about money," Ellen commented. "I broached the subject while you were out. She won't take money, says she has no use for it, but she wants us to do a few little jobs for her because she's getting on a bit."

"She had no difficulty carrying your two heavy suitcases," Paul pointed out.

"Perhaps she's strong, but at her age she can't be very agile, and she's not very tall. I see no reason why we shouldn't help her. She's been kind to us."

"Yes, Ellen, I agree, I was just pointing out that the old biddy is as strong as the proverbial ox."

"I'm ready for bed," said Dave, getting up. "I'll have to go to the village to see about an alternator tomorrow."

"Yes. We'll do her jobs while you sort that out. Come on, get a candle and I'll show you our rooms." They trooped up the stairs and were soon sound asleep.

Chapter 3

Ellen woke with a start. *Boom! Boom! Boom!* She looked around but could see nothing in the near total darkness. On her right she could just make out an eerie glow around the edge of the curtains. In her panic she didn't know where she was and shook Dave violently. *Boom! Boom! Boom!* Louder this time, pounding on the door.

"Rise and shine, dearies," came the voice from the other side. "Time to get up."

"What's going on?" Dave muttered, still half asleep.

"I thought we were going to be murdered in our sleep. I must have been dreaming." Ellen gave him a kiss and a hug, then lay back and laughed quietly. She thought about what had happened yesterday - the breakdown, the old farmhouse, their genial hostess - and silently chastised herself for being so silly.

"Open the curtains, love, I want to see the time," said Dave, groping for his wristwatch. Ellen got out of bed and pulled one curtain back letting the daylight flood in through the small window. "It's only half past six." He groaned and flopped back down.

"Come on, we might as well get up now." Ellen dragged the bedding off him. "No doubt there'll be another mug of tea waiting for us. I don't think I've ever had so much tea in such a short space of time as we did last night. The old girl must be hooked on caffeine or quinine, or whatever's in it." She drew the other curtain and stood looking out of the window at the vegetable plot they had staggered through the previous night. On the right stood a couple of stone out-buildings with slate roofs and rickety wooden doors. The small hill that screened the house from

66

the road curved round to the left. "This view probably hasn't changed much in the last two hundred years," she thought. A sudden gasp from Dave as he splashed the cold water from the bowl onto his face brought her back to the present. She turned quickly, then winced. The bed wasn't long enough, and she had backache to prove it.

In the other room Sarah and Paul had slept peacefully and comfortably all night and were feeling relaxed and refreshed. Sarah leant on the narrow windowsill, admiring the view. Rolling hills stretched to the horizon in varying shades of green and purple, with the occasional streak of grey where the rock broke the surface. Here and there, small clumps of trees and bushes gave shelter to birds and rabbits. About half a mile away white sheep with black faces chewed at the coarse grass. There were no signs of modern civilisation anywhere. She stood absorbed in the beauty of the Yorkshire countryside - so different from the view from her window at home. This is where she belonged. Paul put his arms around her slender waist and kissed her tenderly on the cheek.

"I know just what you're thinking," he whispered. "One day, when we're rich, we'll get a cottage up here somewhere. I promise." She turned to him, wrapped her arms round his neck and kissed him. They held each other, gazing out of the window for a few moments, then Paul broke the silence. "Come on, get dressed. With a bit of luck there'll be a mug of tea waiting for us downstairs."

"Well, good morning," announced Ellen. "We are so grateful you are able to grace us with your presence at long last. We've been up for hours, but you've probably had more important things to do."

"Take no notice. We've been down about ten minutes." Dave grinned. "She's in a foul mood because her back hurts." He was doing some bending and stretching exercises. "My back hurts too, but I'm doing something about it."

"I would do some exercises if the right facilities were available, but I won't go about smelling all day, and I've absolutely no intention whatsoever of sitting in a tin bath in front of the fire with you lot making comments about my bulges."

"Get your tea while it's still hot, young Sarah and Paul," said Ma with a friendly smile. She turned to Ellen. "If you needs a bath you can have one. I'll make sure nobody gets in 'til you're decent. Just say the word and I'll put the kettle on."

"Not more tea! We've just had a cup!"

"Don't be daft! I'll put kettle on for your bath, deary, unless you want a cold one."

"Oh! Sorry, I didn't realise. How silly of me!"

"Well look, you four run along and have a little walk while I see to breakfast, then if your back still hurts we'll see about a bath. Alright?"

"Good idea! Back soon, Ma." Ellen grabbed her jacket and put it on as she strode away. "Come on, you three," she called over her shoulder, "we haven't got all day!" Ma winked at Dave; he grinned and followed Ellen. Paul and Sarah gulped down their tea then trotted off after them. They walked round to the other side of the farmhouse, then stood for a few moments listening to the silence. Ellen put her arm round Dave's waist and rested her head lovingly on his arm.

"Isn't it beautiful?" she said softly.

"Almost as beautiful as you," he replied, reaching his long arm round her broad shoulders and giving her a squeeze. This was the Ellen that only Dave saw - soft, gentle, quiet, - this was why he loved her so much. To everyone else she was the brash domineering Amazon, more manly than some men, with only her excellent clothes sense and considerable ability with make-up reminding them that she was an attractive and artistic young lady, but to Dave she was his little woman, in need of love and care. Not that Dave was at all chauvanistic. He firmly believed in equality of the sexes and wasn't bothered that Ellen was on a much higher salary, but he always saw himself as his wife's protector, her knight in shining armour. She reached up and kissed him, then, remembering that they weren't alone, pulled away from his strong arm, laced her fingers between his, and set off slowly and deliberately across the stony grass, pulling him along gently. Sarah watched and smiled. She too had had the occasional glimpse of her big friend's alter ego. Sarah tightened her grip on Paul's hand. They looked at each other, smiled, and followed Ellen and Dave. Sarah was quite happy to have a more gentle public image than her friend. She didn't like the idea of appearing to be what she wasn't, but she was in a career where appearances were less important. Despite her pretty face and attractive figure her colleagues looked upon her as a person rather than a woman, and she liked it that way. She had a keen logical mind which won her the respect of even the most condescending of city gents, ensuring rapid promotion to become the youngest Senior Analyst in the history of the company. Ellen stopped and turned to face them. "I say, this is marvellous! I must use this place in an advert. It would have to be food or drink. With clothing the models have to move about, and our lot wouldn't be able to walk without stumbling in this heather. You know how useless those dreadful people are."

"I think this should be protected from your crowd," Paul protested. "They'd just trample over everything and leave litter everywhere."

"You're right, but that would deprive my public of this breathtaking view."

"No it wouldn't. I intend to come back here and do a few paintings." They strolled on, Ellen and Paul discussing, sometimes heatedly, the merits of a city film crew in the countryside. They reached the sheep, whose chewing reminded them of breakfast.

"I'm hungry. I think it's time we went back," said Sarah.

"Yes," said Dave. "I've worked up quite an appetite. How's your back, Ellen?"

"Much better, thanks. Let's go back."

Ma was busy dishing up the breakfast when they got back.

"I could eat a horse," declared Dave.

"There's no horse here," said Ma. "Only what's left of George. Sit down and eat before it gets cold."

"What about you?" asked Sarah. "You've only set four places."

"Oh, I've had enough. I don't need as much as you youngsters. Tuck in, now, there's more if you want it." They had fried eggs, ham, and mushrooms, all home produce of course, with great slabs of home-baked bread, and the obligatory mug of tea. Ma fussed around them, offering more as soon as a bare patch of plate appeared, topping up their tea, and threatening they wouldn't grow unless they ate more. Eventually they were all full, even Dave, who had a reputation for never leaving anything.

"He's better to keep a week than a fortnight!" Ma commented. "No wonder he's grown so well. You'd come to no harm to follow his example, you little ones." She said to Paul and Sarah, wagging her finger jokingly.

"Well, it's quarter past eight," said Dave, "I'd better see about our alternator. Back as soon as poss." He kissed Ellen then left, his long legs taking him out of sight in no time.

"Right. Let's get these dishes done then we'll set about earning our keep," said Ellen, rising to her feet.

"Leave them to me," said Ma. "You must do the things I find difficult. Any old woman can wash dishes. Come outside." They followed her out into the garden, and across to the small out-house. Inside were some saws and axes, and Paul was instructed to select one of each. He picked up the biggest axe.

"Now don't be silly, that's for your big friend. Your arms are too short for that one. Try this one, if it feels comfortable." She pointed at another. "That's better. Bring them and follow me." She led them to the other end of the house where two tall but slender trees stood propped up against the wall. "These came down in the last gales, so I fetched them here. Your job, Paul, is to chop them up into logs like you saw on the fire. I'll be back to see how you're doing, and mind you don't hurt yourself."

"Okay, leave it to me." he replied, wondering how long it would take.

"Ellen, two jobs for you, 'cause you're a big strong lass with Yorkshire blood in them veins." She gave Ellen a coil of thin rope from a hook on the wall. "This is my washing

71

line. It needs to go from this post to that. Paul and Sarah have their backsides too close to the ground, like me, so it's up to you, and when you're done, get all my knives and axes and sickles from kitchen and tool-shed and sharpen them. There's a stone on a treadle in the barn. Young Sarah, you come back inside." Ellen made short work of the washing line, then collected the knives from the kitchen. She dragged the old barn door open and set to work with the stone. Pumping the treadle with one foot while balancing on the other was hard work, but she soon got a rhythm going, and sang quietly to herself as she worked. She could hear Paul chopping and sawing, and wondered what Sarah was doing.

Dave covered the five miles to the village in a little over an hour. There was a garage with two petrol pumps, a church next to it, a shop across the road, which was also the village post office, an old stone pub beside the shop, and about twenty houses and cottages. He went into the garage and rang the bell on the counter. A man came through the door from the workshop and smiled warmly.

"Can I 'elp?" he asked.

"Do you do parts?" asked Dave.

"Aye, lad, we do. What're you after?"

"An alternator for a Hyundai."

"Alternators we got, but for Land Rovers and tractors mainly. What is it for again?"

"Hyundai."

"Just a minute, our Brian's better wi' these foreign names." He opened a hatch to the workshop and called through it. "Brian, can you come 'ere a minute? Got a chap wants an alternator for an 'Igh-n-Dry or summat." Brian entered, wiping his hands on a rag.

"Morning, young feller. What is't you want?"

"An alternator for a Hyundai." Brian scratched his head.

"We've none of them. Come through and see what we've got. Do you think one off a Land Rover would do?" He led Dave to the store room. Dave examined what was available but shook his head.

"These are too big. I could make one work, but none of them would fit into the space under the bonnet. Is there anywhere else might have one?"

"We can get you one. I'll give Jimmy a ring." He picked up the phone and dialled a number scribbled on the wall. "Is Jimmy there? ... Jimmy, its Brian Pickering. Look, I've a strapping great lad in 'ere wants an alternator for a Hyundai. You got one? ... Good. 'Ow much? ... Let's 'ave it then, as soon as you can." Dave was nodding, grinning, and silently indicating agreement with the price Brian was scrawling on a piece of paper.

"What? Just a minute, Jimmy." He laid the phone on the counter and stormed through to the workshop. "John, Jimmy says we 'aven't paid 'im for the last three deliveries. What's goin' on? I told you always to pay Jimmy Cox on time, didn't I?" Dave heard John muttering apologetically. Brian returned shaking his head. "What do you do with 'im, eh? 'Ow can I be expected to run a business when my useless stupid brother can't pay our biggest supplier on time? 'E's as much brain as one of our dad's sheep." He picked up the phone. "Jimmy? Sorry about that. You know what a pillock our John is. Look, I'll 'ave a cheque ready for your driver to collect. ... Aye, and next time I'll see you're

73

paid, 'cause I'll do it myself. That lad is about as much use as an ashtray on a motorbike. ... Righto, thanks." He put the phone down and smiled at Dave who was trying very hard not to grin too much. "It'll be here ten o'clock Monday." Dave was shocked. His broad grin disappeared.

"But I wanted it today! Where's it coming from?"

"Middlesbrough, but they never deliver Saturdays, 'cause their lads finish at dinner time and wouldn't get back soon enough."

"Isn't there anywhere else?"

"Well, there's Billy Anderson in Leeds, but 'e's the same," he said, scratching his head and staring into the distance, "and old Albert - no, 'e doesn't keep much for foreign cars. No, you'll have to wait 'til Monday." Dave paid a deposit and turned to leave. "Where are you staying?" Brian asked.

"At the old farmhouse about five miles away."

"With old Fred Robson and his cats?"

"No, with an old lady, calls herself 'Ma'."

"Can't say I knows 'er. Where did you say?"

"About five miles away. An old farmhouse sheltered from the road by a funny shaped hill."

"John! Come here!" he called. John appeared through the workshop door. "Young Mr Roberts 'ere says 'e's staying at the Shepperton farm. I thought that were derelict."

"No, I told you." John planted his hands on his hips in an 'I told you so but you wouldn't listen' manner. "About this time last year - I remember it 'cause it were just afore our Mark told us he'd put Angela in the family way - they'd been up there courtin' and they saw a light on, and some old wife invited them in, but they ran off 'cause Angela were scared."

"It doesn't make sense." Brian shook his head. "I were up there just before Easter 'elpin' our dad when tractor broke down, and it were derelict then. Looked as though it 'adn't been lived in for 'undred years or more."

"Well, our Mark might be daft, but 'e's no liar, and other young folk 'ave seen lights up there."

"So you don't know who lives there?" Dave enquired.

"No," John replied. "Used to belong to the Sheppertons, but that were a long time ago. Granddad knew them. Says they kept themselves to themselves – only saw them two or three times a year to bring pigs 'n' sheep to market. Nobody knows when they died - no funeral or burial or nothin'. Just stopped comin' to market, and nobody bothered 'cause nobody liked them. Kids were scared of them. Vicar went up there but never got in. Chased off by dogs. Old women in the village said she were a witch, and I believes them."

"You're an old woman if you believe such nonsense, John. Our dad always said I were the one with the brains," laughed Brian. "Now get some work done. I'm still mad about you not payin' Jimmy Cox." Dave grinned and left. He could still hear them heatedly discussing the merits of paying Jimmy Cox as he crossed the road to the shop. He bought a box of chocolates for Ma, a few sweets for himself and the others, and a roll of two-ply super-soft luxury toilet tissue for Ellen who had complained so bitterly about the squares of old newspaper, then, with the voices of Brian and John still raised in disagreement, he set off back.

"Sit at table, Sarah, and get comfortable." Ma opened a drawer and took out a small wooden box. Inside were a few reels of cotton and a pin-cushion with several needles and pins. She went out through the door that led to the stairs, then came back a minute later, her arms full of dark blue material. "These are my winter curtains. They need rings sewing on," she explained to Sarah. She went to another drawer and located a brown paper bag containing some brass rings. She explained where to put them, and Sarah set to work. Ma washed the breakfast dishes then made a pot of tea. She took two mugs out for Paul and Ellen, then brought another two over to the table and sat opposite Sarah.

"I thought you wanted us to do things you couldn't," said Sarah between sips of tea. "I'd have thought this would be child's play to you."

"Arthritis, love. Winter would be over before I finished these. When I were your age this would've been child's play, but I can't sew for more than a couple of minutes at a time now." She flexed her fingers stiffly and grimaced at the pain.

"Anyway, I'll be finished soon, then perhaps I can help Paul or Ellen with something a bit more energetic. I'm quite strong, even though I'm small, and I'm very fit."

"Oh, no, Sarah. We can't have you doing anything like that. Not in your condition!" Sarah froze, her mouth hanging open. She tried to speak, but no sound came. She slowly put the sewing down on the table, stared into the fire for a few moments, then looked back to Ma's smiling face. She couldn't decide whether there was a glint of evil in those sparkling eyes.

"But how do you know? I'm not even sure myself yet."

"I knows all sorts of things without being told, deary. Now not a word to the others, not even Paul just for the time being. When they go out after dinner you stay here with me, and we'll have a little talk."

"But we'll be going home after lunch. It'll not take Dave and me long to fix the car."

"We'll see." Ma patted Sarah gently on the arm as she rose to her feet. "I'll make a start on dinner. You finish my sewing and we'll have our chat this afternoon. Don't fret, now."

Chapter 4

Dave trudged over the brow of the hill and stopped to admire the view. His eyes roamed slowly across the timeless scene, and he thought about having to stay until Monday. It seemed quite a good idea now, even though he had been horrified at the prospect little more than an hour earlier. In fact, Dave wouldn't mind staying here forever. He was much less dependent on modern luxuries than the others, although he could easily imagine Sarah being content in this environment. He could work as a handyman, repair cars and tractors, radios and washing machines, and he could help with the harvest and sheep-shearing. What he couldn't imagine was Ellen settling down to that sort of life, having children, keeping chickens, doing without her sauna and sun-bed. She was definitely not farmer's-wife material. No, this place would have to wait until they could afford to have a purpose-built hi-tech house with all ameneties included. He grinned, shook his head slowly, then set off down the hill to the barn where the noise of the grinding wheel was the nearest sign of activity. He stood watching Ellen labouring over her task, humming gently, and oblivious of his presence. She seemed happy in her work, and Dave began to think he had misjudged her. He stepped forward, casting a shadow across the wheel.

"Oh!" Ellen jumped, dropping the axe, which fell to the ground and embedded its corner in the earth floor less than an inch from her foot. "You clumsy oaf! Look what you made me do." Her fright turned to anger, then back to fright again, as she realised what might have happened. Tears welled up in her eyes and Dave quickly stepped across the fallen axe to comfort her. "I could have lost a foot then," she sobbed against his shoulder. Dave held her tightly and said nothing. "I'm sorry, Dave." She kissed him. "I'll have to sit down." Her legs had turned to jelly. Dave helped her over to a bale of straw then sat beside her, his arm around her heaving shoulders. They sat without speaking for a short while, then Dave wiped her tears with his big handkerchief, and supporting her round the waist with his big strong arm, he helped her to the farmhouse. Ma had already put the kettle on. Sarah sat at the table, ashen-faced, as Dave helped Ellen through the door. Ellen's mishap caused such distraction that they didn't notice Sarah's disturbed expression. The sudden flurry of activity jolted Sarah back to life. She got up and went across to where Ma was already helping Dave lower Ellen to the sofa.

"She's had a bit of an accident." Dave said quietly. "There's no harm done, but she's a bit shaken - her legs are a bit wobbly. A mug of tea and a little rest and she'll be fine."

"Kettle's about boiled," Ma announced. "Sarah, see if Ellen wants more cushions and get her settled while I make tea. Them axes can be dangerous." Ellen's plight made Sarah forget her own worries. She made Ellen comfortable then ran to the pump room to get a cup of water for her to sip until the tea was ready. Dave knelt beside his wife, stroking her hair and holding her hand. He didn't speak, but he didn't have to. She looked into his gentle calm eyes and felt secure and relaxed. She smiled weakly and ruffled his hair.

"Thanks, Dave," she whispered. "I'll be alright in a few minutes, but I'd appreciate it if you could finish off the axes." Dave grinned and slowly rose to his feet. Ma poured out the tea.

"Come on, Ma, show me what's what with these axes. I'll finish them."

"I'll just take this mug of tea to Paul. Let's leave the girls alone together." Ma followed Dave out into the garden. Ellen told Sarah what had happened. They sat staring into the fire for a while, then Ellen broke the silence.

"I was just beginning to really like this place, even though it hasn't a proper bathroom or anything, just beginning to feel at home, when this happened!" They flung their arms around each other and cried quietly for a few moments. Ellen extricated herself from Sarah's arms, blew her nose, wiped her tears away, then said, in quite a business-like manner, "Drink your tea - it's getting cold." Sarah knew her big friend was more or less back to normal now. She smiled broadly, then they both burst out laughing. Ellen gave Sarah a hug then they drank their tea and chatted about axes and curtain rings. Sarah decided not to mention her pregnancy, or Ma's knowledge of it, until they were away from here. After all, it could've been a guess, or in these country areas the old women might even be experts at spotting such things. A farmer's wife sees pregnant animals as an everyday event, so Sarah decided not to let it spoil what was left of the holiday. She was still a little uneasy about the evil glint in Ma's eyes, but perhaps being pregnant made her somewhat oversensitive.

Paul was glad of the tea and a rest. He had been working hard, and the sweat ran down his muscular chest and arms in tiny rivulets. He sat on the pile of logs and chatted to Ma and Dave about the difficulties he was having. Ma laughed and told him he was trying too hard.

"Slow down a bit. Try not to chop it in two with a single blow. You've got good strong arms there, but there's no need to go at it like a bull at a gate. You'll do yourself an injury. Take it easy."

"Look, Paul, if you like, I'll finish the logs and you do something less energetic," Dave volunteered.

"But I thought you'd want to get started on the car," Paul said.

"Er, no. There's a slight problem there. The garage can't get the part until Monday."

"Monday! I intended to spend Monday in bed recovering from the holiday!"

"No chance of that. The part should arrive in the village at about ten, so if all goes well we'll get home at about six." He turned to Ma. "Can we stay a bit longer? We'll do some other jobs for you."

"Of course you can." Ma smiled. "I've not much else needs doing, but you're welcome to stay in any case."
"Thanks, Ma. I'd better break the news to the girls."

"Rather you than me, mate." Paul laughed. Dave related the details of Ellen's near accident to Ma and Paul while they drank their tea. Ma's face remained calm throughout. When Dave had finished she took the empty mugs away, and left the two men to their logs. Dave removed his shirt, then wielded the axe, while Paul tidied up what had already been chopped.

"Funny, but it seems to me Ma knew all about it before I said a word. She even knew it was an axe when I first took Ellen in, even though we hadn't mentioned it," Dave said between logs.

"Not necessarily anything to worry about, Dave," Paul answered after giving it some thought. "She knew Ellen was doing axes and knives, and was much more likely to have difficulty with an axe. I know Ellen's rather strong for a woman, but some of those axes are very heavy."

"Yes, but her face never changed while I was telling you both, whereas yours showed shock, surprise, concern, all sorts of emotions. There's something not right about that old woman."

"Don't worry, Dave, it's probably just the difference between us city boys and these country folk getting under your skin a bit. They'd probably say the same about us if they saw us dashing across the road at Holborn Circus and leaping in and out of cabs and wine-bars. They'd be standing on the kerb saying, 'There's summat not right 'bout them folk. 'Tain't natural to cross roads like that,' and it's the same here - we're out of our normal environment, so we're bound to feel a bit edgy."

"I suppose you're right, Paul. When we get home to our black cabs and Evening Standard and the rotten old Northern Line we'll look back on all this and laugh."

"Monday! Didn't you tell him that's not good enough? We need it today. There must be another garage somewhere."

"Relax, Ellen," said Paul. "This is the country. There's only one of everything around here. There was absolutely no point at all in Dave upsetting the garage people with threats and demands. We'll have to wait until Monday. Ma has generously offered us accommodation, and we all like it here, so ranting and raving at poor old Dave is a waste of time and energy."

"You'll stay as long as needs be, and that's the end of it. Sit down. Dinner's ready, if it's good enough, that is. Get knives and forks out of the drawer instead of standing there shouting."

"Sorry, Ma. I didn't wish to appear ungrateful. It's just that we had planned to have a day off before we go back to work." Ellen distributed the cutlery.

"There's plenty of nice countryside around here," Ma told them. "You could spend a month here and still not see it all." They nodded agreement as they tucked in to another huge meal. By the time they had finished they were convinced that staying a few more days would be most acceptable. They sat drinking tea around the fire.

"The village is quite picturesque," said Dave. "Perhaps we could have a walk down there this afternoon."

"Good idea," said Ellen. "I want a postcard of this place. I assume there's a souvenir shop..."

"Well, there's a shop, and I think it sells postcards. That reminds me. Back in a min." Dave got up and went outside. He came back carrying a brown paper bag. "Forgot all about this with all the fuss over Ellen's little mishap. I bought us all some sweets, soft loo roll for Ellen" he grinned as Ellen blushed. "And a present for Ma for looking after us all so well." He took a large box of chocolates from the bag and handed it across to Ma, who giggled with embarrassment.

"Oh, you shouldn't have wasted your money, but thank you anyway. I'm glad of the company. You're the first visitors I've had for a long time. It's nice to have someone to talk to." Dave finished his tea, then looked across at Sarah.

"Are you okay, Sarah?" he asked. "You've hardly said anything all day, and you look a bit pale."

"Oh, er, yes, I'm just feeling a little bit under the weather," Sarah answered hesitantly.

"Well, you don't look too good." Dave was obviously concerned for his friend. "What's up? I hope it's nothing serious."

"Come on," Ellen butted in loudly. "Let's go for a walk down to the village. Are you staying here, Sarah?"

"Er, yes. You three go. I'll stay here for a rest."

"I'll look after Sarah," Ma said firmly. "You go and enjoy yourselves. You've worked hard this morning."

"Are you sure you'll be alright?" Paul asked Sarah quietly.

"Yes, it's nothing. Don't worry about me." She kissed him then they left.

"You sit there and finish your tea while I wash the pots, then we'll have a little chat in the front parlour." Ma smiled. Sarah didn't like that smile. She wished she'd asked Paul to stay, but at the time she somehow wasn't able to do it. She drank the tea and shuddered.

Chapter 5

Ellen, Dave, and Paul walked up the hill in silence, paused at the top to admire the view, then trotted gently down the other side. They stumbled across the heather at the foot of the hill, then Dave spoke as they reached the road.

"I'm not happy about Sarah. There's something wrong."

"You great fool!" Ellen chided him. "She's probably having 'women's problems' and is too embarrassed to say."

"It is about the right time, but it's not like Sarah to feel embarrassed about that sort of thing," Paul pointed out.

"I know," said Ellen, "but perhaps with Ma being there, you know, being from a different generation, there are things they don't talk about."

"You mean she was embarrassed for Ma?"

"Not exactly, but that's about as close as you'll get. Men never will understand properly. There are things of that nature I can talk about freely with friends of my own age that I wouldn't even consider discussing with an older person. Anyway, I think Sarah is in good hands, and she'll be right as rain when we get back." Ellen strode off ahead of them, indicating that the conversation was over. Dave and Paul looked at each other and shrugged their shoulders.

"I suppose she's right, Dave."

"She usually is." They quickly caught up with her and chatted about inconsequential matters for the rest of the journey, occasionally stopping at particularly scenic spots, and resting briefly on tree stumps or flat rocks. Paul kept pointing out good scenes for paintings, to the eventual annoyance of the other two. They reached the village after almost two hours and went into the shop. Ellen twisted her face at the meagre selection of postcards, but bought some

85

nonetheless. They also purchased some cakes and biscuits to supplement their wholesome but sometimes bland meals, and some sweets for the journey back. Dave looked at his watch.

"The pub might still be open. I don't know what hours are like round here, but I could murder a pint."

"It stays open if there's customers," the shop assistant told them. "It sometimes stays open if there isn't. If it's shut, come back here and I'll have a word with landlord."

The pub was open. They went in and Dave ordered the drinks while Paul and Ellen chose a table near the fire. Despite the bright sunshine, there was a chill in the wind, and they were glad of the warmth. They sipped their drinks and looked around them. The pub was old and traditional, with a big square bar in one corner. Ancient farm implements hung from the walls, horse brasses decorated the wooden beams, even the other customers looked as though they belonged to the past. Two old men were leaning on the bar staring ahead, silent but for the occasional cough as they sucked on their pipes and sipped their ale thoughtfully. Another old man sat in the corner near the fire, apparently asleep, with a half-empty glass of ale on the table before him. The click and rattle of the pool table from the next room were not enough to disturb the tranquillity. The three friends sat gazing into the fire nursing their glasses of beer and at peace with the world. The door burst open and a man in his late forties strode in and slammed the door behind him.

"Pint, please, Joe." Dave, recognising the voice, turned and attracted his attention. It was John from the garage.

"'Ello there, Mr Roberts, mind if I join you?" Dave introduced him to Ellen and Paul. As he sat down he waved to the old man in the corner. "'Ello, Granddad. 'Ow you keepin'?" John had raised his voice almost to a shout to address the old man.

"Could be better, lad, but could be a damn sight worse. I'll not grumble when there's folk in a worse way."

"That's my Granddad. 'E's oldest bloke in village. 'E's the one as knew Sheppertons," John whispered loudly. "Funny place, Shepperton Farm," he went on, still keeping his voice low, as though discussing some secret. "Almost as if there's two. My lad Mark and 'is wife Angela, although they weren't wed then, both saw a light on and spoke to an old lady there. Lots of young folk say the same. All older folk, like our Brian, they all says it's derelict and no signs o' life. I never goes near, just in case it's 'aunted. Not that I believe in that sort of thing, you know, but you can't be too careful."

"What's all this about?" Ellen asked, puzzled.

"Sorry, forgot to tell you," Dave apologised. "Your accident sent it clean out of my head. John was telling me yesterday that the old farmhouse where we're staying used to belong to a rather odd couple a long time ago, who disappeared without trace. Since then, some people have seen an old lady there, but others, like John's brother, Brian, have been up there and claim it's in such a state it can't have been lived in for a very long time."

"Aye, and none of them'd touched a drop of drink, so I believe all of them, 'cause they're all honest folk."

"But John, you can't possibly believe all of them," Paul said. "Either the farm's occupied, or it's derelict. You can't have it both ways."

"I believes them all. I reckon the old woman were a witch, and could make things seem what they're not. Not

that I believes in magic, you understand, only simple folk
believes in magic, but folk what've told me about it is the
sort I'd trust to the ends of the Earth." Ellen and Dave
looked at each other, trying very hard not to laugh, while
Paul objected to John's reasoning.

"No, John, it's not possible. If what you say is true,
then you must believe in magic as well, or it doesn't make
any sense."

"That's just it! It don't make no sense! That's what I'm
trying to tell you." John was becoming exasperated by
Paul's failure to grasp the simple facts. "It don't make
sense, but it's true, right enough. Come over and meet
Granddad. 'E'll tell you all about it. All you 'as to do is buy
'im a drink and 'e'll tell all there is to be told." Paul was
despatched to the bar while John introduced Dave and
Ellen to Granddad. "This is Mr and Mrs Roberts, from
London," John shouted.

"Please, Dave and Ellen," Ellen insisted.
"This is Dave and Ellen from London, Granddad. That's
their friend Paul at bar." He pointed to Paul as Ellen
blushed. Surely the whole of Yorkshire knew their names
now. Perhaps she should contact the Noise Abatement
Society about this. Granddad nodded in greeting as they
made themselves comfortable round his table. "They're
staying at Shepperton Farm and want to know about old Mr
and Mrs Shepperton." At this all sound in the pub ceased,
except for the ticking of the old clock above the bar and the
cracking of the wood in the fire. Ellen and Dave looked
across the room. The barman and the two old men were
looking at them with stern, almost menacing expressions.
Three people from the other room had poked their heads
round the door to stare at them. The silence lasted a couple

of seconds, but to Ellen it felt like an hour. Everyone instantaneously carried on with their former activities, except for the two old men, who finished their drinks hurriedly and left rather abruptly. John went on.

"You knew Sheppertons, didn't you?"

Granddad cuffed him playfully. "You knows I never knew them. I'm not as old as that. But I does know all about them, but I can't tell, 'cause I've a sore throat today."

"Pity. Paul were buying you a drink, but if you've a sore throat you'll not be wantin' it."

"Now let's not be 'asty, John. I'll do me best for benefit of your friends. We mustn't be impolite when there's visitors." Granddad cleared his throat and began his tale as soon as he had been refreshed by the brown liquid. He leant forward to speak, adding an atmosphere of mystery to his oft-told story with sharp unexpected glances. "As I've said, I didn't know them, but my father were a lad when they were about. Not that 'about' is the right word, mind, 'cause they didn't mix. They was old already when Dad were very small, so I can't tell about their early life, but old Shepperton used to come down to village twice a year. He'd bring sheep to market, drivin' them down the 'ill as though there were no tomorrow and sell them to first man to offer a decent price. No arguin' or barterin'. No 'angin' around for a better deal. Then he'd be off up the 'ill as fast as 'is legs would go, without speakin' to a soul. Later same day 'e'd be back with a handcart and buy whatever they needed. Pots and pans, cups and saucers, plates and dishes, cloth, nails, tools, and then away up the 'ill again. And 'e could shift! 'E were a great big tall chap, like you, Dave, but painfully thin. So thin that 'e wouldn't 'ave took up no room at all if it 'adn't been for 'is big feet. Well, with 'is great long legs 'e

89

were out of sight in no time. The 'ole rigmarole would be repeated exactly six months later, except with pigs instead of sheep." He paused for a drink. "'E 'ad a foul temper. On one occasion, when 'e were chargin' up 'ill with money from pigs, an old sheepdog got in 'is way. Well, folk said you could 'ear 'im bellowin' from 'ere to Scarborough, and that were a long way in them days, 'cause we 'ad no cars, see. 'E kicked poor dog, and beat it with 'is stick, then 'e picked it up and threw it over wall into a field with one 'and, and they say it went 'undred yards afore it 'it ground. Man 'oo owned dog were mad, and 'is son, great big lad what won money fightin' at fairs, he flew at old Shepperton, but Shepperton out with 'is fist, catching 'im on chin, and knocked 'im out. At first they all feared 'e were dead, but after a while 'e got up and wandered about, dazed. Shepperton were out of sight in minutes, of course. Poor old dog were dead, though, but that night, about midnight, there were a terrible noise in village. All dogs took to 'owlin' and woke everybody up. They stopped as sudden as they'd started, but by then 'ole village were out in street. Man 'oose dog it were found a parcel on doorstep. There were enough money in it to buy two sheepdogs, and a note. Parson were sent for, on account of bein' able to read, and he said note expressed contrition. Aye, contrition, that were word used. Contrition for death of animal, and 'oped money would compensate. Ever since, all children in village, whenever they saw 'im comin' down 'ill, ran and 'id behind their mothers' skirts, and there were a few grown-ups weren't too proud to make sure they was out of the way." Granddad drained his glass and sat back in the chair.

"Well?" Ellen asked, after a moment of silence.

"Well what?" Granddad asked.

"Is that it?"

"Is that what?"

"You haven't said anything about Mrs Shepperton yet."

"That's right, lass."

"And are you going to?"

"Well, I would like to, but my throat's givin' out."

"Dave. More beer for Granddad, or we'll never find out about Mrs Shepperton." Granddad smiled as Dave went to the bar.

"You catch on quick for a southerner. I'd swear you were from Yorkshire if it weren't for your funny way of talkin'." Ellen clenched her teeth and said nothing. Refreshed again, Granddad was able to continue the history lesson. "Mrs Shepperton were a different kettle of fish. She were only seen once. She were round and fat and not very tall. She were a cheery sort, with rosy cheeks and a happy smile. She came down one spring morning. Shepperton had broken 'is leg, and she needed some iodine. One or two folk offered to go back with 'er to see to 'is leg, but she'd 'ave none of it. Insisted she knew what were best for bad legs and needed more iodine. Nobody in village 'ad any, so a man were sent on 'orseback to next village for some. While she were waitin' for 'im she sat outside pub and told children stories, and gave mothers advice about sick children, and gave farmers advice about sick animals, and made 'erself very popular with everybody in village. When rider got back she paid for iodine and gave 'im a shillin' for 'is trouble. Well, that were a lot, then, so everybody wanted to 'elp with Shepperton's bad leg, but she insisted they couldn't." He paused to relight his pipe. "So! You might think that folk wanted to see 'er again, seein' as she were pleasant and generous and gave good advice. Well, just as she were leavin' the village one of the farmers were drivin' his sheep from one field to another, and as soon as they saw 'er they took fright. They ran backwards and forwards like animals possessed, some 'urt themselves on bushes and fences, some ran off never to be seen again, some just lay down and died, and the dogs set up such an 'owl that folk 'ad to cover their ears 'cause it were so unbearable. She turned and shook 'er fist at the dogs, and with an evil expression on 'er face, she vanished. Just disappeared. The racket stopped immediately, and the dogs lay down just like cats in front of the fire, all peaceful and quiet. Well, this bein' farmin' country, folks lays a lot of store by their animals. Beasts knows when there's evil about. They 'as like a sixth sense, so seein' as the animals was all upset by the old woman, nobody would go near 'er, no matter 'ow kind she seemed. Anyway, that were the first and last time she came down that my dad knows of." He drained his glass again and sat back in the chair.

"Is there more?" asked Ellen.

"Aye, lass, there's more."

"Another drink?"

"Why, that's very kind." She got up. "Nay, lass," he called her back. "Women can't buy drinks in 'ere."

"And why not?" she asked, indignantly.

"Because landlord'll not serve thee. Sit down. It's about time our John bought a round. Get up, you tight devil. It's no wonder our Brian complains so much. Go and get drinks, lad." He pushed John towards the bar. John reluctantly bought the drinks, making sure noone saw how much money he had in his pocket. When they were all settled again Granddad leant forward once more to complete his tale. "Strangest thing about Sheppertons were what 'appened to them, or more to the point, what didn't 'appen. Next time dad saw old Shepperton were the last. It were day for 'im to bring pigs to market, and 'e didn't show up. Not at first, anyhow. Business were all but done when 'e comes limpin' down 'ill with pigs runnin' in front. 'Is leg obviously 'adn't mended straight, and 'e could only get about slowly. 'E sold pigs and made 'is way back up 'ill, a tired old crippled man. One kind soul offered to 'elp 'im 'ome, but the old man shouted and cursed, and threatened 'im with 'is stick, so 'e decided against 'elpin'. That's the last time anybody saw old Shepperton. 'E didn't come back with 'is 'andcart that day, and because of the threats, nobody felt inclined to go up there. Six months later, 'e were due down with 'is sheep, and 'e didn't turn up. It were a disappointment in more ways than one. 'E sold 'is pigs and sheep at different times of year to other farmers, for one thing, so 'e was always guaranteed a decent price, and for another, 'is animals was good animals. Always heavier than others, plenty of meat on them. Now, I don't know whether this were due to time of year, or because of summat 'is wife did to them, but them sheep and pigs was always better than anybody's. Apart from that, most wanted to see what 'is leg were like and if 'e'd bring 'andcart. A week went by, and parson decided it were 'is duty, as a man of God, to see if they needed 'elp, so one day 'e went up there, despite the threats. Well, 'e got over the top of that funny little 'ill, and couldn't see signs of life, so 'e went down into garden. Just as 'e set foot on garden path there's a great barkin' and 'owlin' and shoutin' such that poor parson thought 'ell 'ad opened up. The old woman were stood at door shoutin' and cursin' and shakin' an axe at 'im, and there was two great big dogs with fierce teeth boundin' across the garden at 'im.

'E reckoned they was the size of 'orses, with burnin' eyes, paws like shovels, and teeth that would take a man's leg off. Parson turned and ran for 'is life! As 'e got to top of little 'ill, noise stopped. 'E turned round, and old woman and dogs 'ad vanished. Parson didn't feel inclined to investigate further. 'E ran all the way back to village, and you knows 'ow far that is, ran into church and prayed there all night, not darin' to come out 'til full daylight. Many years later a party of men, and I were one, went up there and found nothin'. Well almost nothin'. The old farm was still there, but no signs of people or animals at all, except for a few bones from a pig by the kitchen fire. Some of the older chaps, me bein' just a young lad, about eighteen, they reckoned from the tools and the state of the 'ouse and that, they said nobody 'ad lived there for an 'undred years." He lit his pipe again as they sat silently waiting.

"More beer?" asked Ellen.

"There's no more to tell, lass." He shook his head slowly as he spoke. "No more that's believable, that is. A few weak-minded folk claim to 'ave seen things, but I'll not repeat them, 'cause I doesn't believe them. Some reckons she were a witch. I'll go along with that. I've no reason to doubt it, but that's the end of my story, and it's all as true as I'm sitting 'ere now."

"But what happened to them?" Ellen asked.

"Witches being what they are, anything could've 'appened to 'er. As for 'im, rumour 'as it - and I keeps an open mind on subject - rumour 'as it Ma Shepperton turned old George Shepperton into a pig and ate 'im."

Chapter 6

Ellen and Dave looked at each other, their mouths hanging open. Paul, who was in the middle of having a drink, froze. He looked at Granddad, then Ellen, then Dave, then back to Granddad, while his body remained motionless. He put his drink down on the table, frowned at it for a moment, then leant forward and looked Granddad in the face.

"What do you mean?" he asked quietly.

"She turned 'im into a pig and ate him," Granddad replied, slowly and deliberately.

"That's what you said. What do you mean?" Paul fixed him with an icy stare. Granddad shifted uncomfortably in his seat.

"I'm not sure as I understand what you're askin'," he replied cautiously.

"Do you mean that by witchcraft, or magic, or whatever, she turned her husband, a human being, into a pig? And having done this, she slaughtered him?"

"Yes!" replied Granddad, glad to be back on familiar ground. "She magicked 'im into a pink animal with four legs and curly tail, took axe to 'im in the old barn, cured 'im, then, when 'e were ready, 'ad 'im for supper." He was feeling more confident now.

"Why?"

"What?" Granddad's confidence disappeared again.

"Why did she kill her husband? If she wasn't happily married, why did she wait so long?"

"You're askin' questions that no livin' soul can answer, lad. If I knew such things, why, I'd write a book and make a fortune. Them as knows answers is long dead. One thing's for sure, though. You can look at every 'eadstone in churchyard, and you'll not find 'Shepperton' on any of them. There was no human remains of either. No funeral, no burial, they disappeared without trace. When I went up to the farm all them years ago, well, it were like they'd never existed. 'Ouse 'adn't been lived in for donkeys' years, and only bones to be seen were pig's. I've told all I know, and a bit of what you might call speculation, but that's it. I'll say no more." Dave and Ellen had remained motionless and speechless during this exchange. Ellen nudged Dave, almost spilling his beer.

"Close your mouth, dear, we are not codfish." She turned to Granddad. "Thankyou ever so much for telling us all this. We're very grateful. It's a fascinating story, but we must be getting back now. It'll soon be time for tea." She emptied her glass quickly and rose to leave.

"Fancy a game of pool?" Dave asked.

"No. We're going now. Come on, you two." She smiled quickly at Granddad and John and left. Dave and Paul gulped down their drinks and followed.

"She's a Yorkshire lass if ever there was one." Granddad winked knowingly at John.

"Where's the fire, Ellen?" Paul asked, irritated by her sudden exit. "I was in the mood for a few games of pool."

"We've got to get back. Sarah's up there alone. What if Ma's the witch? Come on, hurry up." She set off at a brisk trot up the hill followed closely by Paul.

"Never thought about that. I hope she's all right," Paul panted as he jogged alongside.

"Just a minute! Stop! Come back here!" Dave called them back. "Did I just hear what I thought I heard? Do you two expect me to believe that Ma is nearly two hundred years old? Do you believe in witchcraft? I certainly don't, and I thought you both had more sense. It's a nice creepy story to tell around the candle in a power cut, and some of it may be true, but that's in the past. Sarah is in no danger from witchcraft."

"Hang on a minute, Dave," Paul spluttered angrily. "Two or three times since we arrived you've said to me you weren't happy about the place, and you've twice expressed concern about Sarah. I don't believe in magic or any other such rubbish, but I do believe that Sarah may be in danger."

"Yes, and so do I," joined in Ellen. "It's all your fault for not servicing the car when you promised to. Sarah's my friend and I'm going to do everything in my power to make sure she's safe."

"Safe from what?" Dave asked, a little disgruntled at being reminded about his earlier misgivings, to say nothing of being blamed for the breakdown again. "Will we get back to find she's been turned into a pig? It's a good thing she isn't a Jew or a Muslim! What harm can she come to? Just stop and think for a second."

"Well, I suppose we are being a bit silly," admitted Paul sheepishly. "But when Ellen put the idea into my head I got carried away. You're right, Dave. She's in more danger from nuclear attack than she is from witchcraft."

"Don't you be so sure!" Ellen objected. "I don't believe in witchcraft, but I don't disbelieve it either. I know I'm not a scientist and don't know what is or isn't possible, but I like to keep an open mind about what can't be proven. Call me old-fashioned if you want, but I'm going to make sure Sarah's alright." She set off at a jog again. Dave and Paul looked at each other, shrugged their shoulders, and set off after her. All three were very fit because they regularly played sports and took exercise, so they covered the distance in forty minutes despite the hill and the strengthening wind against them. By the time they caught site of the farmhouse they were exhausted. It was a little after six o'clock, and though it was still daylight, dark clouds came scudding across the sky from the north. Ellen threw herself to the ground at the top of the little hill. "We'd better rest here for a few minutes to get our breath back," she gasped. "We can keep an eye on the farmhouse without being seen."

"For God's sake, Ellen, this isn't a commando raid," Dave protested. "Sarah will be perfectly safe and well. At the moment she's probably in better shape than we are."

"You did say you weren't happy about the old trout, Dave," Paul reminded him.

"Yes, but I didn't think of witchcraft as a likely source of peril. I thought she may have been spying on us, intending to run off with our money and plastic while we were asleep, or something. Being turned into a fried breakfast never crossed my mind."

"I wish you'd take this more seriously, Dave, Sarah's life could be in danger!" Ellen scolded.

"Dave's right, Ellen, this witchcraft thing is a bit ludicrous," Paul commented.

"So why did you come with me? Why didn't you go back to the pub for your game of pool?"

"Er, actually, you told us to come, we weren't given an option, Ellen, and besides, we wanted to make sure you didn't come to any harm up here on your own," Dave answered, trying to justify his actions, but knowing that he would come off second best.

"Harm? Harm? Pray tell from what? From ghoulies and ghosties and lang-leggity beasties? That's fine after what you said just now about the sheer lunacy of anyone feeble-minded enough to believe that there may be just the tiniest remotest possibility that witchcraft is not an old wives' tale."

"No, Ellen, from rapists and wild dogs and drug pushers, actually!" Dave's voice was raised to a shout – a rare event.

"Ridiculous. You know damn well that I'm an expert at self-defence for one thing, stronger than most men for another, and you're forgetting that this isn't London. Watch my lips. This isn't London! You're pathetic. You haven't the guts to admit that you could be wrong but if the truth were told you're probably more worried about Sarah than I am. Sometimes I think you're always more worried about her than me. You never say anything if I'm a bit under the weather but you're the first to notice if Sarah's just a fraction off-colour."

"Hey! Hey! Cool it, you two." Paul saw that things were in danger of getting out of hand. "Don't be silly, Ellen. You're just a little overwrought, probably with concern. Now I'll wander off for a couple of minutes while you sort out this nonsense, then we'll go inside and make sure Sarah's okay, and we'll have a bite to eat and a mug of tea and everything will be fine. I'm going down the hill to the barn door. Meet me there when you're ready." Paul strolled away. They watched until he reached the foot of the hill then they turned to each other. Ellen burst into tears and threw herself into Dave's open arms.

"I'm so sorry, Dave. I said some ridiculous things. I didn't mean any of it. I know you love me. I can be so stupid at times."

"Don't worry, I love you too. Sarah's a good friend, but that's all. I never think of her any other way. She's one of the lads as far as I'm concerned."

"But she's such a natural beauty. She doesn't need make-up and she'd look good in the grubbiest of old rags. I have to work really hard at my appearance in order to look only half as good. It's so unfair."

"Nonsense. You're a very attractive girl." Dave kissed her, then took out his handkerchief to wipe away her tears. He'd done a lot of that these last few days. Perhaps Ellen was losing a grip on her hard image because she'd been away from work for so long. She patched up her smudged make-up then they went down to where Paul was waiting.

"You two okay now?" he asked tentatively.

"Of course we are." Dave grinned and put his arm round Ellen's shoulders. She smiled at him and nodded to Paul.

"Good. Let's go in, then."

They didn't knock; they just opened the door and walked in. Sarah was in the big armchair by the fire, her feet tucked under her, a shawl round her shoulders. She held a mug in her hands from which she sipped occasionally. As the others entered she looked up at them and smiled weakly. Ma was pouring the tea.

"Good. I've just made some tea. Sit down and have a drink while I get us something to eat. Have you been crying, deary? Is something wrong?" She examined Ellen's face. Ellen blushed and turned her face away.

100

"I just got a little overemotional, but I'm okay now," she said, feeling flustered. Did it show that much? She thought she'd done a pretty professional job with her make-up.

"Good. We'll have ham and cheese and strawberry jam. Sarah will help me. You three get warmed up by the fire. It's quite chilly for the time of year." Sarah rose silently and followed Ma into the pantry.

"Dave!" Ellen whispered loudly. "Is my face a mess?"

"No. Looks fine to me."

"You're no help at all. Paul, where do I need touching up?"

"I agree with Dave. I'd never have known you'd been crying if you hadn't admitted it. I don't know how she could tell." Sarah and Ma returned laden with food. They set about preparing the meal without a word to the others.

"Feeling better now?" Paul asked Sarah.

"Yes, better, thanks."

"She's just a bit out of sorts," Ma chimed in before Sarah had a chance to say any more. "Nothing to worry about. She's had some of my good herbal tea, and an early night will do her the world of good. Mind you, if it's as cold as this tomorrow I'm keeping her in. Best not to take too many chances. Now, get stuck in to these lovely sandwiches Sarah's made while I make another pot of tea." Sarah passed round plates of food and jars of pickle and mustard. She smiled as they ate enthusiastically. She didn't eat anything herself, but returned to her chair and sipped at the drink again, staring silently into the fire. It was almost dark when they finished the meal. Ma lit the big oil lamp and put it in its usual place on the kitchen table. Sarah helped Ma clear away what was left, then Ma announced she was off to bed.

"And it's about time you went up, young Sarah. Say goodnight and I'll see you to bed." Sarah said her goodnights feebly and bent down for Paul to kiss her cheek. Her face was cold, and her eyes lacked their usual sparkle, but Paul put this down to whatever was wrong, and thought no more about it. Ma ushered her out of the room. She reminded them to turn off the lamp, then disappeared up the stairs. The others sat in silence until they could no longer hear her chatting to Sarah.

"I hope it isn't anything serious." Paul broke the silence. "Her face was cold, and she didn't look her usual self."

"I've seen Sarah when she's ill quite a few times, and she always looks like that." Ellen and Sarah had been neighbours for three years before Ellen married Dave. They spent a lot of time together because they had similar interests, and they didn't fit in with the other people in the block. "This is the first time she's been ill since you married, isn't it, Paul?"

"Yes, it is. We've both been in excellent health for a long time. In fact, this is her first illness since we first met." Paul smiled to himself as he remembered being introduced to Sarah at Dave and Ellen's engagement party, and a few months later asking her to marry him as they danced together at their friends' wedding.

"Well, we've nothing to worry about. She's a tough old thing. She'll be fine by Monday," Ellen announced.

"I'm not so sure," said Dave, quietly.

"It's probably just a chill," Ellen went on. "You both got quite a soaking when you were messing about with the car on Friday night."

"It may be a chill, but I think there's more to it than that."

"As Ellen said earlier, it's probably a bad period or something," Paul reminded him.

"No, I think there's something Sarah's not telling. Ever since we got back Ma has spoken for her. Sarah hasn't said anything other than to answer questions, and even then, not always. You can't shut her up usually. I think Sarah is hiding something, and Ma is behind it. It's as though Ma has some strange power over her."

"Well knock me down with a feather! Am I awake or asleep?" Ellen pinched herself. "Ow! No, I'm not dreaming. Definitely awake. Dave, I don't know how you can sit there and say these things after what you said when we left the pub. Paul and I had lost our marbles then, but it's quite alright for you to talk about 'strange powers' even though you have only the flimsiest of evidence. Well, I'm not going to stand for it. Either you stop this ridiculous nonsense and apologise to Paul and me, or I'm off to bed and you can sleep down here tonight. Do I make myself clear?"

"Perfectly clear. I'm sorry, I didn't mean it to sound like that. I apologise."

"Apology accepted. Sarah always goes quiet when she's unwell. There's nothing to worry about. Let's change the subject." They had a look at the map and discussed what they might do tomorrow. On the far side of the village there was a footpath leading to some high ground, so they decided to go in search of it after lunch, weather permitting.

103

As the morning would have to be given up to more jobs for Ma, they thought an early night would not go amiss. Ellen and Dave visited the toilet then went up, leaving Paul on the sofa, gazing into the fire, fondly remembering doing his duty as Dave's best man and dancing all night with Ellen's chief bridesmaid. He followed them up half an hour later.

Paul was in the middle of cleaning his teeth when he suddenly realised he hadn't turned out the lamp. He quickly finished them, then went downstairs to turn it off.

"Paul!" He felt his heart miss a beat. He froze for a moment, then pulled himself together.

"I, er, forgot the lamp. Came back down to turn it off, but as you're here I'll leave it." He turned to go.

"Come here, Paul." Ma's voice drew him towards her. He wanted to go back upstairs but couldn't resist the summons. How did she know it was him? He was sure she couldn't see the door from where she sat. He shuffled over to the sofa and sat down. Ma looked at him curiously, as though they had only just met and she was examining his face for tell-tale signs of some personality defect or a traumatic childhood. After a short while, she spoke to him. She spoke softly and gently, and smiled kindly, but he didn't like the look in her eyes. "Your wife is not well. We need to talk about her. Tomorrow, when the others go out, you stay behind. We'll talk then."

"But if the weather's bad they're staying in."

"When they go out tomorrow afternoon, we'll talk. Not a word to anyone about this. Not even Sarah. She needs rest." Paul rose silently and went to bed.

Chapter 7

The next morning they were wakened by Ma banging on the door again. Ellen slid out of bed and pulled back the curtain. The daylight streamed in and she shut her eyes quickly. She slowly opened them again and looked outside. The sun was already in view from this side of the house, so they must have had a later call. She sat on the bed and prodded Dave into life.

"What sort of day is it?" he enquired from beneath the blankets.

"Blue sky, no clouds, sunny, just right for a relaxing walk to that place we found on the map last night."

"How's your back today?"

"Actually," she stood up and swung her hips a couple of times. "Actually, it's fine. I must've lain differently."

"Not surprised. You slept diagonally last night and kept pushing me out. It's a wonder I got any sleep at all," Dave complained. He buried himself in the bed while Ellen washed and dressed.

"I think I'll wear my denim skirt today. I haven't worn it since we arrived, and it's practical for doing odd jobs and for walking. It'll go well with my brown sweater, don't you think?" Dave didn't answer. She turned to see him laying across the bed asleep. She grabbed a foot and tugged. He spluttered into life again and crawled to the foot of the bed. He sat her on his lap and kissed her.

"Get dressed, Dave, it's after breakfast time already. We've jobs to do to earn our keep, and I want to be finished before lunch so that we don't waste half the afternoon on such a glorious day as this." She dressed quickly, then, after waking Dave again, went downstairs.

105

Paul and Sarah had got up in silence. Sarah sat dreamily on the bed gazing out of the window while Paul washed.

"Are you feeling better today, love?" he asked.

"Yes, better, thanks," she replied.

"What do you think it is? A chill or something?"

"Yes, a chill, perhaps." Paul put his arm around her shoulders and withdrew it immediately.

"You're like ice! Put some warm clothes on instead of just sitting there." He pulled a thick sweater from their bag and handed it to her. She put it on, slowly and laboriously. "Hurry up and get washed. I'm going down for breakfast." He left the room and hurried down the stairs, humming to himself. Ma was distributing the fried meal onto three plates as Paul entered.

"I've not done any for Sarah," she said. "I'll do her some porridge instead."

"Good idea. She doesn't look like having much of an appetite. What do you think is wrong with her?"

"Later, young Paul, later. When the others are out, we'll talk in the front parlour." Just as Ma finished speaking Ellen bounded into the kitchen, followed by Dave. "No back problems this morning, I see!" Ma laughed.

"No. I haven't felt better for months. Dave didn't sleep well, though." Ellen pointed at Dave who was yawning and rubbing his eyes. "Still, he'll probably be alright after a brisk walk." Sarah wandered in, wearing the sweater and a pair of jeans. She smiled weakly and made her way over to the armchair by the fire. "Good morning, Sarah," Ellen smiled cheerfully and went across to her. "How are you today?" Sarah looked up at her and smiled.

"She's a bit better," Paul answered for her.

"Yes, better, thanks," echoed Sarah.

"But she's still not well," he went on. "I think she should have a good rest today. It'll give her a better chance of surviving the long journey tomorrow."

"Come along, you three, breakfast's getting cold." Ma fussed around, ushering them to their seats. "Sarah and me'll have some porridge later. I'll give her some herbal tea to get her going." She disappeared into the pantry and returned with a big mug into which she poured some boiling water, added honey from a pot on the table, then gave it to Sarah, and wrapped the shawl round her shoulders. Sarah sipped the brew obediently. "When you've finished get yourselves out for a breath of fresh air, but don't go far. It's not long to dinner, 'cause I let you lie too long," she instructed the others. "I'll see to young Sarah here."

"But what about earning our keep?" asked Ellen. "Don't you have some jobs for us?"

"Nay, lass. Not on Sabbath. Day of rest, you know. We only do things as can't be put off, like cooking and caring for sick. You can do some tomorrow, if you want, while Dave's mending your carriage." Ellen and Paul glanced at each other and suppressed their laughter. Dave was watching Sarah intently.

"Let's have that walk now," he said abruptly and went outside.

"Bye, love," Paul said as he bent to kiss her.

"Yes, bye," she answered feebly.

Dave strode off along the route of Saturday morning's walk, hands thrust deep into his pockets, head down, and with huge quick strides. Ellen and Paul called on him to slow down, but he ignored them. Eventually they caught up, and Ellen grasped his arm firmly and pulled him round to face them.

"What on earth is wrong, Dave? I've never seen you like this before. Is it something I've said?" Ellen asked with a look of concern. Dave sat cross-legged on the damp grass and covered his face with his big hands.

"No, it's not you, love," he said at last. He grasped her hand and squeezed it gently. "No, it's Sarah. She's more than just ill. Ma's done something to her and I can't work out what it is."

"Look, Dave," Paul placed his hand on Dave's shoulder. "We talked about this last night. There's nothing to worry about. Ellen says Sarah's always like this when she's ill, and she's known Sarah longer than you and me put together. The only thing to worry about is how many times we'll have to stop on the way home tomorrow, and if she gets too bad we'll stay somewhere for a few days and get the train home. You and Ellen needn't worry."

"I'm not worrying," said Ellen indignantly.

"What's wrong with you?" Dave shouted, leaping to his feet. "Are you both blind?" He went a few steps and stood with his back to them, hands on hips, his head thrown back. Ellen looked at Paul with a worried expression. Paul went round to face Dave while Ellen grasped his arm.

"This afternoon, when you go out, I'll stay in with Sarah. That way I'll see if there's anything untoward going on. It'll give you two some time alone together as well. The four of us living in each other's pockets for a fortnight is bound to have put a bit of a strain on us all. Ellen and I have got to know each other much better, so we're noticing things which we previously didn't. The same probably applies to you and Sarah - you've become very close friends. Ellen says this is quite normal behaviour for Sarah when she's ill. That's right, isn't it?"

"Oh, yes! When she lived next door to me there was one occasion I thought she was on drugs or something, she acted so strangely, but it was just a dose of 'flu'."

"Perhaps I am a bit on edge. You're probably right." Dave grinned and put his hands round their shoulders. "But I'm glad you've decided to stay in, Paul. I'm still not sure about Ma. Let's go back now."

"Dave, if Ma wanted to harm us, she's had plenty of chances. She could've poisoned us on Friday night, but we're still here."

"Yes, Ellen, you're right, as usual. I'm being silly, aren't I?"

"Just like Ellen and I were at the pub, Dave." They all laughed. They slowly made their way back to the house. Dave had covered quite a distance in his agitated state, and it was approaching noon when they opened the kitchen door.

"That smells good, Ma," Dave said, sniffing the air. "I can hardly wait for lunch."

"Dinner's nearly ready," Ma replied with a broad smile. Sit yourselves down, I'll not keep you waiting longer than needs be. Sarah, pop into pantry for salt and pepper, love. Now, mind your heads, it's hot and I've got short arms." Ma deposited a Yorkshire pudding on each plate and put a big jug of gravy in the middle of the table. She sat down and picked up her knife and fork. "Well, are you going to eat, or not?"

"Of course we are." Dave said, grinning from ear to ear. "It's just that we've never seen Yorkshire puddings this size before."

"No," Ellen joined in. "We usually have small ones, with our meat and veg."

"Anything smaller than this isn't a proper Yorkshire pudding," said Ma, indignantly. "You'll have meat and vegetables next. There's no room on the plate for them." Dave enthusiastically demolished the Yorkshire Pudding which must have been about ten inches across and five inches high at the edge. When the others had caught up, Ma brought in another two to share out, but only Dave and Paul took up the offer.

"These are the best Yorkshire puddings I've ever tasted, Ma," Paul said, as he finished his second one. "I could quite easily make a meal of a few of those with a drop of gravy. I wouldn't need anything else."

"I agree," Dave grinned. "We must have your recipe. They're delicious."

"Yes, I enjoyed them, too," Ellen added. "What about you, Sarah?"

"Yes, very nice," she smiled. Sarah had eaten with the others for the first time since her illness, and Paul was relieved that she was beginning to show signs of normality. She had hardly spoken to any of them, other than to answer questions, and Paul was wondering if Dave had been right after all, but her empty plate put his mind at rest. Her smile seemed a little less vacant now, and she was warmer to touch, although still much colder than usual. Paul thought about his impending talk with Ma about Sarah's health, and tried to think what it could be she wanted to tell him that was so important that the others must be kept in the dark, but he couldn't latch on to anything which seemed even remotely possible. He decided to forget about it until later. Perhaps it was something quite trivial which Ma felt embarrassed about. He remembered Ellen's remarks about the older generations and felt sure that must be it. Ma brought in tureens of mashed potato, turnip, parsnips and carrots, and dished them out generously, then produced a plate of roast lamb, and gave them each a few thick slices. She topped up the gravy pot from a pan and sat down to eat. They ate in silence, but for the occasional compliment, then, when they had finished, sat back in their seats, and heaped praises on the embarrassed cook. Ma giggled coyly, then rose to her feet while Ellen gathered the plates.

"Who's for pudding?" she asked innocently.

"Good grief! There's more?" said Ellen in disbelief. "I can feel my clothes getting tighter already!"

"I've made a lovely sponge pudding. You'll enjoy it," Ma said as she hunted in a cupboard for some bowls. "Get the spoons out, Ellen, and pass me that big one."

A few minutes later they were tucking into the hot pudding. Dave finished well ahead of the others and had a second helping. Eventually they could eat no more, and all agreed it had been an excellent meal. Even Sarah, who had passed the entire meal in silence, expressed her gratitude, but not in her usual flamboyant style. They retired to the sofa and armchairs for tea and sat gazing contentedly into the fire for a while. Paul broke the calm by getting up and collecting the empty mugs.

"You two go on out and have a walk," he said to Ellen and Dave. "Sarah and I will do the dishes for Ma. She's a lot better now, but I don't think it would be wise to go out today, it's a bit too chilly."

"You leave the dishes to me, Paul." Ma told him. "I'll do them. It keeps me busy. You're on holiday, anyway." Paul acknowledged defeat and sat down again. He put his arm round Sarah's shoulders while Ellen and Dave put their jackets on. Sarah smiled at him.

"See you later," she called meekly as they left. Ma pulled a thick blanket from a cupboard and passed it to Paul.

"Wrap this round Sarah and put another log on the fire. I'll be finished clearing up soon, then we'll have our little chat. Make sure she's comfy." Paul did as instructed, and when he looked up Ma was standing by the door to the stairs, hands on hips, with a strange look on her face. He couldn't decide whether it was a smile or a scowl, and he felt sure she seemed bigger, too, but perhaps it was just that she seemed that way in comparison to the small door. Her eyes sparkled as she spoke. "Now then, Paul, come into the parlour." Paul followed her to the foot of the stairs, then through a door on the right which he hadn't previously noticed. He hesitated as he felt the cold stale air meet his face. "Hurry up! We've got a lot to get through." Paul wondered what she meant, and began to feel uneasy, but he couldn't turn back. His feet took him into the front room even though he didn't want to go.

Chapter 8

Hand in hand Ellen and Dave trudged across the vegetable garden and up the hill. They paused at the top to admire the view, then trotted down the other side. As they reached the heather Ellen stopped and pulled Dave back. She hugged him and they kissed passionately. They sat down on the dry grass and held each other tightly for a few moments, then Ellen looked into Dave's eyes and smiled sweetly.

"It's good to be alone together at last," she said. "I'm glad they stayed in. Not that I want Sarah to be ill, of course, but it was becoming a bit of a strain being with them all the time."

"Yes, I know what you mean," Dave grinned at her. He put his arm round her shoulders and they sat for a while watching the birds and rabbits, then they got up and slowly made their way across the heather to the road. They strolled down the long hill into the village, along the main street, and past the pub. The churchyard had a wooden seat, where they sat and listened to the birds for about ten minutes. Dave pulled a bag of sweets from his jacket pocket and began to eat.

"You pig! I don't know how you can eat anything after that huge dinner!" Ellen scolded. Dave just grinned and carried on eating. He offered her the bag. She shook her head in disgust and got up. The gravestones were grouped in families, and Ellen wandered from one cluster to the next, unable to find any signs of the Sheppertons. She strolled round the church twice, making sure she hadn't missed any, then returned to the seat where Dave had finished his sweets. "Perhaps they are buried somewhere else," she contemplated. "There aren't any signs of the

Shepperton family, so they must've come from another place originally, and might have wanted to go back home for their final resting place." She held out a hand and pulled Dave to his feet. "Come on, get the map out, let's find that hill." She led him to the gate and stopped. They kissed in the shadow of a big yew tree, then ambled away from the village. At a crossroads Dave stopped and consulted the map.

"I think we need to go left here," he said slowly. Ellen gave a sharp cry which made Dave look up. He felt a vice-like grip at his elbow and turned his head to see the two old men from the pub, one grasping his arm, the other holding Ellen's. They did not look very friendly.

"What's going on?" Ellen demanded, trying to break free. "Let go of me, or you'll regret it. I'm an expert at self-defence."

"We'll not harm you," one of them said. "There's no need to worry. We just want to talk."

"What about?" asked Dave. He struggled against his captor but was unable to release the sinewy hand.

"Just want to put the record straight," the other answered. "Granny Carter wants to see you. Come with us."

"Who's Granny Carter?" Ellen demanded, still struggling.

"She's our mother," replied one of the men. "But everybody round here calls her Granny Carter. My name's Tom. This is my brother, Bert. Now if you'll come with us, please." They had no choice but to go along with them. The two men never relaxed their grip once. They led them back towards the village, then turned right through a gap in the hedge into a little garden with a picturesque cottage that

114

wouldn't have been out of place on a calendar or a box of chocolates. As they neared the door, it swung open, and they were gently pushed inside by Tom and Bert. They found themselves in a dark hall lit only by the daylight from the front door. The door swung shut, plunging the hall into total darkness. A door opened at the other end, silhouetting a tiny figure, who beckoned to them.

"This way. Come on through," she said quietly, and disappeared into the room. They followed her into a large kitchen not unlike that at the farm. Electrical appliances and running water were the only substantial difference. Tom and Bert followed, and seated them on the sofa round the fire, then busied themselves making tea. Their mysterious hostess sat in an armchair and smiled at them. She was short and thin, slightly round-shouldered, with grey hair tied in a bun. Her long black dress came down almost to her ankles, and a white shawl covered her shoulders. Her eyes twinkled as she smiled benignly. "My boys told me you were hearing about the Sheppertons from old Pickering, so I told them to bring you here so I could make sure you heard something nearer the truth. I don't like folk to go away with their heads full of lies about our village and its history, so I always make sure I say my piece. Speak the truth and shame the devil. That's what I always say. There's some round here will tell you anything for a free drink, but not us Carters. No, we're as honest as the day is long. Oh, here's Bert with the tea, and Tom with some biscuits. Help yourselves, don't be shy now." Granny Carter had spoken without pausing for breath, despite Ellen's attempts to interrupt. She now paused to take her teacup from Bert, so Ellen took the opportunity.

115

"Well I think it's a bit much, really. There are laws against kidnap, you know. All we wanted was to have a little walk in the countryside when we were accosted by your sons and brought here against our will. How do we know what you'll tell is true, anyway? You might have poisoned our tea in order to steal our money, for all we know."

"We'll not poison you!" Granny Carter was obviously offended by the suggestion. "We'll not take your money, either! We're honest folk and always have been." She glared at Ellen. "My boys wouldn't harm a fly. Everybody knows that. Who'd believe that a great strapping couple like you could be taken against their will by these two? They're both over seventy. Now if you've calmed down, I'll tell you what you want to know about old Mrs Shepperton."

"Look, we're sorry. Ellen didn't mean to offend you," Dave said. "It's just that we weren't asked if we wanted to come here, we were brought here. If Tom and Bert had explained, well, we'd have been more than happy to come and listen. Now that we're here, we're all ears. Please, tell us what you know about the Sheppertons. I'm Dave, by the way, and this is my wife, Ellen." He stood up and held out his hand. Granny Carter shook it firmly, then held hers out to Ellen, who reciprocated and smiled.

"Sorry about that," she said. "In London people behave somewhat differently to here."

"You're drinking my tea, so you can't have meant it, can you?" They all chuckled at this, and any hint of hostility vanished. "You see, them Pickerings, they're new to the village. Old Granddad Pickering was the first to be born here. They're from further east, towards the coast. Us Carters, we've been here since the first houses was built so

116

we know what's what. Old Pickering just tells the interesting bits, and even then he often gets it wrong. I don't suppose he told you about what Ma Shepperton did for the womenfolk of the village, did he?"

"He told us she gave advice on caring for sick children," Ellen pointed out.

"He probably doesn't even know. The Sheppertons were long gone before I was born, but my mother benefitted greatly from Ma's help and advice. Things are different now, but in them days a woman's duty was to have babies and to bring them up, and if a couple had been married for a year and there were no signs of little ones, well, tongues would wag, if you know what I mean. The couple's parents might have words with each other, each blaming the other side of the family, and there's many a feud started that way. Well, if a young wife were having difficulty falling wrong, she would go to see Ma Shepperton for help. My mother had her first because of Ma's influence. She was a wonderful old soul to the young women of this village, and it's a disgrace that old Pickering should say any different. She would give you herbal mixtures to make you more fertile, feel your belly to see if there were anything wrong, give advice about ... well I'll not go into that in mixed company, but she'd give good advice, and she was never known to fail. When you were expecting she'd make sure all was as it should be, and she'd help with the birth as well. Why, half the village wouldn't be here today if it weren't for her medicines and skills."

"Granddad Pickering didn't mention any of this," Dave remarked. "He said she was a witch."

"That she was, Dave, that she was, but not all witches is bad, you know."

117

"So you believe in witchcraft?" Ellen asked.

"Yes. Of course. Don't you?"

"I'm not sure, but Dave certainly doesn't. He says it doesn't hold water when compared with his scientific training and knowledge, but I like to keep an open mind on such things. Please tell us more about the Sheppertons. What about Mr Shepperton? Granddad Pickering said he was a bit unfriendly."

"Unfriendly he wasn't. Just a bit quiet, a bit shy, didn't mix easily. A bit like Tom and Bert here, but nobody would call them unfriendly. I must admit, he gave the impression that he was a bit sour in the village, but those that met him at home on his farm said he was a different man. Kind, gentle, wonderful with animals, just like a Yorkshire St Francis. His animals always grew bigger and better than the other farmers, partly because of his kindness towards them, and partly because of Ma's ... let's say her involvement." Dave and Ellen had looked round at Tom and Bert at the mention of their names. They were standing with their backs to the dresser and were leaning against it. Friendly was one word which didn't immediately spring to mind. They had their arms firmly folded, and watched the young couple with dour faces, occasionally fidgeting. Granny Carter turned to them. "Don't shuffle like that when we've got company. Show some respect for our visitors." She turned back to her guests. "I'm sorry about them. I won't let them smoke in the kitchen, you see. Front parlour's not big enough for five, especially when four of them's on the large side, not wanting to be rude, of course, but you're not exactly small."

Ellen turned to the brothers. "If you want to smoke, we don't mind if you want to go outside. Please don't let us stop you." They glanced at Granny, who nodded her permission.

"Thankyou kindly," said Bert as he left through the back door, closely followed by Tom. Ellen felt more relaxed now that they were gone and spoke to Granny again.

"Granddad Pickering told us about an incident with a dog. Is there any truth in it?"

"Oh, yes. Jack Cooper's old dog, Patch. Well, sadly to say, George did kill the poor beast, but it was an accident. He never hurt an animal in his life, apart from slaughtering, you understand, other than old Patch. He were heartbroken when he realised what he'd done, but it were too late then. Mind you, I reckon he didn't regret landing one on Jack's brainless son, Billy. Not for one minute would I believe that! The boy made money out of violence, and violence was something George hated. But I suppose he was caught unawares and wasn't as quick thinking as he might have been. Yes, he killed the poor dog. Poor old George." She sat back and stared into the distance with a vacant expression, as though reliving history.

"You obviously remember it well," Dave said. She rounded on him, instantly back in the present.

"I wasn't born then! I've already told you that. How could I remember it?" She was leaning forward, her contorted face thrust into his. Dave sat back quickly, momentarily frightened by this sudden display of aggression. She slowly returned to her original position, shocked at her own behaviour. After smoothing her ruffled dress and hair, she apologised profusely. "It's a family failing - temper. All the women in my family have hot tempers. I control mine as best as I can, but now and again

119

it slips out, particularly when I'm caught off guard. Would you like some more tea?" She got up and went to the table. She stood with her back to them for a few seconds pulling herself together, then returned with the teapot and milk jug. Both accepted the tea, Dave because he liked it, and Ellen because she didn't want to see the old lady angry again.

"We've heard about George having a bad leg. Do you know what happened?" Dave asked cautiously after Granny had settled herself.

"That was a tragic accident, that was. He was sharpening some axes, in the barn, when the big axe flew out of his hands and struck him on the ankle. His ankle was shattered, but he was lucky. The corner of the axe just missed his foot. He had huge feet, did George, and it missed taking his toe off by a couple of inches. His ankle didn't mend properly, despite Ma's efforts, 'cause she were an expert at women's troubles, but not so strong on things like broken bones, you see, and he was a cripple from that day on." Ellen had turned pale. She looked at Dave, who sat in silence, studying the old woman's face.

"Come on, Dave, it's time we were getting back for tea," she said hurriedly. Dave glanced at his watch and nodded.

"Yes, we must be going," he said, grasping Ellen's trembling hand. "But I would like to ask a question before we go. What happened to them? Ellen's looked in the churchyard, and there's no sign of them there."

"Why, bless my soul! She was a witch! I've told you that already, and so has old Pickering. Witches don't die! They just, well, they go on forever, sort of, in their own way. They disappear, then come back when they're needed, if they're good witches like Ma Shepperton, that is."

"Okay, so what about George?"

"He was her 'familiar'. That's like a kindred spirit that goes about with her. Most witches have cats or crows as familiars, but they say, and I believe them, they say she turned him into a pig. Now then, you're welcome to stay longer, but if you must go for tea, you must go. Where are you staying?"

"At Shepperton Farm."

"And who are you staying with, you and your friends?"

"An old lady, calls herself 'Ma'. Didn't tell us her name." Granny Carter's eyes twinkled as she described Ma as well as though she were in the same room. Dave and Ellen stood speechless, nodding in agreement with the description. Eventually Granny threw herself back into the chair and uttered something between a laugh and a cackle. She mopped her brow and smiled, with an evil twinkle in her eye.

"Mercy me! She's back! Ma Shepperton has come back to the village, like she said she would. You and Sarah will be pregnant before the year's out. You mark my words."

"Dave, get me out of here," Ellen whispered, clutching Dave's arm in panic. "Please, get me out of here, quickly." She was almost hysterical, so Dave quickly thanked Granny Carter for her hospitality, and they left. They marched up the hill to the church, where Ellen flung her arms around Dave and burst into tears. Dave stood in silence with his arms round her shoulders for five minutes, while she sobbed bitterly against his chest. She looked up at him. "Dave, I'm scared. I don't like all this witchcraft business."

"I don't believe in witchcraft, at least I think I don't, but I know what you mean. I don't like it either."

"That business with the axe ..."

"That could be coincidence. What worries me is that she knew Sarah's name without us mentioning it. I don't remember Sarah being mentioned in the pub either. Noone, other than Ma, knows Sarah's with us, and Ma hasn't been on her own long enough to get down to the village and back, unless she went out in the middle of the night of course, and ..."

"Oh, shut up about bloody Sarah!" Ellen burst into tears again. Dave led her into the churchyard where they sat on the wooden seat until Ellen had calmed down.

"Sorry, love, I'm just trying to work out which bits don't add up."

"You and your analytical mind! Sometimes I think you've spent too much time with those computers and you're becoming like them." She got up and wandered through the gravestones. Dave opened his mouth to speak, but decided silence was the better option. He fidgeted for a moment, then resorted to a bag of sweets for comfort. Ellen returned to the seat a few minutes later. She sat beside him and took his hand in hers and leant against him.

"Feeling better now?"

"Yes, thanks. I suppose it could all be coincidence. We could have mentioned Sarah in conversation in the pub. Perhaps one of the Carters visited the farm when we were out. I'm being silly. Tell me I'm being silly and I'll feel a lot better."

"No, there's still one thing I'm not happy about. She was talking as though she had actually been there and met them, but when I suggested that she flew off the handle and jumped down my throat. There must be something I don't believe is true, but I'm not certain what it is."

"When you've eliminated the impossible, then what remains must be true, no matter how improbable. Come along, Watson. Mrs Hudson will have our tea ready!" She rose and hauled him to his feet. "I'm being silly, and as a result you're being over-cautious. Let's go back now, and we'll not tell the others what's happened until we're safely back in London." So saying she took his hand and led him out to the road and back up the hill.

Chapter 9

They wandered slowly through the village, now much quieter than yesterday, enjoying the scenery. By the time they had reached the other side Ellen was much calmer. She thought about the events of the last two days and examined her own attitude. She was quite surprised by her own reactions, now that she thought about it. Her mother had always criticised her for being unemotional and independent, insisting that she would "never find a man unless she changed her ways" and never failing to remind her that she would like to be a Grandmother. Ellen had always insisted that she didn't want children, and that her strong domineering character was essential to success in her career; she had always despised her schoolfriends who had given up promising futures to become 'baby factories' and stay at home like good little wives doing the housework and watching afternoon television. She felt guilty in a way about openly showing emotion in front of her friends, and it had happened more than once recently. Sarah had a similar but less aggressive outlook, and looked up to Ellen, or so Ellen thought, as a shining example of how to be a successful career woman. Ellen thought she was letting the side down by behaving like a silly blonde in a forties movie. What really worried Ellen was that she didn't feel that the way she had been behaving was wrong; she only knew that it was uncharacteristic. It felt quite normal. Perhaps her hard-faced image was beginning to wear thin. Dave and Sarah both knew what she was really like, so why shouldn't the rest of the world? Why should she carry on with this charade that had been so useful for the last fifteen years?

"I don't know!" she muttered under her breath.

"What don't you know, love?" Dave enquired.

"Eh? Oh, I'm not really sure I know anything, Dave. This holiday has been ... well, different. I've enjoyed it, but these last few days ... I haven't been feeling myself. Emotionally, I mean. It's been a good break, and very refreshing, both physically and mentally, but I've been more than just a little confused about some things."

"Yes, I know," Dave said quietly. He put an arm around her waist and looked into her surprised face. "You're certainly not the girl I married," he grinned at her, "but I like you better like this.   I only wish you'd show your real self more often." Ellen looked away and put her free hand to her forehead.

"I'm sorry, Dave," she said after a few seconds. "I'm ..."

"Don't say a word. You'll only confuse yourself more. This country life has done you the world of good, but it's not your home. When we get back to London, back on our home ground, you'll be able to think more clearly. Until then, just carry on enjoying the break."

"Yes, you're right. The pace of life here isn't agreeing with me." They stopped walking and Dave kissed her tenderly. Ellen smiled at him lovingly, then they set off up the long hill back towards the old farm. As they caught sight of the farmhouse they both suddenly remembered the strange events of the afternoon. There were no signs of life, but this was to be expected. Ma had expressly forbidden any non-essential work, so they assumed Paul and Sarah would either be out for a walk or resting by the fire. They went in to find their friends on the sofa with a couple of paperbacks, while their hostess slept in the armchair.

"Well, have you been up to anything interesting? Are you feeling better, Sarah?" Ellen asked, cheerfully.

"Yes, better, thanks." Sarah answered.

"What have you been doing?   Have you been out at all? It's a beautiful day."

"No, we stayed in," Paul said, and carried on reading. Ellen turned to Dave, who returned her glance and shrugged his shoulders. She turned back to them.

"We've been down to the other end of the village and had tea with Granny Carter."

"Tea. That's nice," Paul commented without looking up from his book.

"It's nice to know we've been missed." Ellen began to sound annoyed. She handed her jacket to Dave who hung it up with his behind the door. "I'm going upstairs for a wash." This brought no response. She stormed up the stairs and slammed the bedroom door. The sudden noise disturbed Ma, who rubbed her eyes then got up.

"So! Been down to the village, have we? You'll be hungry then. Granny Carter's a good soul, but she's not one for feeding folk. I suppose all you got was a mug of tea and a couple of biscuits. I'd better see to sorting something out for you to eat. It wouldn't do for you to die on me, would it now?" She winked at Dave who suddenly felt uncomfortable. "Sarah, let's you and me get tea ready." Sarah closed her book immediately and followed Ma through to the pantry. Dave sat next to Paul and attempted conversation.

"What've you been doing? Reading?"

"Yes, reading."

"Been out anywhere? Done anything else?"

"No, nothing else."

"Are you alright, mate? Hope you haven't caught what Sarah had."

"No, I'm alright." Dave knocked the book from Paul's hands and shook him by the shoulders. He frowned at Paul, who seemed completely unperturbed by this sudden attack.

"No, you're not alright, and I want to know what's going on." Paul looked up at him with sleepy eyes and smiled dreamily.

"Relax, Dave. I'm alright." Dave still wasn't satisfied, but didn't know what to do next, so he released his grip on Paul and went upstairs to talk to Ellen.

Ellen was having a wash when Dave burst in and sat down heavily on the end of the bed. He perched his chin on his hands and looked at Ellen.

"What's up with you?" she asked, continuing to wash.

"It's Paul and Sarah. Ma's got both of them now. She's done something to them while we were out. It'll be us next."

"You're getting carried away, Dave." She carried on washing, then looked up. "Anyway, remember what Granny Carter said, Mrs Shepperton was into obstetrics. She wasn't very good when it came to men. If Ma is a witch, if she is Mrs Shepperton, the only thing we need worry about is me becoming pregnant. I've been thinking about it while I've been up here."

"You're not taking me seriously. I don't believe for one minute that Ma is the Shepperton woman, but I do believe that she is up to something. Perhaps she's been giving them drugs or something."

"You could have something there. Sarah is the type to experiment, but I wouldn't have thought Paul would be interested. Anyway, neither of them smoke, and hyperdermics don't exactly grow on trees, especially round here."

"No. It's completely out of character for Paul to willingly try anything like that, but suppose she gave them magic mushrooms or something. Paul could have downed a plateful without realising."

"Yes, you're obviously intent on building up quite a solid argument, but there's one thing missing. What is her motive? Why, if your theory is correct, does she want to get them, and presumably us as well, high as kites? She's already refused our money, so what is it? This is where your reasoning falls down." Dave got up and walked across to the window. He looked out, as though searching for inspiration.

"Yes, you're right. No motive. I don't understand."

"I think you're worrying needlessly. There's nothing wrong with Sarah apart from a chill, and Paul's just having an off day. Anyway, I'm the one that worries. You're supposed to be the calm one." They both laughed. Ellen slid her arms around Dave's waist. He turned around and kissed her. There was a knock at the door.

"Tea's ready!" Paul's voice sounded quite normal.

"We'll be down in a minute," Ellen called to him. "Paul is fine. It's you who's been at 'certain substances'," she teased. The expression on Dave's face told her that he wasn't amused. "Sorry, only joking. Let's go down for tea, and I promise I'll not have too many mushrooms."

They entered the kitchen to be met by a table full of food; sandwiches, biscuits, home-made cakes and scones, pots and jars of pickle, jam, mustard, but not a mushroom

128

to be seen anywhere. Ma, Sarah, and Paul were already sitting at the table with full plates and big mugs of tea.

"Come along," Ma greeted them. "There's plenty to eat. You'll be hungry after your long walk. Tuck in." She smiled cheerfully at them as they took their seats and began to eat. Dave was still not happy and sat with a dour face. His usual big appetite was noticeable by its absence. Ma eyed him for a few minutes as he picked at his food in a disinterested manner, then she said, "What's wrong with you, Dave? Your plate's normally empty by now. Are you feeling under the weather or something?"

"No, I'm fine, thanks." The last thing he wanted to do was to let her know he was on to her. If he was to discover her motive he must appear completely unsuspicious at all times. "I've just been thinking about something. That's all," he said. "Thinking about repairing the car tomorrow." He set about eating, but didn't enjoy the food as much as usual, even though it was excellent. Ellen quickly cottoned on and did her bit by distracting Ma.

"These scones are beautiful. Do you have some secret ingredient?" she asked.

"No, dearie, nothing out of the ordinary," she smiled knowingly. "There's nothing fancy about any of my cooking. It's just the way my mother taught me. Good ingredients, cleanliness, and care over the preparation are all that's needed to make good scones."

"Well I think there must be something. Whenever I make scones they are horrid. Not that I make them very often, but I never have much success. The last lot I made were so bad that even Dave wouldn't eat them!" Ellen and Ma laughed heartily at this. Ellen kicked Dave under the table, and he joined in. Sarah and Paul chuckled weakly.

129

The meal dragged on, with Ellen doing most of the talking to keep Ma occupied. Eventually they finished and Ma got up to make a fresh pot of tea. "For God's sake, try and be a bit more lively!" Ellen whispered angrily to Dave. "I'm running out of things to talk about. If we sit and say nothing she'll think something's up, and the way you ate your food didn't help either."

"I'm trying to think!" Dave whispered back.

"There'll be plenty of time for that after she's gone to bed. Try to act normal." Ma returned with the kettle full of water, and put it on the fire, then began clearing the table. She asked Paul and Sarah to help, which they did obediently. Five minutes later they were all sat around the fire with mugs of hot tea. Dave was still not his usual cheerful self, so once again Ellen lead the conversation to keep Ma occupied. "They tell me that country folk are experts when it comes to the weather, Ma. What do you expect tomorrow to be like? We've a long drive ahead of us."

"Let me see," Ma grunted, levering herself out of her chair and strolling to the kitchen window. "There'll be no clouds tonight," she said slowly, "and there's no wind to speak of so I reckon it'll be much the same as today - dry and bright." She made her way back to her chair, patting Dave on the shoulder as she passed him. He shuddered and shifted uncomfortably in his seat. "I suppose you'll   be wanting an early start," she said as she leaned back in the chair. She winked at Dave, knowingly.

"Er, yes," Dave spluttered. "We have a long way to go, and I have the car to fix tomorrow as well. And I'm not sure I can count on any help from Sarah."

"Well, I'll not keep you up any longer than necessary. I'm off to bed, and you'd be well advised to do the same." She smiled and bade them all a good night, then disappeared up the stairs. They sat in silence for a moment, then Dave relaxed into the chair a bit more.

"Thank goodness she's gone!" he muttered quietly. Ellen rounded on him.

"Thank goodness she's gone? I don't know how you can say such a thing! I was the one doing all the hard work! I was the one that kept the old biddy occupied while you did your best to make her suspicious! I was the one that distracted her so that she wouldn't see you behaving like an absolute moron! And you've got the nerve to say to me 'thank goodness she's gone' as though you'd acted completely naturally all evening! You're pathetic." Ellen folded her arms firmly and looked away from Dave who cowered under this tirade. Sarah and Paul sat unperturbed through the whole exchange, almost as though it wasn't actually happening. Dave noticed this and touched Ellen's knee. She turned abruptly, ready to launch another attack, until she saw where Dave was looking. Her mouth hung open as she looked back to Dave's anxious face. Dave addressed them quietly, trying not to let his voice show the fear that engulfed him. Under normal circumstances they would both be chuckling at this disagreement.

"Sarah, Paul, are you alright?"

"Yes, of course we are," Paul replied dreamily. "We're fine, aren't we, Sarah?"

"Yes, fine," said Sarah, feebly. Ellen now began to understand Dave's concern. She regularly sounded off at her husband, but this usually provoked hysterical laughter from Sarah, and complaints about the noise from Paul. This

131

passive acceptance of her attack was totally out of character for both of them.

"You'd better get an early night," she told them firmly. "We've a long trip and you both look tired."

"Yes," answered Sarah. "We're both tired." They slowly got up, visited the toilet, then went upstairs. Ellen and Dave sat in silence, watching them cautiously, hardly daring to speak until they heard the bedroom door close.

"What are we going to do? I'd like to get out of here now, but we can't leave our friends like this, and in their present state we couldn't possibly get them away without waking Ma," Ellen whispered loudly to Dave. Dave sat back with his hands behind his head and stared at the ceiling.

"Well," he paused, and curled his bottom lip up over his top lip thoughtfully. "Well, I'm not sure there's anything we can do, short of breaking the law. Nothing constructive, anyway." He sat forward and held up his hand to count the options as he raised them. "We could go now and leave them here. Not an option." Ellen shook her head in agreement. "We could go now and take them with us, but I can't see us getting far." Ellen agreed. "We could tie the old girl up or something, which would get us out of this mess, but it's not really on with what is, after all, circumstantial evidence, and we'd be brewing up quite a bit of grief for ourselves, especially if she were to take ill as a result. Not really an option." Ellen was about to scold him for not taking their predicament seriously, but she realised he wasn't joking. Dave sat back in his seat and folded his arms. "Or we can stay the night and leave tomorrow as soon as I get the car fixed, which I can't start until the part arrives at ten o'clock." Ellen stared at him in silence.

"That's the best we can do," he said after a short while. He looked so calm about the whole thing while Ellen was on the verge of panic.

"Do something, Dave, do something," she blurted out as she burst into tears. Dave stood up and gently helped her to her feet. He wrapped his strong arms around her heaving shoulders and stared into the distance.

"Don't worry," he said eventually. "Nothing will happen to you while I'm around."

Chapter 10

Ellen and Dave woke early, still tired after a restless night. She grasped his hand and held it firmly. He looked at her and smiled broadly.

"Well, we're still alive," he said. "It all seems so strange. Last night I wanted to get away, and now it all seems, well, normal, I suppose, and I don't really feel in a hurry to leave."

"Yes, I know what you mean," Ellen murmured thoughtfully. "When I think back to last night, the things we said, it all looks so utterly ridiculous. We must have been mad. The only odd thing was that Paul and Sarah ignored me blowing my top. Sarah and I have known each other for a long time, and she's always poked fun at my fiery temper. I wish I knew what's wrong with her. If I knew she was ill that would account for everything, and I wouldn't bother thinking about witches and things."

"Yes, I agree. Paul's calmness could be just because he's been in the country too long." Dave turned onto his side and put his arm around Ellen's waist. He kissed her and looked into her eyes. "We're still alive, after all. Let's forget the witch idea and concentrate on getting home to civilisation." They kissed again then lay gazing at the ceiling.

Downstairs Ma was busy with breakfast. She bustled about fetching plates, mugs, food, then trotted upstairs to bang on the bedroom doors. The sudden noise made Ellen jump. She giggled as she rose to her feet. They washed and dressed quickly and went down to find Sarah and Paul already eating.

134

"Good morning! You both look much better than you did last night," Ellen said, jovially. "Good morning, Ma. Our last meal here. It looks as delicious as it smells."

"Sit yourselves down," ordered Ma. "Tuck in. There's more if you want it. Dave will need feeding well if he's to fix your machine. Tea'll be ready in a minute." She disappeared into the pantry.

"Did you sleep well?" Dave asked Paul.

"Yes, like a log," Paul answered flatly.

"Like a log," echoed Sarah. Ellen and Dave glanced at each other knowingly. Dave consulted his watch then sat down at the table.

"I'll just have a bite to eat then I'll be off down to the village for our alternator. Are you up to giving me a hand, Sarah?"

"Yes, I'll..."

"Of course she can't!" Ma interrupted fiercely. "She's had a nasty chill. Anybody can see she still needs rest. If you can't do it yourself you'll have to get the man from the village to help you."

"Okay, I'll manage by myself," Dave apologised quickly. "I was only asking." He glanced at Ellen who just shrugged her shoulders and carried on eating. They finished the meal then all sat round the fire with mugs of tea. Paul and Sarah's behaviour, while still not back to normal, now gave Ellen and Dave much less cause for concern. Ellen said little, hoping that one of them would start up a conversation, but Ma ensured that there were no long silences, and Paul and Sarah were both quick to agree with whoever spoke last, or else to make some neutral comment. Ellen looked at her watch then spoke to Dave.

135

"You'd better be off now. Do you want me to come with you?"

"No, there's no need. You can help clear the dishes then pack our case." Dave emptied his mug then retrieved his jacket from the peg. Ellen got up and went over to straighten his collar.

"I'd like to come with you," she whispered with her back to the others.

"Are you worried again?" Dave asked, quietly.

"Yes ... no ... I mean, not actually worried, but I don't feel entirely comfortable."

Dave bade the others farewell then left, pulling Ellen behind him. He shut the cottage door and looked at Ellen. "I thought you were convinced we'd been the victims of over-active imaginations. They're alright. Sarah's just a bit under the weather, and Paul's actually learned to relax. There's nothing to worry about."

"Perhaps you're right," Ellen replied, looking down and shuffling her feet nervously. She raised her head and beamed at Dave. "What a silly cow I am. I'll see if Ma needs any more chores doing." She pecked him on the cheek and he strode away. When he was out of sight she went back inside where Ma and Sarah had almost finished the washing-up. "Do you need any help with anything before we go?" she asked sweetly.

"No, dearie," said Ma as she put the finishing touches to the dishes. She looked up at Ellen with a mischievous glint in her eye. "There's nothing you can do for me, but there is something I can do for you. I think we need to have a little chat, don't you?" Ellen bolted for the door.

"Dave - don't leave me here. Come back!" She got halfway across the vegetable patch, but her feet wouldn't go

136

any further. She looked around to see Ma standing in the doorway.

"Come here, dearie, we need to have a chat." Ellen slowly turned and made her way back to the cottage. She didn't want to go in, but her feet were beyond her control. "Come on into the front parlour. I need to talk to you about your friends. No need to be scared." Ellen obeyed. As Ma opened the parlour door a shiver ran along Ellen's spine. She looked across to where Sarah and Paul were standing by the fire, grinning stupidly at her. She tried to stand still, but her feet took her into the parlour.

In a little over an hour Dave was at the garage. He rang the bell on the counter, and Brian's head appeared through the hatch.

"Good morning," Brian said. "It's Mr Roberts, isn't it?"

"Yes," Dave replied. "I'm here for my alternator."

"Oh, you're a bit early for that. It'll be here in about half an hour. Would you like a cup of tea while you wait?" Dave nodded. "John! Put kettle on for some tea. Young Mr Roberts is a bit soon," he shouted to his brother. A few minutes later John appeared with a tray bearing three mugs of tea and a packet of biscuits.

"Granddad were telling us all about you," said John through a mouthful of biscuit. "He says you visited Granny Carter and she filled your heads full of nonsense. You don't want to believe her. She's a bit, you know, a few sandwiches short of a picnic. She'll say anything to make Granddad out a liar."

"Now John," Brian butted in. "You mustn't say such things, even if they're true." He winked at Dave knowingly.

"Well, what she said did contradict a lot of what your Grandfather said, but I'm not in a position to say who was telling the truth. If, that is, either of them was," Dave commented. John became angry.

"Are you calling our Granddad a liar?"

"No, of course not, but I've no proof one way or the other."

"Alright, then, but my advice is to get away from that farm as quick as you like, and if ever you comes this way again, call in here, and we'll tell you who has lodgings." Dave was about to reply when a van drew up outside.

"Look sharp, John, here's Mr Roberts' alternator. He'll be wanting to get away quick, just like you said," said Brian, as he rose to greet the driver. "Now then, Tommy, what news?"

"What news do you want?" Tommy asked with a smile.

"Oh, any news'll do. Any gossip? Any road news? This young man's going back to London today."

"Well, a bit of both, but I'm a bit thirsty, if you know what I mean," he winked.

"John, tea for Tommy. There should be some in the pot." John brought the tea. Tommy emptied the mug in one draught, then handed the mug back to John, who brought more.

"Now then, where shall we start? Well, there's fog on the A1 and M18, if you're going that way, but that's about all on the roads, except for roadworks on the A19, but you'll not be going that way. As for real news, there's a few young lasses found themselves in the family way unexpectedly in the villages around here. All of them, so they say, had been up to the old farm bank holiday weekend, the one that's supposed to be haunted. Not that I believes in such things, of course. If you ask me, they were a bit clumsy with 'precautions', perhaps after a drop too much drink, but there we are. That's all there is for now. I'd better be off. I'm due in Scarborough in ten minutes! No chance of that. Come to the van and I'll get your parts." He drained his second mug of tea and went about making his delivery. Dave anxiously examined the alternator, then paid for it and left. By the time he reached the top of the hill he was sweating profusely, but he set to work straight away, and soon had the car in full working order. He wiped the grime from his hands as best as he could, then made for the farm.

"Hi! I'm back," Dave announced as he strode in through the open door.

"Upon my word!" Ma greeted him. "You didn't take long."

"Would've been back sooner, but I had to wait for the part at the garage. I'd better have a wash." He held up his grimy hands for all to see, grinning. Paul, Sarah, and Ellen all smiled. "Are you alright, Ellen? You look a bit tired."

"Yes, Dave, I'm a bit tired," she replied.

"Your friends are eager to be off, so I'll make one last pot of tea, then you can go," Ma said as she put the kettle on the fire.

"Good idea. The car's all fixed, so Paul and I can load the cases while it's brewing. Come on, Paul." Dave disappeared upstairs then struggled down with two big suitcases. Paul followed with their modest holdall. They set off along the garden path, then up the hill. As they reached the top Dave became aware of Paul stumbling behind him. "Are you managing okay?" he asked over his shoulder.

"Yes, just a bit tired," Paul answered. Dave looked round to see Paul staggering like a drunk.

"Here, let me help." Dave put his cases down and held his friend by the arm. He took Paul's bag, which wasn't heavy, and guided him through the heather to the car. He sat Paul in the front seat while he retrieved his abandoned cases and packed it all into the boot. "What's up? Are you ill?" He looked into Paul's eyes, as he had many times on the rugby field when he'd taken a knock. "If I didn't know better I'd swear you were concussed, mate. Perhaps we'd better find a doctor. How do you feel?"

"I'm just a bit tired. Nothing to worry about." Dave knew that something must be wrong. Back home Paul was forever worrying about his health. The 'A to Z of Illness and Disease' was very well used in the Chambers house.

"Come on," Dave grunted as he lifted Paul out of the car. "I'm taking you back to the cottage, then we'll decide what's what." Ignoring Paul's protests he carried him back to the farm and deposited him onto the settee. He explained to Ma what had happened.

"I think he's got a bit of a chill. Just like young Sarah, but not as bad. You can stay here longer if you want, you know." Ma brought a mug of tea for Paul, who was recovering quickly. "You'll need a sit down too. You carried him a long way." She thrust tea and scones toward Dave who ate and drank gratefully.

"Thanks, but we need to get home today. Anyway, he seems a lot better already," Dave replied.

Twenty minutes later they were saying goodbye to Ma. Dave thanked her for her hospitality, then they set off along the little path, and up the hill. As they reached the top the

140

others began to lag behind Dave, who didn't notice until he'd reached the car. He stood watching them as they made heavy work of the walk across the heather. He couldn't make up his mind about Ma; she had seemed perfectly normal that morning, and did nothing to prevent their departure, but the evidence before him was that his wife and friends were not their usual selves. Then again, one thing they had learnt this holiday was how to relax, so perhaps they were not quite as sharp as they had been. All the same, Dave resolved to get home as soon as possible.

"Come on," he called to them. They looked up and smiled, then continued at the same pace. Eventually they were all seated comfortably in the car, and Dave was zooming along the country lane. They sat in silence, without complaint about the bumpy road or Dave's driving. "Well, I've enjoyed the break, but I'll be glad to be home," Dave commented.

"Yes, I agree," Ellen answered.

"Can't wait to be back in my own bed again," Dave went on. "Looking forward to a good hot curry tonight."

"Good idea, hot curry," Ellen replied. Dave glanced at her. She was staring ahead as though in a trance.

"One thing's for certain," he said firmly. "If you're no different by the time we get home, I'm taking you to the doctor. I think you're not well." Dave knew something was amiss when Ellen didn't object. She always insisted that seeing the doctor was her own decision, and nothing to do with Dave or anyone else. Dave drove on, wondering what to do. He was torn between stopping to look for help (although how the Yorkshire Constabulary would be able to help he hadn't worked out yet) and getting as far from the old farm in as short a time as possible. Before he could decide they were on the M18, so he decided to press on to the next services then stop to stretch his legs and have some food and drink. The fog, which had been little more than a mist when they first joined the main road, was now quite thick, and worsening. "I think we'd better stop soon and have a break until the fog lifts a bit. Is that okay?" he asked.

"That's okay," said Ellen and Paul, almost together. After about fifteen minutes they were down to a crawl, and Dave was considering stopping on the hard shoulder, when he saw the signs for Woodall services. He breathed a sigh of relief and indicated left. It seemed like miles before the slip road came into view, but Dave just put it down to the fog giving a false impression of the distance and their speed. He eased over to the left and began to look for the car park. The fog hung motionless around them as though they were not moving. Dave drove on slowly, peering through the gloom, hoping he wouldn't hit anything. Suddenly the fog began to swirl, then a few minutes later cleared a little, so that Dave could just make out the shapes of a few trees and bushes. Eventually he could see a building straight ahead. He stopped the car and got out, his mouth open in disbelief.

"What on earth?" Before him stood the old farmhouse. He got out of the car and looked around. There was no sign of the motorway; indeed, no sign of any road – the car stood in the vegetable plot. The others got out and stood together. Dave turned to speak to them, but he was interrupted before he had begun.

"Hello, dearies." Dave froze. He slowly turned to see Ma a few feet away. Sarah, Paul, and Ellen walked over to her, and stood behind her, smiling weakly. Dave's surprise turned to anger.

"What's going on? I demand an explanation. You can't keep us here - we're going home..." Ma held up her hand and he fell silent.

"You are home, Dave," she said slowly and deliberately.

"What do you mean? Our homes are in London."

"This is your home now." She smiled with that glint in her eye that sent shivers up Dave's spine.

"I don't understand," he said. The others shuffled their feet, trying to suppress giggles. "How did we get back here?"

"You never left. You died here, all of you."

"Died here?"

"Yes, your friends were easy, you were more difficult, but a little something in your tea did the trick." She laughed heartily at Dave, who fell to his knees with his face in his hands. Then he threw back his head and screamed hysterically, tears running down his face. The others stood and watched, smiling weakly.

The Big House

Chapter 1

Maddie lay in bed, looking up at the ceiling. What was today going to bring? Another day of not knowing what to do? Another day of staring at the blank page on the computer? Another day of trying to avoid Imogen, her agent? 'Thought for the Day' came on, so she listened, hoping for inspiration. None came. Maddie was an author; she wrote books for children. Her mentor had told her years ago that there was always a market for children's fiction, especially young children, primary school age. And he had been right. Her first book had done well; Imogen had at least three publishers wanting it. That had been *Toby and Jocasta go to the Museum*. A sort of posh version *of Janet and John*. Imogen was ecstatic about it. "The publishers are over the moon because they can more than double the price because it's very up-market and the riff-raff won't buy it because it's too expensive and sounds a bit tedious," she had said when she talked money with Maddie. The next time they met for a working lunch Maddie came up with the idea of '*Toby and Jocasta at the National Trust Property*' after too much wine. Imogen squealed with delight and they were asked to leave the restaurant, but the book was a huge success. A few similar-sounding titles followed, *Toby and Jocasta Dine at the Stately Home, Toby and Jocasta in the Crypt of the Cathedral*, and six or seven more. Then Maddie couldn't think of a good title. The actual content of the book was easy; it was for young children after all, but the title had to grab the 'I'm seriously more posh than you' parent by the credit card, and she couldn't think of a good one. The news was even more tedious than usual and didn't help her plight, so she

146

climbed out of bed and got washed and dressed. T-shirt and jeans were good enough for sitting about the house not working, and she wasn't expecting visitors, nor could she be bothered to go out. She had to find a title. The royalties from the other books kept body and soul together and a roof over her head, but very little else. She wanted to go away for a few days, but couldn't stretch the finances that far until the advance on the next book arrived, which it wouldn't if there wasn't a next book. The phone rang. Would it be Imogen again? No, it was too early in the morning for her. Better answer it in case there's an idea in it.

"Hello?"

"Maddie, sweetie, it's Lizzie. How are you? I've got a suggestion for you. You'll love it. It's just what you need. I saw you looking a bit forlorn the other day and I thought 'I know just what Maddie needs' when it just fell into my lap. Do you want to know now or shall we meet for lunch? No, lunch is far too far away. I'll tell you now. Do you fancy a cheap holiday at a gorgeous place in the country? I know how much you like the countryside and you haven't been away for ages and ages."

Maddie butted in. "Stop, Lizzie, stop. Or at least slow down. I don't know where you get the energy. Yes, a holiday sounds great but I've got absolutely no pound notes at the mo."

"No probs, darling. This is free. Tell you what, I'll meet you at that new coffee shop on the high street in ten. What's it called? Lattissimo or something. See you in ten." The phone went dead. This sounded like a good idea, a free holiday in the countryside. But this was Lizzie. Things are never straight forward with Lizzie. There must be something odd about it or she wouldn't be interested. Anyway, no harm in finding out, and Lizzie always insisted on paying for the coffee and cake. No - cakes, plural. One was never enough for Lizzie. And if they talked for long enough it might turn into lunch. Lizzie would pay for that too. She didn't sponge off Lizzie; no, it was more like sponging off Lizzie's dad. But the family were so rich they didn't care and were happy to spread the wealth a bit. A lot really. Better put some proper clothes on. Lizzie was always immaculately dressed. So Maddie dug a smart blouse and skirt from the back of the wardrobe and changed quickly and headed off down the high street. When she got there Lizzie was already at the door, gesticulating wildly.

"Come on, sweetie, I'm suffering withdrawals. Haven't had coffee since breakfast." Maddie smiled and waved back and quickened her pace. They selected a booth in the corner furthest from the door. Lizzie ordered coffee and various cakes. The waitress brought the order and Lizzie's eyes lit up. "Ooh, lovely. Tuck in, sweetie, get what you want and I'll have the rest." Maddie had just finished breakfast less than half an hour ago, but cake was cake, and she didn't want to offend Lizzie. Halfway through the second cake Lizzie stopped and looked Maddie in the eye. "I'll tell you about it. It's lovely really, but a bit strange. Well, some peeps would think it's a lot strange, but I've been doing it for some time and I'm used to it now." Maddie felt the colour drain from her face. If Lizzie thought it was strange, it must be very strange.

"Okay, give me the facts, but slowly please, so I can take it all in." Lizzie finished the cake she was eating, then sat back and looked serious.

"It's a question of inheritance, sweetie. Have you heard me talk about Aunt Emily?" Maddie shook her head. "Well, I have to visit her for a holiday once a year so she doesn't cut me out of her will. That would be seriously bad news, because she has more money than the Pope. No, that's wrong, more money than ... than ..." Lizzie was struggling here so Maddie helped her out. It isn't every day Lizzie is lost for words.

"Than a very rich person?" volunteered Maddie.

"That'll do. More money than a very rich person. So I go once a year with Maggie. You remember Maggie? My younger sister? Were you at her wedding? Posh do, white ties, ball gowns and pearls, remember? Anyway, Aunt Emily, who is actually Great Aunt Emily but we just refer to her as Aunt Emily, doesn't like men so Maggie can't go, so Aunt Emily suggested I bring along a close friend and I couldn't think of any friend closer than you. So how about it?" Lizzie leant forward, expecting an immediate answer. When an immediate answer didn't come she attacked the next cake. "Well?" she said through a mouthful of cream.

"Let me get this straight," said Maddie, slowly. "We go on holiday in Aunt Emily's house, with Aunt Emily, and that's all there is to it. No catches, no ifs or buts, no strings attached, a free holiday?"

"I won't say there are *no* strings attached, but they are only little strings, easy to comply with, and it is totally free, nothing to pay, Aunty's staff will do all the food and they put on a rather excellent spread and they do all the cleaning and stuff, all we have to do is entertain Aunty in the mornings and the afternoons are ours to do what we want provided we don't leave the grounds." Maddie's eyes opened wide.

"Staff? Grounds? Okay, what's the catch? How do we 'entertain' Aunty?"

"Yes, it's a big place – she wouldn't manage without staff because she's in a wheelchair. Entertaining her is easy. One morning we do sport and she watches, one morning we do music and she listens, one morning we play snooker or ping pong or something and she watches, one morning we read a book to her and she listens. What could be easier? The only drawback, which isn't really a drawback, is there's no TV or radio or WiFi or modern stuff like that, but she wouldn't object to you using your laptop, in the afternoons, of course, if you wanted to do a bit of work. And there's a well-stocked library too, I know you like that sort of thing, but I don't but whatever."

"We entertain Aunt Emily every morning and that's the only drawback?"

"More or less. She's a stickler for being totally proper, so it's full tennis whites for tennis, posh frock and heels for dinner, and smart casual for everything else. And when I say smart casual, I mean very smart casual. Ladies don't wear trousers or expose too much leg or cleavage. Think of it as dressing up for a posh do in the old days and you'd be in the right ball-park. And that's another thing – modern expressions, especially American, are totes verboten. And she has no sense of humour; absolutely none, so she would be offended if you tried to crack a joke or use irony or satire. Serious is the order of the day." She stuffed half a cake into her mouth and looked at Maddie appealingly.

"So you want me to go on a free holiday with your mentally disturbed ancient relative so you don't go up the wall?"

"For the inheritance, sweetie. When she pops the clog I'll drop you a few shillings if you'll do this for me." A wide smile spread across her face, partly hidden by cream. Maddie laughed.

"Okay, I'll do it for you, not for the money, although that would be nice, but because you are my best friend."

"Bonzer!" shouted Lizzie, and the coffee bar staff and customers all turned round to see what was happening. "Sorry, bonzer!" she whispered. They finished their cakes and coffee and set off towards Maddie's flat. On the way Lizzie filled Maddie in on dates and times, and they agreed Lizzie would pick her up the following Sunday afternoon.

Chapter 2

Sunday arrived and Maddie spent much of the afternoon
packing her case, folding the clothes around tissue paper so
they didn't crease, seeing as Aunty was such a stickler. She
had to buy a few things in case her 'smart-casuals' weren't
smart enough and her tennis whites weren't white enough,
but she had done her best, and if Aunt Emily wanted to
complain, tough. She decided to travel in one set of her
smart casuals – didn't want to give a bad first impression –
then change into proper casuals, T-shirt and jeans, after
they had been 'dismissed' for the day. Lizzie was due at
four, but Maddie realised that she didn't actually know
where they were going. Never mind, Lizzie had been there
many times, and her driving was quite good, very good for
one so scatty, so there shouldn't be anything to worry
about. Lizzie arrived at three, which caught Maddie on the
hop. Lizzie wasn't given to punctuality, so that gave
Maddie an idea that if Aunty had such an effect her, well,
she must be a very strong woman. Or was it just because
she was so rich? Maddie put her case in the boot and
climbed into the little car, not easy in that skirt, and greeted
Lizzie with a smile and a peck on the cheek.

"By the way, sweetie, Aunty doesn't kiss people, and
doesn't expect them to kiss anyone they aren't married to,
and even then, not in public." As they drove away Maddie
wondered what the week was going to be like and began to
doubt her wisdom at agreeing to it. Lizzie noticed the look
on her face. "Don't worry, it will be alright."

"So where are we actually going?"

"That's another thing; sentences don't begin with 'so'.
We're going somewhere up north. I'm never sure where,

but I've never got lost in the eight years I've been doing this. It's somewhere in Northumberland, but so far from anywhere that the place name is meaningless because it is absolutely squillions of miles from everywhere. Get the map book from the glove compartment and turn to page sixty-eight. In the middle of the page there's a big expanse of green with a little white road going through it, and near the road there's a little black dot. That's where it is. Don't know why it's called a glove compartment – I've never kept gloves in it."

"I think in the old days when cars had just been invented the people wore gloves because it was so cold on account of the cars not having a roof and stuff."

Lizzie considered this for a moment. "J good thinking, old girl. Never thought of that."

"So what time, sorry, *at* what time do you think we'll get there? Northumberland's quite a way, and there aren't any main roads on page sixty-eight."

Lizzie giggled. "About nine, I think. Aunty will have gone to her room by then, so Jane will give us a light supper. Hope you are hungry – 'light' is a technical term, not a description." She giggled again. "Best not to stop for a bite on the way or we'll be overwhelmed, and Aunty hates waste and Jane will give her a blow-by-blow account of our left-overs."

Lizzie told Maddie what she had been up to at work, which nightclubs she had been to, what she saw at the cinema and theatre, and all manner of things which Maddie didn't really take in. At one point Maddie dropped off to sleep and woke up an hour later, but Lizzie didn't notice. Eventually they left the motorway and an hour later turned off the main road onto what looked like a farm track.

Maddie was kept awake by the bumpy road which seemed to get worse the further they went along it. "Nearly there, sweetie. About twenty mins." And sure enough, twenty minutes later they turned off into a large gravelled area in front of a substantial house. House wasn't the word. Mansion. They pulled up by the main entrance and got out. They hauled the suitcases out of the boot and went up the steps. Jane, a middle-aged woman, soberly dressed, with dark hair going grey, greeted them at the door. She didn't speak.

"Hello, Jane," called Lizzie cheerfully. Jane smiled and curtsied. "This is my friend, Madeleine." Jane curtsied again and turned away to lead them into the hall. Maddie had never seen anything like it. It was considerably more posh than the stately home in her book. They followed Jane up the grand staircase and along a corridor. At the first door on the right they stopped and waited while Jane unlocked it. Lizzie went in, and Maddie went to follow but Jane put her hand up and wagged her finger from side to side, then turned and took Maddie further along the corridor and unlocked another room, two along from Lizzie's. Maddie went in and her jaw dropped. She had seen pictures of the royal family's rooms, but this surpassed them all. She turned to thank Jane but Jane had disappeared. She put her suitcase on the little rack and unpacked some of her clothes. She stopped when there was a knock at the door. In came Lizzie, beaming.

"What d'you think? Knew you'd like it. Isn't it totes amazeballs? Come on, supper time. I'm malnutrished." She turned and trotted off, not giving Maddie time to answer. Maddie followed and soon caught up. They went down the grand staircase to the dining room which had a huge table and chairs for about a dozen. The table was set for two at one end, with an assortment of cold meats, various breads, cream cakes, and five or six different cheeses on the sideboard. There was a choice of tea, coffee or fruit juice, but of Jane there was no sign. Lizzie picked up her plate and piled it high with bread and meat and flung herself into a chair at the table. Maddie did the same and they ate in silence for about ten minutes.

"This is excellent," said Maddie. "I'm glad you talked me into it. Amazing room, amazing food, amazing."

"Yes, it's always the same. Better than you would get at a top hotel. Sorry, can't talk at the moment. Need to eat." Maddie laughed. Lizzie kept going back for more bread and meat, then cakes, then she picked at the cheeses, washed down with tea and fruit juice. "Can't drink coffee at this time of the day or I won't sleep. Dad always reckoned it was nothing to do with the coffee – he just thought I was overactive." Maddie burst out laughing; Lizzie stopped eating and looked at her, shocked. "What's funny?" she asked.

"The idea of your dad thinking you were overactive. It's ridiculous."

"Quite. Anyway, I think I'm done. Are you? Let's take our tea up to our rooms. Do you want to come up to mine for a chat? I'm done in by all that driving. I can show you round the place tomorrow." Without waiting for an answer she topped her cup up and walked off. Maddie followed her up the stairs with tea in one hand and a small plate of cheese and biscuits in the other. They settled comfortable armchairs in Lizzie's room, which was even more luxurious than Maddie's. They sipped their tea while Maddie munched on the last of her cheese and biscuits.

155

"I'll give you a knock at twenty past eight. Breakfast is at half past and Aunty wouldn't like us to be late. Monday is usually something relaxing like snooker or reading, so smart casual until dinner, then it's posh frock and heels. Aunty will join us for all the meals, but she won't eat anything. She eats in her room because she has to be fed and doesn't want anyone to think she's not in charge. Riding accident when she was about twenty. No use in her lower body and her upper body isn't brilliant. But her mind is sharp. Nothing gets past her. Never married – the boyfriend was killed in the same accident. They jumped the same fence at the same time and landed badly with the horses falling on top of them." Maddie winced. "Well, sweetie, I'm putting you out now. I need to be alert for Aunty tomorrow." Maddie turned to go. "By the way, do not leave your room during the night." Lizzie grinned wickedly.

"Well, I'm not expecting to, seeing as there's a perfectly good *en suite*, but why not?"

Lizzie beckoned her back into the room and gestured to a seat, leaning forward so she could whisper. "They say, but I've never experienced it in all the years I've been coming here, they say there are strange movements in the dark."

"Movements? What do you mean?"

"Images of those long gone have been seen to walk the corridors. Maggie says she saw one, and my cousins who sometimes stay here, Anthea and Geraldine, they've seen them more than once." She sat back abruptly. "But I've never seen anything. Then again, I've never left my room at night." She giggled. "But I have heard noises."

Maddie wasn't sure if this was a serious warning or a mischievous prank. She tried not to look worried. "The noises could be the staff, couldn't they?" she suggested.

Lizzie shook her head. "Jane is the only one you see, and she doesn't make a sound. Silent as the grave." She paused. "And Aunty lives in the North Wing – opposite end of the house."

"Servant's quarters?"

Lizzie shook her head. "Back of the house, and in the attic. Noone would have any reason whatsoever to come along here other than for cleaning, which Aunty would never ever allow while guests were in." Maddie turned and slowly walked to the door. "Good night, sweetie," Lizzie called in her usual cheerful voice as though the last few sentences had never been spoken. "Sweet dreams. See you in the morning."

"Yes, sweet dreams. See you in the morning." Maddie left the room and walked the ten yards to her own room and gingerly opened the door. She turned the light on, and everything was normal. Was Lizzie winding her up? Was there a ghostly problem? She undressed, cleaned her teeth, and got into her nightdress. She had brought a book but decided against reading. She climbed into the huge comfortable bed and turned out the light. Within minutes she was fast asleep.

Chapter 3

"Maddie, sweetie, it's time to go down to breakfast and you're still in bed!" Maddie woke with a start to find Lizzie shaking her wildly. "Aunty doesn't put up with tardiness. Get up now and get dressed immediately and brush your hair. We've got less than ten mins to get down there!" Maddie jumped out of bed to find herself alone in the room. She glanced at the clock on the mantelpiece and could just make it out through the gloom. Five forty-five. Could that be right? She reached for her wristwatch, which had luminous hands. Five forty-five. She fell back onto the bed and stared at the ceiling for a little while, then decided to get up. Pointless going back to sleep just to be late. She finished unpacking her case, which she had totally forgotten about in the worry about the ghostly apparitions, and had a long luxurious bath, then sorted out her clothes for the early part of the day. She had remembered to pack her hair dryer, which she didn't always, so her hair was dry in good time. She opened the curtains to discover there had been rain overnight, but the ground was drying quite quickly. The book she was reading was on the dressing table, so she read a few pages but couldn't really get into it, so she flopped into the armchair and thought about last night. No ghostly apparitions, but she hadn't left her room. No noises either. Perhaps it was Lizzie's idea of a joke. Eventually she decided to walk along to Lizzie's room, as it was almost time. She knocked on the door.

"Come in," came the voice from the other side. She went in to find Lizzie looking a bit dishevelled and definitely not ready. "Don't get in the way. Aunty will be furious if we're late." Maddie perched on the end of the

158

dressing table stool and waited while Lizzie flew about pulling clothes on and brushing her hair. She stopped suddenly. "Will I do?" she asked, with a big smile.

"Yes, you'll do. Bra strap showing." Lizzie put that right and they went downstairs and along the corridor into the dining room. The table was set for two at opposite sides of the end, with just a placemat at the table end, the missing chair put by the wall. Maddie sat down. Lizzie gesticulated.

"Get up!" she whispered loudly. Maddie stood. Aunty came in in her electric wheelchair, closely followed by Jane. She manoeuvred into the space at the end of the table and smiled benignly. She was a slim woman in her nineties with a grey bun, wearing a matching jumper and cardigan in pale blue which were plain but obviously very expensive. Around her neck she wore a thin gold chain with a locket. Her lower half was covered by a narrow-striped tartan rug. She had a wristwatch on one wrist and a delicate bracelet on the other. She wore gold-rimmed spectacles.

"Good morning, ladies," she said, nodding to each in turn. "Please sit." The girls sat down.

"Good morning, Aunty, you are looking well," said Lizzie with a smile.

"Good morning, er, Aunty," began Maddie.

"What?" snapped Aunty. "Don't be ridiculous! I am not your aunt. As far as I am aware we are not related in any way." Maddie was a bit flustered.

"Sorry, I wasn't sure what to call you."

"What to call me?" Aunty said, raising her eyebrows and shaking her head slowly. "I think you mean how to address me."

"Yes, sorry, how to address you," said Maddie apologetically.

"Don't apologise all the time. It is unbecoming. I understand your predicament, as Elizabeth hasn't introduced you." She glared at Lizzie.

"Sorry, Aunty, this is my dear friend Madeleine."

"How do you do," smiled Aunty. "I'm sorry, I can't offer you my hand; it doesn't function."

"How do you do," replied Maddie, remembering what Lizzie had told her about this being the correct response.

"You are welcome here as my guest." She smiled again. "During your stay you will address me as 'ma'am' and I will address you as 'miss'. I think that most appropriate considering our age difference."

"Thankyou. Yes, of course," replied Maddie. "Good idea."

"It is not a good idea. It is the correct form for a new acquaintance."

"Of course, sorry."

"Apologising again. Do stop it." Aunty bowed her head and mumbled a short prayer than looked up. Jane left the room silently and unobtrusively; Maddie didn't see her go. "You may begin. I trust Elizabeth has explained that I eat in private but attend meals as a matter of courtesy."

"Yes, fully," Maddie replied, then she got up to help herself from the sideboard, which had bacon, sausages, fried eggs, all on plate warmers, and cereal, toast and marmalade, tea and coffee, and fruit juice. It looked a lot, but there was exactly the right amount for two people. They ate in silence. While they were drinking coffee at the end of the meal Aunty spoke again.

"The weather is unpredictable today."

"Yes," replied Maddie. "I see it rained through the night."

"Quite. This morning we will spend some time reading, and if I am not too tired, perhaps some music."

"Certainly, Aunty," said Lizzie. This was the first time she had spoken since introducing Maddie. When Maddie realised this she was quite dumbfounded. Lizzie with the batteries taken out. Aunty was obviously very much in charge and Lizzie knew it.

"Good. The drawing room at ten fifteen. Thankyou, ladies." Lizzie stood and Maddie followed suit as soon as she realised. Aunty left the room. The girls sat back down.

"She's a good old stick really, just a little particular," said Lizzie with a smile. Maddie nodded.

"I could get used to her, but she keeps you on your toes, doesn't she?"

"Come on, I'll show you the drawing room. Nice room – you'll like it." The drawing room was the next room but one. It was elegantly furnished with a few bookcases at one end and a baby Grand piano at the other, with some cupboards behind it. In the middle was a chesterfield with its back to the window, and a fireplace on the opposite wall. At each end of the chesterfield was a small table, one bearing *The Complete Works of William Shakespeare*, and the other a novel – *The Lonely Daughter by Alice Cumberstone*, which Maddie had never heard of. "Oh, no!" exclaimed Lizzie. "Not more Shakespeare! Aunty does love Shakespeare."

"That's okay," smiled Maddie. "I love Shakespeare." She picked up the volume and flicked through it. It was in near perfect condition but had obviously been well used as there were about a dozen bookmarks in it.

"See that chap in the painting? He's an ancestor. Most of the peeps in the paintings are ancestors. It can be a bit creepy being watched by your family all the time. This rug is genuine Persian. Great, great, great Granddad, - is that the right number of greats? Well, however many greats, he brought it back from the war. Not sure which war. Doesn't matter, but it's the real thing. And those African masks either side of the fireplace were brought back from the war, different war, but not sure which one, by a great, great, random number of greats Granddad. Not the same one as the carpet, but you get the drift." Lizzie prattled on about the contents of the room until she realised Maddie wasn't listening. "I say, sweetie, try and keep up. I thought you were interested in this stuff." Maddie was staring at a painting of a young couple holding the reins of horses.

"Oh, sorry, Lizzie, I was captivated by this painting. It's her, isn't it?" Lizzie came over to join her. "I mean, it can't be. Can it?"

"Haven't a clue, sweetie. Why can it not be her?"

"Well if she's about ninety-five, is that about right?" Lizzie nodded. "The woman in this painting is about twenty-something, yes?"

"If you say so, sweetie."

"So this would be around the outbreak of the Second World War." Lizzie paused to do the maths in her head, then she nodded.

"Yes, your point being?"

"Look at the clothes. These clothes are definitely not thirties or forties. These clothes are most certainly Victorian." Lizzie studied the painting for a moment.

"See what you mean, but perhaps that isn't her. I agree it looks like her, and she was keen on horses, but it could

162

be her Grandmother, couldn't it? Do you look like your Grandmother? They say I do, but I never was big on resemblances. Yes, must be her Grandmother. Anyway, this Grandfather clock used to belong to the Duke of Derbyshire or somewhere. Big pal of some ancient ancestor. Gave it as a wedding present." She glanced at her watch. "Gosh, look at the time!" She smoothed her skirt and blouse, straightened her hair, and sat on the chesterfield, keeping well away from the Shakespeare. Maddie did the same and got settled just as Aunty arrived. They stood while she adjusted the position of the wheelchair opposite the chesterfield, but at a slight angle so the sun wasn't shining too directly onto her.

"Please sit." They sat and made themselves comfortable. "I think we'll start with some Shakespeare. Sonnet fifteen today; it's about growing old, which is appropriate as we are all growing old. Which one of you is going to read? Or do I have to decide?" Maddie raised her hand.

"I would like to read, if that's acceptable," she said, remembering at the last second not to say 'okay'. Aunty smiled.

"Of course it is. Thankyou. You may begin when you are ready." Maddie found the page and sat on the edge of the seat in order to straighten her back and raised her head. She read it with great expression and clarity and when she reached the end remained stock-still for a few moments to maintain the atmosphere she had created. Aunty had smiled throughout, and at the end a tear made its way down her cheek. Lizzie got up to wipe it away.

"Thankyou, Elizabeth, and thankyou, miss. That is, I must say, the most beautiful reading of that particular

163

sonnet I have ever heard. You have a great gift. Are you willing to read another?" Maddie nodded.

"Of course, I'd be delighted to. Do you have one in mind?"

"Twenty-three is another favourite. It reminds me of my youth." Maddie found the page and read. Again, Aunty was enraptured. Maddie read three more before Aunty became flustered. "Oh, Elizabeth, oh, I'm so sorry. You've been crowded out by your friend. Not that it's her fault, it's mine for being so self-indulgent. Please accept my apologies." Lizzie, flapped a hand.

"No, Aunty, I fully understand. Madeleine reads so beautifully, and much better than I can. I'm happy for her to continue. It really is a great pleasure."

"Well, if you really don't mind," She turned to Maddie. "And if you don't mind reading more, miss, I would be grateful if you could. The novel can wait for another day."

Maddie smiled. "No, it's a pleasure. I love Shakespeare."

"Tell me, miss, if you don't mind me asking, what is your occupation?"

"I'm a writer. I write children's books."

"Well done, young lady. That's what we need in the world today, more writers for children. Tell me one of your titles."

"Toby and Jocasta at the Museum." Maddie smiled, embarrassed. She always thought the title was a little pretentious, but it had served its purpose.

"Toby and Jocasta at the Museum," Aunty repeated. "Good to make plain the nature of the protagonists from the outset. I approve." She stared into space for a few moments, smiling. "Come, are you willing to read

164

another?" she said, returning to the present. Maddie read another three, then Aunty said she must stop. "I would like to listen to you reading all day, but I am tiring myself too much. I must return to my room and rest for a while before lunch. Thankyou ladies." They stood solemnly and remained still until Aunty had left the room. Lizzie ran across and closed the door quietly. She ran back, beaming and threw her arms around Maddie.

"Well done, sweetie, you were brill. The old girl is as happy as a pig in poo. You've really made her day." Maddie blushed.

"Sorry to crowd you out. You didn't get a chance to read."

"No probs, sweetie, I'm not as good as you and I don't really enjoy it that much. I remember this damned book from when I was here last year." She picked up the novel and held it up briefly before throwing it back down onto the side table. "Boring as hell. Do you remember those tedious books we read at school? *Silas Marner* and *The Mayor of Casterbridge*? Well they were real action movies compared to this. To be honest I think Aunty found it a bit tedious – I'm sure I caught her almost nodding off when I was reading to her. Or perhaps it was the way I was reading it. But honestly, the best reader in the world, someone like you, couldn't make this thing sound exciting. Anyway, now that we have a bit of time I have a question for you. What on earth did you think you were doing waking me up at quarter to six?"

Maddie's jaw dropped. "What? No, you woke me at quarter to six. I was fast asleep in bed when you rushed in and told me to get up or we'd be late for breakfast then you disappeared before I had a chance to move."

"No, you're getting it all wrong. You woke me, at that exact same time, with the exact same message, and disappeared ..." A look of horror spread across their faces. "Oh, sweetie!" She grasped Maddie's hand. "What's going on? Did you really not wake me at quarter to six? Then who did?" They both sat down heavily on the chesterfield and looked at each other. After a short silence Lizzie spoke, with a tremble in her voice. "Perhaps," she said hesitantly, "perhaps it was just a dream." Another silence, then Maddie spoke.

"Are you telling me we had the same dream, at the same time? No, sister. I don't believe that. That's the sort of thing that only happens in books, and I am most definitely not in a book." She turned to look Lizzie full in the face. "There's something strange in this house and I'm going to find out what it is. The thing, whatever it is, didn't harm either of us, so in theory, there's nothing to worry about, other than losing a bit of sleep. I'll think about it later and decide what we're going to do."

"We?"

"Okay, decide what *I'm* going to do, if you're scared of this potentially harmless thing."

"It's not that I'm scared," said Lizzie, slightly offended.

"What, then?"

"Okay, I might be just a little bit scared. But you're better at thinking than I am, so let me know what you think later on." She glanced at the clock. "Come on, it's almost lunchtime." They made their way to the dining room where a light lunch was already set out on the sideboard: sandwiches with egg, cucumber, etc, various salads, and individual sponge cakes and petits fours, and tea. They

166

stood by their chairs waiting for Aunty to arrive. Aunty came in, followed by Jane, and gave them permission to sit. After they had eaten she turned to Maddie.

"I can't thank you enough, miss, for those sonnets. I do hope you won't object to reading some more later in the week."

Maddie smiled. "I'd love to, as long a Lizzie doesn't mind." Lizzie cringed.

"I think you mean 'Elizabeth'," said Aunty glaring over the top of her glasses.

"Yes, of course, Elizabeth." Maddie blushed and looked down.

"No, I am happy to sit and listen," volunteered Lizzie.

"Quite. Your time is your own this afternoon and this evening, but I will see you both at dinner at seven," she said, ignoring Maddie's embarrassment. "Thankyou, ladies." They stood and she left the room; Jane had already disappeared silently. They looked at each other. Maddie smiled. Lizzie didn't know whether to smile or not.

"Come on," said Maddie. "Let's do something – take your mind off it for now. Leave the thinking to me. It's a nice day; is there anything to do outside?"

"If we take a stroll around the house while the weather's fine, that'll bring us back here about an hour before dinner. Remember we have to dress for dinner; posh frock and heels."

"Okay, come on. Let's walk off some of that excellent lunch. I'm going to be a bit too round by the time we get home." They set off walking at a gentle pace. Lizzie pointed up at various windows, with a running commentary.

"That's the library, that's my room, that's yours, and, oh! I thought I saw someone move in that window! That room isn't normally occupied. That one, two along from your room, do you see? Oh, whoever it was has gone now." She stopped walking and continued to stare up at the window.

"Jane's room?" suggested Maddie. Lizzie shook her head.

"No, Jane's rooms are directly above Aunty's. That wing is just for guests, but we are the only guests this week."

"Could it be the cleaners? Preparing it for next week?"

"Yes, suppose so. I've never seen any staff except Jane, so I wouldn't know what they look like. Yes, that's probably the answer." They continued walking, but Lizzie's mind wasn't at rest about the figure in the window. She took up her commentary again. They rounded the end of the building and Maddie just stopped, her eyes wide and her mouth open.

"Wow! A proper grass tennis court!" There in front of them was a fenced-off area containing two grass courts with a couple of benches at the side. "I've never played on grass before. This is going to be absolutely amazing." She jumped up and down with excitement a couple of times. "Will Aunty come out to watch us?" Lizzie shook her head.

"No, Aunty never ever leaves the house." She pointed at a ground floor window. "She watches from there, with binoculars. Poor old thing, I don't know why she doesn't come out, but she never does, not for anything."

"What if she took ill?"

"She has a private doctor who comes out to the house. Dentist, hairdresser, manicurist, dressmaker, they all come to the house. She hasn't set foot outside since before I was born. Not that she can 'set foot', but you know what I mean. Probably not since she got home after the accident, I would imagine." They carried on around the house, stopping occasionally to admire the gardens. The path took them back to the front of the house, at the other end. Lizzie pointed again. "Those eight windows are Aunty's rooms. Noone is allowed in, except Jane, of course, and people like the doctor and so on. And those rooms above are Jane's rooms, but I'm not sure how many. We're not allowed in any of them, including the corridors and stairs. That wing is totes verboten to normal visitors." She checked her watch as they approached the door. It was a big house with extensive grounds, so the walk had taken them up to six o'clock. "Time to get ready for dinner. I'll give you a knock at ten to."

Dinner took the same form as the other meals. Everything was laid out on the sideboard: a tureen of asparagus soup, a joint of roast beef, tureens of vegetables, a gravy boat, little covered dishes of sauces, and individual trifles, three wines - two white and one red, coffee, a bottle of ruby port and a bottle of dry, pale sherry, the soup and main course items on hot plates, the white wines in coolers. After inviting them to sit Aunty addressed Maddie.

"There is sherry if you would like an aperitif while Elizabeth is serving the soup."

"Thankyou. That would be lovely." She got up and poured glasses of sherry for herself and for Lizzie. Lizzie poured the soup and took the bowls to the table.

"Don't forget the wine, Elizabeth." Lizzie looked flustered.

169

"I'm sorry, Aunty, I can't remember which wine goes with the soup, I rarely have a three-course dinner at home."

Aunty shook her head. "Memory like a sieve. The soup is asparagus, so which wine would we have?" Maddie mouthed the answer across to her.

"Medium dry white, Aunty?"

"That's right. Pour some for your friend and yourself, if you want it." She looked enquiringly at Maddie, who nodded.

"Yes, please." Lizzie proceeded with the wine, and they ate in silence. After the soup Maddie cleared the bowls away to the other end of the sideboard while Lizzie carved the beef. Maddie helped with carrying the vegetable tureens and gravy and sauces across to the table while Lizzie went to pour the wine. Aunty could see she was hesitating.

"Red wine with beef," she said. "Red wine with beef. No, not those glasses. Dear me, I thought you would know by now, the number of times you've been here. The smaller glasses are for the dessert wine. These are basic facts. Try to remember for the rest of the week." Lizzie was getting flustered so Maddie went over to carry the wine to the table. Spilling the wine would be the last straw. After the main course, again Maddie cleared away, while Lizzie dished out the trifle and poured the wine.

"Sweet wine for pudding," she beamed.

"That wasn't difficult – it's the only one left," sneered Aunty. "And trifle isn't pudding – it is dessert."

"Sorry, Aunty." After the meal they had a glass of port, then Aunty left the room and they had a cup of coffee. Maddie laughed once Aunty was out of earshot.

"It's alright for you," Lizzie scowled. "You are the golden girl – I am the useless niece."

"Come on, Lizzie, after everything you told me to do and not do I would have thought you'd have brushed up on etiquette. Most of it is quite basic." They took their cups of coffee into the drawing room where Maddie looked at more of the family paintings while Lizzie sulked on the chesterfield. They returned their cups to the dining room to find that everything had been cleared away, even though they hadn't heard any staff moving about.

"That's a pity," said Lizzie. "I was going to have another glass of something. Never mind. What shall we do now?"

"Do you want to show me the library? Or have you had enough of books for one day?"

"Okay," said Lizzie. "It's a nice room for me to just sit in while you look at the books. And there are more paintings up there too." The library was well stocked, but all the books were old, and Maddie decided a detailed examination could wait until later in the week. They sat for a while, Lizzie unusually quiet, then they went along to their rooms. After chatting about inconsequential matters for thirty minutes or so Lizzie decided to call it a day, and hoped tomorrow was going to be a bit less of a 'things going wrong' kind of day. Maddie said goodnight and returned to her room. What was going to happen through the night? Would she have to wait until quarter to six to find out? Could she stay awake that long? Would she be an absolute wreck the next morning if she did? She changed into her nightdress and put on a dressing gown and slippers and sat in the armchair. She had a little torch which she always carried when she stayed at unfamiliar places, and had a notebook and pencil ready. She soon dropped off. Just after two she heard a noise in the corridor. It sounded very much like someone walking past. Ten minutes later she heard it again. It obviously wasn't Lizzie because Lizzie would have knocked and come in. When the footsteps went past for the third time she tried to open the door without making a sound, but the knob creaked. The footsteps stopped immediately. Should she open the door now? Would she end up face to face with someone - or something - menacing? Judging from when the footsteps stopped it must be right outside her door. Nothing else for it, she pulled the door open, but the corridor seemed deserted. She put the torch on and shone it both ways. Nothing. Imagining things? Perhaps. She closed the door gently and went to bed.

Chapter 4

Maddie woke and looked at the clock. Seven thirty. No more ghostly goings on through the night. She washed and dressed and went along to Lizzie's room.

"You look tired, girl," said Maddie as she sat down in the armchair.

"Not surprised," Lizzie answered, with no life in her voice. "Didn't get a wink of sleep worrying about the night visitors."

"So you heard them too. What did you think?"

"Heard them? I heard nothing. I stayed awake all night because I daren't go to sleep. What are you talking about?" Maddie told her about the mysterious footsteps. Lizzie stared at her in disbelief.

"Never mind that now. Look at the time. Breakfast!" Lizzie jumped out of bed and washed and dressed and brushed her hair. "We'll talk about this later." They made it to the dining room just before Aunty arrived. She invited them to sit, and breakfast took much the same form as Monday. After the meal Aunty smiled and said, "Anyone for tennis?"

"Wouldn't that be nice." Maddie replied without thinking.

"What? 'Wouldn't that be nice'? What does that mean?"

"Sorry, it's a line from a song. 'Anyone for tennis, wouldn't that be nice' - long time ago – political connotations. One of my father's favourite bands – Cream."

"Cream?" said Aunty. "Is that an appropriate name for a band?"

"Sorry, ma'am, a pop group."

"Ah, I see. Cream? Would that be single, double or whipped?" She gave it a moment to sink in. Lizzie and Maddie glanced at each other, wondering whether to laugh or not. Aunty chuckled. "Ha-ha. Ha-ha. I made a witty remark." The girls laughed, not so much at the remark, more at the ridiculousness of the situation. "That's the first witticism I've done for many years. Don't expect another one soon." This made them laugh more. "That's enough. This is not a house of frivolity. Settle down." This made them want to laugh even more, but they managed to control themselves. "What I was saying was today would be a good day for tennis, considering the weather and the state of the ground. Be out there and warmed up by ten. I'll watch from the house. You will stop at eleven thirty so that you have time to shower and be ready for lunch. Thankyou, ladies." They stood and she left. Once she had gone a little way along the corridor Lizzie ran across and closed the door. They collapsed into each other's arms and burst out laughing quite uncontrollably.

"I don't know how I kept it in," said Lizzie after they had settled a bit. "I was almost wetting myself."

"Elizabeth!" said Maddie sternly. "Young ladies do not wet themselves. Not in this house." And they collapsed in more fits of laughter. Lizzie started to look serious.

"Come on, let's get changed. There's not much time." They ran to their rooms and emerged some minutes later in tennis whites and made their way downstairs. Lizzie retrieved rackets and balls from a cupboard as they went out by the side door. Nine forty-five. Just in time for a quick warm-up before Aunty started watching at ten. The grass was in perfect condition and had obviously been mown just a day or two before. The net was up, and at the correct height (Lizzie checked) even though it hadn't been there when they passed that way yesterday. Aunty watched from the window which Jane had opened so that she could shout 'Bravo!' when there was a particularly good shot. Lizzie won the set by six games to two, but both enjoyed it, as did Aunty, who shouted encouragement throughout. Jane stood behind her and just to the side, impassive. At eleven thirty Aunty called to them to stop just as they were starting the second set. They were both grateful for this, as neither had done much sport for a while and both were out of condition. They waved at Aunty as they made their way back in through the side door and went straight up to their rooms. Showered and dressed, they came down to the dining room to find Aunty already there.

"Sorry we're late," said Maddie. "Getting showered and changed took longer than we expected."

"Think nothing of it. You both played well and I enjoyed it very much indeed. And I wouldn't want you taking lunch soiled from your exertions." She seemed much more cheerful than yesterday. After lunch she reminded them dinner was at seven and the rest of the time was their own. They took their cups of tea to the drawing room and sat in silence for a moment. Maddie was the first to speak.

"Let me get this straight. You stayed awake all night last night, but you didn't hear the footsteps. Is that right?" Lizzie nodded. "It was about two, then ten mins later, and another ten after that. And you didn't hear anything? They weren't quiet – it didn't sound like anyone creeping about trying to go unnoticed."

Lizzie shook her head. "No, I heard absolutely nothing, and I was deffo awake at two because I was watching the

175

clock thinking how the time dragged when nothing's happening."

Maddie shook her head. "I don't understand this. Last night I heard something you didn't, the night before we each did something to the other and don't remember doing it. Strange."

"That's if we actually did it," said Lizzie. "We might have dreamt it."

"Yes, we might, but I find that difficult to accept – that we would have the same dream at the same time. And while we're in here with a bit of time, I'm going to take a closer look at that painting, to see if there are any clues." She drained her cup and put it down and walked across to the painting. Lizzie remained on the chesterfield and looked at it from a distance. Maddie spotted something and moved closer to have a look.

"What is it?" asked Lizzie.

"I think it's a date, but very difficult to make out. Looks like eighteen ninety-eight. Come and have a look – see what you think." Lizzie got up and went over.

"Yes, I think you're right, but it is very unclear. Could be eighteen eighty-eight, but I think ninety-eight is more likely. And the closer you get the more it looks like Aunty. It must be her, despite what you say about the clothes."

"Usually paintings are better from a distance, but this is definitely her. I'm going to ask her."

Lizzie was horrified. "No, you can't do that! Not Aunty! She'll be, she'll be, oh, I don't know what she'll be, but it won't be good. No, I won't let you ask her. She's my aunt, not yours. Isn't there an etiquette rule against it?"

"Calm down. I won't just come out with it. I won't say 'by the way is that you in the painting?' No, I'll find some words to ask subtly. But you've got to agree the more you look at it the more it looks like her."

Lizzie nodded. She looked up at the clock. "Yes, can't disagree. We've almost two hours before dinner. What shall we do?"

"I would like to have a look along our corridor, see if there's any signs of the mysterious footsteps. What are the other rooms along there?"

"Oh, do we have to? I'm not sure it's a good idea. I don't know what the others are. I've always stayed in the same room, and when Maggie came she stayed in yours."

"Okay, you stay here and I'll go by myself. I wondered from the start why they didn't put me in the room next to yours. I'm off to have a look."

"No, I'll come with you. You've got me scared now. I'm not staying on my own. The thought of Aunty being a hundred and fifty years old is a bit much to take. I mean, it can't be true, can it? Well I'm not going to take the chance." They went upstairs and into the corridor. Lizzie popped her head into her room. She didn't know why she did it, or what she was looking for, but she got a surprise. Her tennis whites were on her bed, freshly laundered and expertly folded up. "Maddie, come and look at this!" she called. Maddie came in and Lizzie pointed at the clothes.

"Er, that's not like you, Lizzie, I mean, not wanting to be rude, but since when were you so tidy?"

"No, I didn't do that, I threw them onto the floor in a hurry to get down to lunch on time and haven't been back until now. Someone's done them for me. I'm grateful, but who did it? We never see the staff, and it's not long since I took them off." Maddie stood looking at them while Lizzie

177

looked round the room to see if anything else had been done. Maddie turned and left suddenly.

"Come on, let's see if mine have been done too." Lizzie followed her. In Maddie's room the situation was the same. The tennis whites were immaculately laundered and folded but nothing else was touched. "Well, it doesn't actually prove anything, but it makes me think we are being watched. To get those done in such a short time and to such quality they must have taken them as soon as we left the rooms. Perhaps it's nothing, but I don't really know." Maddie went back to the corridor and tried the door of the room between hers and Lizzie's. It was locked.

"Well of course it's locked," said Lizzie. "Remember when we arrived, Jane brought us to our rooms and unlocked them to let us in. They were locked before we arrived, so it makes sense that the others were locked too." Maddie let go of the handle in frustration and went along the corridor. The fourth door was locked, and the fifth, and the sixth which was the last one.

"Okay," said Maddie. "You stand in my bedroom window while I go outside."

"What?"

"Stand in my bedroom window so I can see which one it is." And she went downstairs and out onto the gravel forecourt. She waved at Lizzie and Lizzie waved back, then she counted along the windows. Lizzie was in the third window, but there were four more windows. Four windows for three rooms. One room could be bigger of course, but everything inside seemed so equal. She counted along again just to make sure and saw a figure in the second window – the room between hers and Lizzie's. She ran inside and up the stairs and dragged Lizzie out into the corridor, putting her finger to her lips for silence. They went to the next room and Maddie knelt down to look through the keyhole. She couldn't see anyone. She could see the window, but the figure wasn't there. There seemed to be nothing else within view. No furniture, no carpet, no curtains, nothing. Fair enough, that's why she was put in the next room, but who had she seen from outside? She dragged Lizzie back into her room and explained quietly. They sat in silence, Maddie wondering what to do next, and Lizzie wondering what Maddie was thinking about. She tugged at Maddie's sleeve.

"Come on," she whispered. "Time to go down for dinner." They changed and went down and had a good meal, just like yesterday. At the end they stood while Aunty left, then they took their coffees into the drawing room.

"I just don't know what to think," said Maddie. "I want to explore a bit but I don't want to arouse suspicion, or everything will be covered up more. Perhaps we should wait until bedtime." She went back to the painting of the couple with the horses and stared at it for what seemed to Lizzie like hours, but was in fact only about ten minutes. Lizzie began to cry.

"Oh, Maddie, I'm sorry, I should never have brought you here. You are my dearest friend and now we're both going to die and it will all be my fault." Maddie came across and pulled Lizzie's arm sharply.

"Don't be ridiculous. What do you mean? Why are we going to die?"

"Well it always happens in films. Spooky things happen then at the end they are all dead."

"For one thing, we are not in a film, and for another, they don't always end up dead. A knight in shining armour or an old priest or something comes along and saves them. Pull yourself together. If 'it', whatever it is, intended harm it could have done it last night or the night before. Perhaps it's staff wandering about to do their work and scared of being seen and incurring Aunty's wrath. But I want to find out anyway." She let go of the arm and they retired upstairs with their coffees. Maddie went along all the rooms, trying door handles and looking through keyholes, but the other three rooms were all exactly the same as the second; all locked and completely bare. Lizzie sat in her room, not sure whether to cry or not, and most definitely not enthusiastic about exploring. This hadn't happened before; the laundered tennis whites had, both to her and Maggie, but she hadn't returned after such a short time, so they hadn't thought it odd. Not that Maggie was a great thinker. Lizzie was definitely the brains in their family. About ten minutes later Maddie returned, beaming.

"I've got a plan," she said. "I need your help, and bring that little mirror off the dressing table." She pointed at a small mirror in a swivel attachment on a stand. Lizzie reluctantly picked it up and followed out into the corridor. Maddie was just disappearing into her own room and emerged with a similar mirror. Lizzie was puzzled.

"What are we doing now?" she asked. Maddie grinned.

"I'm leaving my door ajar all night, and with these mirrors I'll be able to see what happens out here without moving from the armchair. Put that one down over there, yes, that's the place, now turn it to about sixty degrees so it reflects onto this one just inside my door."

"Oh, Maddie, I can't remember what sixty degrees is. Is this right?"

"No, that's forty-five. Turn it a bit towards my room. That's it. Stop right there. Come on in here." Lizzie came into Maddie's room and sat in the armchair. Looking in the mirror by the door she could see right along the corridor, through the other mirror.

"Oh, sweetie, you are clever, but I'm not sure about leaving the door open all night. Do you think it's wise?"

"As I said earlier, if 'it' wanted to do us in it had two opportunities. And I've got to leave the door open, because last night it disappeared as soon as I made a noise."

Lizzie considered this for a moment. "Ok, as long as you have some weapon or other to defend yourself. Look, there's a brass poker among the fire irons – that'll do, won't it?"

Maddie grinned and Lizzie looked hopeful until she realised Maddie was being sarcastic. "When was the last time you fought off a ghost? Things like that are no good whatsoever. Now if you'd suggested a crucifix or a Bible or a bottle of holy water, well, that might be different."

Lizzie looked around the room anxiously. "But we don't have things like that here," she said, dismayed.

Maddie laughed. "Sorry, Lizzie, just winding you up. No, I don't think I have anything to fear, only fear itself."

"What?"

"Never mind. If you are really genuinely concerned, you can stay in here all night. I'm in the armchair so you can have the bed. But it isn't necessary. I'll be fine." Lizzie was now in a quandary. Should she stay here to look out for her friend, or should she go back to her room, out of harm's way? "If you can't decide, Lizzie, I'd rather you went back to your own room so you don't make a noise and frighten it away." This made her feel a bit easier, as that's what she wanted to do. They sat and chatted for another half hour, then Lizzie retired to her own room, and went to bed, but didn't sleep. Maddie changed into her nightdress, slippers and dressing gown, and sat ready in the armchair. At about two thirty she woke with a start. She could hear the footsteps coming along the corridor. Without moving her body she twisted her head around until she could get a good view through the mirror. What she saw made her gasp, and the apparitions disappeared at the sound. It was the young couple from the painting.

Chapter 5

Lizzie was wakened by Maddie knocking on her door. She had locked it, just in case.

"Why did you lock the door?" Maddie asked, when she was eventually admitted, after questions such as 'Who is it?' and 'What sort of me?' and 'How do I know it's really you?'. Maddie was exasperated.

"Locking the door only succeeded in keeping me out. The ghosts, if that's what they are, wouldn't have been stopped by a lump of wood. Anyway, I suppose you didn't hear a thing."

"Oh, sweetie, no I didn't. What happened? I stayed awake all night, I'm sure I did, and didn't hear anything."

"Well, no, you wouldn't, because they didn't make any noise. They just walked along the corridor, arm in arm, then when I forgot myself and broke the silence they disappeared."

"They? Who are they?"

"'They' are the couple from the painting, in full Victorian dress, but pale and semi-transparent, like you might expect a ghost to be. I need to ask Aunty."

"No, you can't do that! We agreed yesterday, remember?"

"I promise I will be subtle. I don't want to worry her if she knows nothing about it. And by the way, when I first agreed to this 'holiday' you never said there were rumours the place was haunted until we got here, so it's no good being shocked or surprised or anything. Or were you just making that up?"

"No, I hadn't heard or seen anything, but last time Anthea and Geraldine were here Geraldine swore she wouldn't come back because she saw ghosts in the corridors and heard strange noises through the night. I should have listened to her and forget about Aunty's will."

"Are they reliable? Might they have had a drop too much to drink?"

"Geraldine might, but Anthea doesn't drink or do stuff or anything like that. But they can be a bit scatty. I'm the sensible one in the family."

"Dear me! Gosh! Look at the time! We'll be late for breakfast if we don't get a wriggle on." Maddie rushed back to her own room and washed and dressed quickly. She emerged five minutes later to meet Lizzie in the corridor looking a bit dishevelled. "Do something with your hair, girl. You look as though you've had a fright." Lizzie dashed back in and came out with a hairbrush in her hand and sorted her hair out while they went downstairs. Breakfast was uneventful, and at the end Aunty decided on music for the morning activity. They met in the drawing room at ten. Aunty parked her wheelchair near the piano.

"Elizabeth, I would like to hear some Beethoven this morning. You know where the books are; choose your favourite sonata." Lizzie chose number eight, *The Pathetique*, in C minor. Aunty was delighted. "I do love C minor, don't you, miss?" she asked, turning to Maddie.

"I'm not an expert, ma'am, but I have heard others commend it," she answered diplomatically.

"Yes, his best key. All his C minor works stir the soul. Elizabeth plays this one exceptionally well, especially the second movement, which she plays with real passion. Take a seat and we'll listen." Maddie sat in an armchair on the other side of the piano. She picked that one so she could study the painting at the same time. Lizzie made a good start, and Aunty was obviously pleased. The second movement made her close her eyes and hum along gently. The last movement caused Lizzie a few problems because of the speed, but she carried on valiantly to the end.

"I'm sorry, Aunty," she said after she had finished. "I'm a bit out of practice." But the good had already been done.

"Don't worry, dear," said Aunty with a benevolent tone to her voice. "Speed isn't everything, and that second movement, oh, I know it is easier, but the beauty flowing from your fingers! Oh, if only your cousins could play as well as you do!"

"Thankyou, Aunty," she said as she put the books away.

"Now, miss, what are you going to play?" Maddie was a bit flustered. She wasn't expecting this.

"Oh, well, I don't play the piano at all," she said, her head taking a downward direction.

"Don't worry," said Aunty. "Those cupboards contain various instruments. There's a violin, a flute, a clarinet - although I'm not sure it functions as I believe I was the last to play it and that was a very, very long time ago - but the flute and violin have both been played recently. Can you manage either of those?"

"I had flute lessons," Maddie admitted tentatively. "But that was a long time ago, and I wasn't very good."

"Oh." Pause. "Do you sing?"

"No. I'll try the flute, if there's something not too difficult." Lizzie got the flute from one of the cupboards and the music from another, and helped Maddie find the easier books. They settled on the theme from the slow movement of Dvorak's Symphony No. 9, *From the New*

185

World, which had a piano accompaniment part. After a few false starts Maddie played it in an almost recognisable manner. By the time she got to the end she was close to tears. "I'm sorry, I wasn't expecting to play. I did my best, but I don't have the talent that Liz – Elizabeth has. You are obviously a very musical family." Aunty looked a bit downcast. She suddenly looked up.

"Would you prefer to read another sonnet or two?"

Maddie brightened instantly. "Oh, yes," she said gratefully. "Which would you like?" She read three sonnets, then Lizzie played a short piece on the piano, then Aunty needed to rest before lunch. They stood while she left the room, then Maddie burst into tears.

"Oh, that was so embarrassing," she said while Lizzie hugged her and dried her tears. "When you said 'we do music' I didn't realise I was included."

"Sorry, sweetie, I didn't know you didn't play. I remember you having a flute at school. *Mea culpa*. But you more than made up for it with your sonnets. You're deffo onto a winner there."

"Yes, I only had lessons for one year, then the teacher told Mum I should consider a different instrument. I tried the cornet but couldn't get a note out of it so I gave music up totally. And I was so upset I forgot to ask about the painting."

"Leave that for another time," said Lizzie, relieved. She led Maddie back upstairs where she washed her face and tidied up her hair while Lizzie gazed vacantly out of the window. "You know, Geraldine and Anthea had a blazing row about this last time I saw them. They almost came to blows and Anthea said the house was just lonely and needed someone to be nice to it. Geraldine said the

186

house was haunted, but it's a known fact that Geraldine likes her drink so we put it down to that. But let's sit and rest for a little while before we go down to lunch." Lunch was much the same as usual, with Aunty making a fuss about Lizzie's playing and Maddie's reading. Maddie decided to take advantage of her being in such a good mood.

"Ma'am, may I ask a question?" she said.

"Yes, you may, but I won't give you an answer if it would be inappropriate."

"Well, it's about the painting near the piano – the two young people with the horses. I think I see a resemblance – are you related to the young lady?" Aunty looked down and pursed her lips. Lizzie cringed, thinking Maddie had gone too far.

"Actually, yes, I am," she said, looking up again, but staring into the distance. "She died long before Elizabeth was born, as you can see from the clothing, but yes, she is - er, I mean was a family member, but I would rather we didn't talk about it."

"Thankyou," said Maddie. "I didn't mean to pry or bring back sad memories or anything. I just thought she looked like you. I'll ask no more."

"Good. Thankyou, ladies." This was their signal to stand for her departure. When she had gone Lizzie shut the door and rounded on Maddie.

"See, you've upset her now. There was no need for that."

"I didn't mean to upset her, I just wanted to know, now that I've seen them walking about outside my room in the middle of the night."

"Well you know now so can we have no more about it?"

"I won't mention it to Aunty again, but I'm going to watch again tonight. What are we going to do now?"

"You wanted to look in the library, so let's go there." Lizzie stormed off up the stairs and Maddie followed. In the library Lizzie, obviously not pleased with Maddie's opportunistic approach, sat in an armchair and sulked, gazing out of the window. Maddie went to the furthest corner and looked at the books. She pulled a few off the shelves and sat at a table to examine them. Suddenly she sat up.

"Lizzie, come and see this!"

"What?" said Lizzie, still sulking.

"It's the Family Bible. It has names and dates of birth and marriage and death and all sorts of stuff." Lizzie came over and pulled up a chair at the table. "What is Aunty's surname?"

"Garrington-Wylam, with a hyphen. Is she in there?"

"Good question. There's one here, Emily Elizabeth Mary Garrington-Wylam. Does that sound like her?"

Lizzie nodded. "Yes, I think that could be her. Does it say much?"

"Well, there's the thing. Date of birth: 15th April 1880. No date of marriage or death. What do you make of that?"

"I don't know when her birthday is. April rings a bell, but as for the date, haven't a clue. Aren't I terrible?"

"Wake up, dozy. If this is her she must be about a hundred and forty years old! This is surely the young woman in the painting, but is it Aunty? The name is a match, if you've got it right."

"Of course I've got it right, but she might be named after her mother or Grandmother or somebody."

"Well I'm not. My mother is Doris, her mother was Eleanor, and her mother was Euphemia."

Lizzie burst out laughing. "Euphemia? What sort of name is that?"

"It's from the Greek, I understand. We are a family of the classics," Maddie said haughtily, then they both burst out laughing again.

"Well my dad is called George and his dad was George and his dad was George, so finding a name doesn't prove anything."

"Okay, I take your point, but this Emily doesn't have a date of death. All the others do, both before and after. Why doesn't she?"

"Well that proves she isn't the ghost. If she isn't dead there can't be a ghost." Lizzie got up and walked away. She sat by the window with a book which she had randomly picked from the shelf. Maddie looked more closely at the entry in the Family Bible, and picked up a magnifying glass from another table to study it.

"Lizzie! Lizzie, come here and look at this! There has been a date of death, but it's been scratched out, and quite skilfully, too. Someone has decided to hide the facts for some reason or other." Lizzie came over reluctantly and examined the page.

"Yes. So what? We're no further forward."

"Yes, I suppose you're right. It doesn't prove anything. I'll think about this."

"Well I'm going to my room to make myself beautiful for dinner." She left the room. Maddie was disconsolate that she had gone round in circles and proved nothing, but

189

this made her even more determined to solve the puzzle before they went home on Saturday. If there actually was a puzzle, that is. A hidden date of death doesn't prove that a ghost does or does not exist. Is she making something out of nothing? Does Lizzie actually have a point? She decided to forget it for now and went to her room to get ready for dinner. Dinner took its normal course, and Maddie took her coffee back to the drawing room where she sat for some time staring at the young couple while Lizzie tried to engage her in conversation. After a while she apologised to Lizzie and they went up to their rooms. Fifteen minutes later Lizzie knocked on Maddie's door and came in.

"I say, sweetie," Lizzie began, then paused for a second or two, "I've been thinking. I know it isn't my strong suit, but if Aunty isn't dead she wouldn't have a date of death for anyone to rub out in the book. So that means the person in the book can't be Aunty. So it must be someone else, so Aunty and the horse lady can't be the same person. Does that sound right? I know you don't think I'm logical, usually, anyway, but I think I've got it. Someone wanted to hide dead Emily's death. I don't know why, perhaps as part of an insurance scam or something." She smiled broadly, pleased with her logic, and hoped Maddie would agree. Maddie stared at her, then sighed.

"Yes, you've hit the nail on the head. The missing date in the Bible is a red herring. Let's forget it. But I still intend to stand guard tonight and see where the ghosts go to after they pass my door."

"Oh, dear, I was hoping this might be the end of it. I won't sleep knowing you are on detective duty."

"You can sit up with me if you want."

Lizzie was horrified. "No way, sister! I don't want to get mixed up with dead people. It isn't … it isn't … help me out, sweetie."

"It isn't healthy? Isn't natural?"

"That's it. It isn't natural. Suppose, just suppose something goes wrong. How am I going to explain it to your folks when I don't even understand it myself?"

Maddie laughed. "If - and it's a big if - if it goes wrong I think explaining to my folks is going to be the least of your problems."

"How do you mean? The least of my problems? I don't understand."

"If it goes wrong, not sure how it can, but we'll be in the same boat and you won't be here to explain anything."

"That's it. I want no more to do with this. If you want to carry on staying up all night watching corridors and stuff, well, that's your lookout. Don't come crying to me when you are dead."

Maddie would have laughed if Lizzie hadn't been so upset. Lizzie went to her room, got ready for bed, and settled down with a book for a while before turning in. Maddie did much the same but positioned the little mirrors first in case she got caught unawares. She tweaked them a bit and added a third from her handbag so she could see clearly in both directions without leaving the armchair. Midnight came and she put the book down and sat with a glass of water. Two o'clock came and nothing had happened; she was struggling to stay awake, having missed quite a bit of sleep the previous night. At three thirty she jolted into wakefulness as she heard footsteps coming along the wooden floor. The mirrors gave her a clear view. The couple from the painting were strolling along, arm in arm,

191

and went right past and on to the end of the corridor. There they kissed briefly, then the woman went into the end room, and the man came back. This accounted for the ten minute gap on the second night. He went into the second room – the one between hers and Lizzie's. Maddie didn't move a muscle. Then ten minutes later the woman came out of her own room, along the corridor, and into the second room. Silence. Maddie waited another half hour, but nothing happened. She carefully got up and crept along to the second room, not making a sound, and looked through the keyhole. There was nothing to see. Absolutely nothing, just as there had been earlier. No furniture, no carpet or curtains, and no people. She returned to her room and got into bed, listening all the time. There wasn't a sound, and she fell asleep.

Chapter 6

Maddie slept like a log. When she got up she was refreshed and bouncy, unlike Lizzie who was dismal and tired.

"I don't know how you can sleep with all this going on," Lizzie remonstrated. "I was awake all night, worrying about you." Maddie was beaming.

"I know what's going on. Well, I know what was going on over a hundred years ago." Lizzie's face lit up. Maddie recounted the nightly exploits of the young ghosts.

"Oh, how romantic!" Lizzie gasped. "I do hope they didn't get caught."

"Well," said Maddie triumphantly. "That solves the mystery of the footsteps and the ghosts and the painting. And I don't care if it was Aunty. If it was, and she's over a hundred, good for her. That just leaves the mystery of the first night." Lizzie's face darkened.

"But if it was Aunty, how can she be so old? It isn't possible. And what about the first night? Did we dream the same dream?"

"No. I've heard of twins dreaming the same dream, but we aren't even related. I don't believe that idea. I've got to admit, for the time being I'm stumped." She stood hands on hips staring at the floor. Lizzie sat silently, wondering rather than thinking.

"Time for breakfast!" she called suddenly and jumped out of bed and got washed and dressed. They went downstairs and into the dining room.

At the end of breakfast Aunty said, "Snooker this morning, I think. I haven't seen a decent game of snooker for some years. You do play, I take it?" This to Maddie, who nodded her head.

"Yes, my father taught me. But I'm not top notch."

"No matter, as long as you can make a decent fist of it. The snooker room at ten. Thankyou, ladies." They rose and she left. The snooker room was next door to the dining room, but they had to finish their coffee before they went in; drinks were not permitted in the snooker room. Lizzie couldn't remember which ball went on which spot, but Maddie saved the day by setting up the table. They sat and waited. Ten o'clock came and went. At ten fifteen Aunty entered the room; she had been crying, and Lizzie wiped away the tears with a handkerchief.

"What's wrong, Aunty?"

"Please don't fuss. I've had some bad news. Someone has discovered a secret which was so old I thought it wouldn't matter, but as you can see, it is still upsetting. I do so apologise for my late arrival. Let's press on with the game." They played in silence. Maddie's height advantage helped, and she won four frames, before Aunty declared she had watched enough, and left the room. She was still unsettled, and the girls hoped it was nothing to do with them.

At lunch Aunty seemed much brighter and talked about the snooker briefly while the girls sipped their tea. As soon as they were out Maddie went straight to the library and buried herself in the books on the same shelf as the Family Bible. She was looking for records of family history. She didn't know why, and couldn't explain when Lizzie asked, but she wanted to find something. She found nothing, and Lizzie made her put the books back tidily before they went down to dinner. After dinner she asked Aunty about her early life.

"What did you do after leaving school? Did you go on to study further or did you take up employment?" Aunty seemed put out at being asked, but felt obliged to answer, having asked Maddie about her work.

"In those days young ladies weren't permitted to go on to higher education. And no, I didn't take up employment as I was of independent means and would have married if it hadn't been for my accident. I would have been in charge of the household staff, much as I am now, but in greater numbers." Maddie could see she was starting to get upset, so she changed the subject.

"What activity will we have tomorrow morning? I ask so that I can prepare, if necessary."

"It is wise to be prepared. I think, as you read so beautifully, I would like to hear you read, and Elizabeth can play the piano, if neither of you objects." Both girls nodded their approval. "Thankyou, ladies," she said, and they stood while she left.

As soon as she was gone Lizzie turned on Maddie.

"You've gone too far. I forbid you to speak like that to Aunty again. She was already upset when she came in and it was plain to see but you couldn't leave her alone. You took advantage of her distressed state to pry into her life. Poor old thing! You're turning into a monster. You're getting just like the journalists we see on the news, thinking everybody's business is fair game. Well, I won't stand for it. If you do anything like that again to poor old Aunty that's the end of our friendship." She stormed out and went to the drawing room.

Maddie sighed. "Oh, dear," she said out loud, and followed Lizzie. "Look, Lizzie, I'm sorry if you see it that way. I wasn't, well, I'm not sure what I wasn't trying to do, but I didn't mean any harm. There was no malice intended."

"Didn't mean any harm? Didn't mean any harm? That poor old woman, a hundred and something or whatever she is, comes into the room late, which is about as far out of character as is possible for her to get, obviously upset, and you pick over her past. If that's how you behave when you 'don't mean any harm' I'd hate to see you when you're being vindictive." They sat in the drawing room without speaking for about an hour then they went to their rooms. Maddie set the mirrors again and observed exactly the same scenario; he escorted her to her room, they kissed then he returned to his, and she came back ten minutes later. After this Maddie went to sleep and forgot about it.

The next morning they greeted each other frostily, and went down to breakfast. They rose for Aunty's arrival, and she greeted them, and they ate, in silence, as usual.

"Reading and music this morning," Aunty reminded them, and she left. They made their way to the drawing room and Lizzie started berating Maddie again, reminding her that Aunty was not only a dignified elderly lady, but also their hostess for the week. Maddie struck back that she did appreciate the old girl and was only curious about her history. They heard a cough in the doorway, so they stopped arguing and tried to look pleasant. Aunty came in and settled in her usual position by the fireplace. She had obviously heard what had been said but pretended otherwise. Maddie wondered if she should apologise. She turned this over in her mind while Aunty positioned herself, and decided she would, but only if Aunty raised the subject. Aunty had obviously had her face washed and dried, and looked better than she did at breakfast, but there was no sparkle in her eyes. Maddie decided a good reading might help and gathered herself together to do the best reading of sonnets she had ever done. They sat and Aunty took a few minutes to compose herself.

"I think sonnet thirty-seven might be appropriate this morning. Begin when you are ready." Maddie found the page and settled her posture and began reading. About halfway through her voice began to waiver, so she paused to clear her throat then continued from where she had left off. At the end she was close to tears, as was Aunty. "Thankyou, miss," she said after a lengthy pause. "It was very moving, especially after my upsetting news." Maddie took this as a cue.

"I'm sorry if I upset you at dinner yesterday evening," she said, looking suitably contrite. "I didn't mean to; I was just curious, but I shouldn't have asked such questions when you were upset."

"Thankyou, miss, your apology is gracious and settling. My news about the revelation of what has gone on in the distant past is something young people of today might not understand, and so I won't burden you with it, but your apology is thankfully received and calms my heart. Would you like to read another sonnet? Perhaps one more uplifting?" Maddie smiled and nodded. "Perhaps number eighteen?" Maddie smiled; it was a sonnet she knew well. She read it, and another, then Aunty asked Lizzie to play some Mendelssohn, which she did. After another two sonnets Aunty retired to her rooms to rest before lunch. Maddie and Lizzie sat in silence for a few minutes. Lunch followed, then Lizzie and Maddie took another walk around the house and grounds, not saying much. After

197

dinner they went to their rooms. Maddie sat reading her book but couldn't settle. After about half an hour she knocked on Lizzie's door and went in.

"Are you okay, Lizzie?"

"Oh, sweetie, I'm sorry. I was right to tell you off, but I did go too far, didn't I?" Maddie nodded and Lizzie came over and they hugged each other. They chatted about inconsequential matters until ten.

"By the way, Lizzie, I'm not sitting up on guard tonight. I think I've found out about as much as we're going to find out, so I'll give it a rest."

"Oh, thankyou, sweetie. It has been wearing me out. I'll sleep better tonight." They bade goodnight and went to bed.

Chapter 7

"Maddie, sweetie, it's time to go down to breakfast and you're still in bed!" Maddie woke with a start to find Lizzie shaking her wildly, just as she had on Monday morning. But this time there was someone else in the room. She pushed Lizzie aside and tried to see who it was. It looked a bit like Jane, from the size and shape, but it was too dark to be certain. She jumped out of bed and found herself alone in the room. Grabbing her torch she dashed straight out into the corridor, but saw noone. Coming back in, she shone the torch on the clock. Five forty-five.

"Here we go again," she said out loud, even though she was alone in the room. Was she alone in the room? She shone the torch around, quite slowly, making sure she got to every nook and cranny. Yes, she was alone in the room. She breathed a sigh of relief and decided to have a bath. After that she sat in her dressing gown reading her book, then got dressed to go down for breakfast. She popped her head round Lizzie's door. Lizzie wasn't there, nor were any of her things. The room was immaculate, just as it had been when they arrived on Sunday evening. The bed was made, hotel style, and everything was arranged perfectly in the bathroom. She looked out of the window, and Lizzie's car wasn't to be seen. It was normally on the forecourt and had been all week. It was almost as though Lizzie had never been there. Had Lizzie thrown a strop at Maddie's harsh treatment of Aunty? Maddie thought they had made up and that was over and done with. She went downstairs and into the dining room to discover there was only one place set at the table. The usual breakfast fare was there, but only half

199

the usual quantity; only enough for one. When Aunty arrived she greeted Maddie in the usual way.

"Good morning, ma'am. Do you know where Liz - Elizabeth is? She wasn't in her room when I went for her."

"Elizabeth isn't joining us for breakfast this morning," Aunty said, rather coldly, as though they had had a falling out of some sort.

"Where is she? Where's her car? Has she left?"

Aunty stared straight ahead. "You will see her later." Maddie didn't know what to do. "Please begin."

Maddie ate some breakfast but wasn't in the mood for it. She thought it best to eat something in case she needed energy, perhaps to rescue Lizzie, perhaps to escape, perhaps for one of a thousand reasons she hadn't yet considered. While she was drinking her coffee Aunty said, "Thankyou." Maddie rose and Aunty left. After pausing for a moment, not sure what to do or say, Maddie left the dining room to pursue her along the corridor, but she was nowhere in sight. She looked both ways, but it was deserted in both directions. How could Aunty have covered such a distance in such a short time? The electric wheelchair wasn't fast enough to have reached the corner already. She dashed upstairs to look for clues in Lizzie's room, only to find it locked. A glance through the keyhole showed it totally empty, no furniture, no carpets, no curtains, nothing. A tear ran down her cheek. Here she was in a haunted house where even the living are a bit strange, and her best friend had disappeared without trace. She was without means of transport and miles from anywhere, and even if she had her mobile phone (which she'd left in Lizzie's glove compartment because there was no signal), she couldn't tell anyone where she was because she didn't know. Page sixty-eight of Lizzie's map-book – that's all she knew, but that too was in the car. She checked her own room, to make sure she hadn't 'disappeared' too, but all was well there. She sat in the armchair; it gave her a strange feeling of security, even though she didn't know why, which she no longer had in the rest of the house. She decided sitting worrying wasn't going to do any good, so she got up and went out into the corridor to look for footprints and marks of a scuffle or something, because in her heart of hearts she didn't believe Lizzie would just run off and leave her without explanation. If she had a message about a problem at home she would have stuck her head round the door to say 'got to go, explain later' or something. She examined the wooden boards all the way from Lizzie's room to the top of the stairs and saw nothing amiss. The corridor ahead, immediately above Aunty's rooms, led to Jane's rooms, but Lizzie said they weren't allowed to go along there. Well, this was an emergency, so if she encountered Jane she might get a few words of explanation. If Jane could speak, that is, because she hadn't spoken so far. Even when they arrived it was just gestures, and after that she hadn't interacted with them at all. She gingerly walked along the corridor, trying to be silent, still looking for signs of a struggle, or even footprints on the wooden flooring. She knelt down at each door to look through the keyholes; some of them were empty. Three rooms had furniture, nothing out of the ordinary; one was obviously a sitting room, another, an office, and a third, a bedroom. Unlike the corridor where her bedroom was, this one had a door on the end wall, after the last room on the side. This attracted her attention. She went to it and looked through the keyhole. There were people moving about!

Moving silently, but people. She couldn't make out who they were, as the keyhole was rather small. Should she knock? Should she just barge in? The matter was taken out of her hands. The door swung open and Jane beckoned her inside. She stepped into the room and froze. The room was quite big, about twice the size of her bedroom, and on the floor in front of her was a human skeleton. Next to it was another, and a third. Then, horror of horrors, was Lizzie. Was it Lizzie, or was it Lizzie's dead body? Maddie was frozen to the spot. She didn't know what to do. Should she run? But what if Lizzie was still alive? Should she try to rescue her? She looked around but the door had closed behind her. Aunty was there in her wheelchair, with Jane standing behind and slightly to one side. In the other part of the room there was a sort of cloud, a mist, which shimmered as though it was trying to move.

"What's going on? What have you done to Lizzie? I won't take this lying down. I'll fight whatever it is you're doing. I won't let you take my friend like this." Then she stopped speaking in utter amazement. Aunty held up her hand for silence and stood up out of the wheelchair. She walked across to the second skeleton and stood by its feet. Jane took her place by the third. A young man appeared from the misty cloud, the young man from the painting, and stood by the first, then the mist faded away to reveal Lizzie, who went to stand by her body. Lizzie smiled weakly and pointed at the floor next to her own body, and beckoned Maddie to join her.

The next morning Maddie and Lizzie came down to breakfast. They sat in silence until Aunty arrived. They stood until she instructed them to sit and greeted them.

There were no places set at the table, just empty place mats, and there was no food on the sideboard. They sat in silence for about fifteen minutes.

"Reading and music today," said Aunty. "Thankyou." They stood and she left. In the drawing room fifteen minutes later she positioned her wheelchair and said "We will start with reading."

"Which sonnet would you like to hear today, ma'am?" asked Maddie.

"Let's start as we mean to go on. Sonnet number one, please, Madeleine."

PW (in brackets)

Part one

Chapter 1

The blue people carrier drew up outside 8 Sycamore Gardens. The street was a cul-de-sac of about sixteen large houses, all well spaced with manicured lawns, block- paved drives and neat unfenced front gardens. The cars on the drives were all quite new, and all top-of-the-range models. The people who lived here obviously weren't short of a few shillings. Number 8 was the biggest house in the street with neat borders around the lawns and alternating purple and yellow plants exactly equidistantly positioned, as though the gaps had been measured with great precision, perhaps by laser control. The driver, a young woman dressed in a T-shirt, jeans and trainers, with short dark hair and below average height, got out and went to the back of the car. As she opened the boot lid a middle-aged man emerged from the house carrying a large suitcase and a substantial cool box. He put the suitcase down, made a gun shape with his hand as children might in the playground, and shouted, "Hi, Jack!" with a broad grin on his face.

Jack imitated the hand gesture and shouted back, "Take me to Cuba!" and they both exploded into giggles. The two passengers, Helen and Rachel, had got out of the car by now, and rolled their eyes, smiling.

"Don't be so miserable," the man called to them, "the old ones are the best!"

"Sorry, Mr Sutherland," answered Helen, "but that joke is so old it doesn't mean anything to most people these days."

"Yeah, I've often wondered why we say it," replied Jack, "what's it all about?"

"So why do you say it?" asked Helen.

"Dad taught me to say it when I was about five."

"When Mr S was young, people would hijack planes to go to Cuba," Rachel explained with a smile, "Now you can buy a ticket for Cuba from your high-street travel agent. You should pick a more politically controversial country." Mr Sutherland nudged Jack's arm.

"Hi, Jack," he called, making the gun gesture.

"Take me to North Korea!" Jack replied, after a moment of thought.

"Yes, that's better," Rachel answered, "but it doesn't sound so good – not snappy enough."

"That's right," Helen said, "you need a shorter name." Mr Sutherland nudged Jack again.

"Hi, Jack!"

"Take me to Syria!"

"That sounds better," Rachel commented, "but no more, please, or we'll be here all day." Mr Sutherland hugged the women in turn, then his face took on a slightly serious expression.

"Listen, girls, I need to ask a favour. You know my Flora isn't familiar with the countryside and outdoor life; I need you to take good care of her, you know, make sure she doesn't come to any harm." At this point he turned his face away and stared into the distance. "Since Janet, you know, passed away, well, Flora's all I've got. If something happened to her, well, I don't know what I'd do." Rachel put her arms around his shoulders.

"Of course we'll look after her – we always do," she said. He wiped a tear away on his shirt sleeve and turned back to them.

"Yes," Helen spoke up quickly to dispel the situation, "we've got our mobiles, although we're trying to not use them – we're doing an experiment to see if we can manage without technology, like in your day," she grinned wickedly, "and we've got rape alarms and first aid kits, and Rachel has her Bible with her, as usual; she'll pray for Flora."

Mr Sutherland looked earnestly at Rachel. "Will you do that? That would be lovely. Will you pray for me too?"

Rachel hugged him again. "Of course I will," she replied, glancing furtively at Helen who returned the glance. "I pray for you all every day anyway." The atmosphere was broken by a shout from the house.

"Hello! It's me!" Flora strolled along the garden path, arms outstretched. The others went up to her and hugged her lovingly in turn. Mr Sutherland took the suitcase and cool box to the back of the car and Jack stowed them securely.

"New car, Jack?" he asked.

"Yes and no, Mr Sutherland," Jack replied. "I have a new car but this isn't it. I just hired this one for the holiday." They discussed Jack's new car for a few moments, then Mr Sutherland pressed a small roll of notes into Jack's hand.

"Petrol money," he said.

"Thanks," Jack replied, "but we won't need this much."

"If there's any left over, take it as a contribution to the car hire. Nothing's too much for my Flora's happiness." They returned to the others. "The cool box has sandwiches and cakes and biscuits and drinks, and an ice pack, so they should be okay for a couple of days. My advice is to stop for a meal at lunchtime and raid the box for supper, and you should have enough left over for tomorrow, too," said

Mr Sutherland, relieved at the change of mood. After more hugs Flora wrapped her arms around her father and kissed him on the cheek; the women got into the car and it pulled away.

"Flora, you do realise we're going camping, don't you?" Helen asked, "in tents and stuff and no public to notice your image." Flora was wearing top of the range clothes: an expensive white T-shirt decorated with pink hearts and bows, pink jeans, day-glow pink trainers and a handbag which must have cost well in excess of a day's pay, and was in full make-up.

"Yes, I know, but I have to look good for me, and for you girls," she laughed.

"Trying to make us look grotty?" Jack replied.

"No, you can do that without my help," Flora laughed. "You know I don't mean that – you all look lovely. In your own way." The journey passed without incident, catching up on news about work and hobbies. After about two and a half hours they pulled into a car park next to a cafe in open country. The car park had two trucks and about seven or eight cars, but was nowhere near full. Two men sat on the bench outside, having a cigarette.

"This looks okay," said Jack, "and I'm starting to feel weak from malnutrition."

"Me too," said Helen. "Let's follow Dougie's advice and have a substantial meal here, if it looks half-decent."

"Please, Helen," Flora remonstrated, "he's a grown man and old enough to be your father. Call him by his proper name."

"Don't be so old fashioned, Flora, and I'm a grown woman. No disrespect intended. He's a dear man and a friend."

"Come on, you two," Jack called back to them, "or they'll be shut before we order." They went inside and sat at a table near the window, which had a good view over rolling hills and clusters of trees. They glanced through the menu until the waitress came to take their order.

"I'll have the full English breakfast, please, with a mug of tea." Helen was the first to order.

"Same for me," said Jack.

"Do you have a vegetarian option?" Rachel asked. The waitress shook her head.

"No, madam, we don't. We just do ordinary food here. None of that fancy stuff. Basic stuff – that's what folk want on holiday, and the truckers. There's just what's on the menu," she replied curtly. "We don't do that posh stuff 'cos there's no call for it. We must get three or four people every day wanting vegetarian stuff, and I tell them there's no call for it, but they don't listen."

"Okay," said Rachel, "I'll have beans on toast, two fried eggs, a portion of mushrooms and a mug of tea, please."

"See," commented the waitress, "that wasn't that difficult, was it? No need for that fancy stuff." She turned to Flora. "And for madam?"

"I'll have a full English breakfast, but could I have my tea in a cup and saucer instead of a mug please?"

"No, we just do mugs here; tastes the same anyway."

"Well, actually," Flora began, but Rachel nudged her.

"Leave it, Flora, just have the mug and look pleasant," she whispered. The food arrived and they tucked in and carried on their chat while they ate.

"I do hope you've brought some vegetarian sandwiches for Rachel," said Jack through a mouthful of beans.

210

"Jacqueline! Don't speak with food in your mouth!" said Flora in a mock scold, then smiling, she continued, "I expect there will be. Daddy sent Phong to Waitrose with strict instructions."

"Phong?" queried Helen. "Who's Phong?"

"Just the maid," replied Flora casually.

"The maid?" Jack butted in. "How long have you had a maid?" Flora began to look sad.

"When Mummy, you know, passed away, we got Mrs Henderson in as a regular cleaner, but one day she had a fall and broke her leg and her doctor said she should rest for at least six months, because of her age, you know. Well, one of Daddy's colleagues had a maid whose sister was looking for work, and that's how we got Phong."

"What sort of name is Phong?" Helen asked, "Where is she from?" Flora looked embarrassed.

"Phong isn't her name – it's what we call her. Her name is like a bad Scrabble hand. Like Welsh but worse. She's from the Philippines."

"I'm surprised at you, Flora," Jack commented, sitting back, obviously taking the moral high ground. "I didn't think you would take such a racist attitude, not making the effort to get the poor woman's name right, especially when you're fluent in four languages."

"Six, actually, but none of them South-East Asian. No, she wrote her name down in western script and I tried to pronounce it but she would glare at me. She refused to write it in her native script – I think she can't read or write in it. Daddy can't say it either. She would laugh and say 'You are stupid. Just call me Phong' and looked angry while she was laughing at us." Flora was visibly upset by this. Rachel put a comforting arm around her shoulders.

211

"Don't worry," she said, "you're with us now; two weeks without her." Helen and Jack glanced at each other, looking puzzled. Rachel explained. "She's a live-in maid, and you just can't get away from her. She does everything Dougie and Flora do – she sits with them to watch TV, goes with them to the theatre and for a meal out and shopping and everything."

"That's a bit strange," Helen said, "if she's just a maid, I mean." By now Flora was in tears.

"Daddy and I don't get to talk without her being there listening and interrupting and being horrid about everything I say and do. She's deliberately coming between us and I hate her, I hate her and she's a witch." Flora covered her eyes with a handkerchief, sobbing uncontrollably, and Helen and Jack came round to help comfort her.

"Hey, take it easy, Flora," said Jack, feeling uncomfortable and not knowing what to say. "Have a swig of tea and tell us later. Don't let Phong spoil your holiday. Concentrate on what we're doing now." Flora touched Jack's arm.

"Thankyou, Jacqueline," she said, "I know I'm safe with you three. I'll just go to the little girls' room to tidy myself up." So saying she picked up her handbag and dashed off to the toilets.

"Safe with you three?" said Helen in a loud whisper, looking at Rachel inquisitively. "What's that about?" Rachel shifted in her chair uncomfortably.

"I've been there twice since Phong arrived, and I've got to admit, I don't like her; I don't feel comfortable when she's in the room, which is most of the time. Nothing I can put my finger on, but I was pleased to be able to take Flora out and leave Phong with Dougie. I could tell she wanted to come with us, but she didn't want to leave Dougie on his own either. She even tried to tell Dougie to come with us so we could all be together. No wonder she's upset." At this point Flora returned to the table. "I'll tell you more later," Rachel whispered to Helen.

"Has everyone had enough to eat?" asked Jack, trying to lighten the mood. They all nodded, Helen paid the bill and bought a few snacks for later, and they got back into the car. Helen took Flora to one side.

"Listen, you need a break, and this holiday is exactly it. I'm here if you need anyone to talk to, and I'm sure Rachel is too, and Jack, although I admit Jack isn't exactly a talker. We're your friends, and we'll help you."

"Yes, I know, thankyou Helen. I'll try not to be so silly."

"Come on, Flora, you're always silly. That's what makes you so adorable." She kissed Flora on the cheek and got into the car. Flora paused for a moment, wondering if that was an insult or a compliment, and climbed in beside Rachel.

The rest of the journey passed without incident, although the chat was a bit subdued. Jack tried to lighten the mood with obscure jokes, until she and Helen had to concentrate on the journey, Helen navigating in unfamiliar territory.

"Remind me," chirped Flora, obviously feeling a bit better now, "why aren't we using the satnav?"

"This is Helen's experiment," Rachel answered. "If we can manage it, she's going to take her Brownie troop away without technology. She did it last year with the Girl Guides."

"So if the Guides managed, why the question over the Brownies?" Flora asked.

"With the Brownies we have to take a certain number of parents, because of the large number and the young age-group. That's what I'm worried about; I'm sure the Brownies themselves will be fine; I'm not sure about some of the parents. Those that insist on going are the type least able to cope. Those that would be able to cope trust me and their girls and think it would do them good. I must be mad." They all laughed. Helen returned to studying the map. "A bit of hush needed," she insisted. "I think we're nearly there. Look out for a white sign on a stick. Mr White said it would be obvious."

After driving around for half an hour in open countryside with no signs of habitation and retracing their steps three or four times, they saw it. It was exactly as Mr White had described it – a white sign on a stick, but it was in the middle of nowhere surrounded by grass and bushes and the occasional tree.

'This land belongs to Mr and Mrs White of White's Farm. Trespassers will be prosecuted. For permission to stay contact Mr White at the farm.'

Chapter 2

"Let's get the tents up while it's still light and not too windy," said Helen to Jack.

"Okay," Jack replied, looking around. "There's two flat bits just here. Ideal." They proceeded to sort out the tent poles and sheets while Flora and Rachel poked about in the car boot, deciding what they would need that night and what could stay in the car. Jack and Helen took no time at all erecting the tents then they stood leaning against a tree and waited for the other two to finish. Eventually Flora came over, carrying food, and drink and arranged them neatly on the grass in front of the tents.

"Now," said Helen in a commanding tone, "you are small so -" but she didn't get a chance to finish.

"Yes, we are small," Flora retorted quite aggressively. "So what? We are small so that gives you the right to tell us what to do? We are small so you have to make all our decisions? Or were you simply reminding us we are small in case we had forgotten? I don't forget. I am reminded every time I go to the theatre or cinema or any other sort of event where some great big tall person can block my view simply by being tall in front of me. We don't need people to say 'Hello, you are small' because we are reminded every day."

"Yes, that's right," interjected Jack. "Do people come up to you and say 'Hello, you've got big tits'? No, they don't," she said, prodding Helen's ample chest. This infuriated Flora even further.

"Jacqueline! I am trying to make a serious point and all you can do is reduce it to smutty talk about body parts. You are incorrigible." Helen laughed. "And you are just as bad.

215

She wouldn't do it if you didn't encourage her." And Flora stormed off, nearly knocking Rachel over as she emerged from behind the car. Rachel approached the other two.

"You just can't stop yourselves, can you?" Rachel growled. "You know she's a bit upset about this Phong business, and instead of showing some compassion you go out of your way to wind her up." She didn't wait for a reply and turned away in pursuit of Flora. Helen and Jack turned to face each other and tried not to laugh.

"She's right, you know," said Helen, "we are sometimes a bit rough on poor old Flora. She's not like us in some ways."

"Some ways?" queried Jack. "Many ways!" Then, unable to hold it in any longer, they burst out laughing briefly, until they saw Rachel scowling at them from behind the car. They went over to them. "Sorry, Flora, we were just trying to lighten the mood with a bit of humour," Helen said. She hugged Flora and led her back to the tent area.

"Sorry, old girl," said Jack sheepishly. "I didn't mean to upset you. It's just that your sense of humour isn't like mine." Flora accepted their apologies graciously as they sat down around the food.

"I'm sorry, Jacqueline, I don't think I have a sense of humour. I don't understand your jokes and seem to be offended a bit too easily sometimes. I'm sorry, I can't help the way I am." So saying she grasped Rachel's outstretched hand and tried to smile.

"What I was going to say," resumed Helen, slowly but firmly, "was that because you and Jack are short you will have to sleep in the green tent, and Rachel and I will sleep in the brown tent because it is longer." Jack and Flora

216

looked at each other, horrified. "What's wrong with that?" Helen asked, looking from one to the other.

"Well," began Flora slowly, "It's just, well, Jacqueline and I love each other dearly, but we have very little in common. There wouldn't be anything to talk about." Rachel smiled gently at them.

"Give it a go," she said, "and if it doesn't work, we'll do something different tomorrow night. Now let's eat before Jack dies of malnutrition." Jack and Flora tried to smile, and selected food and drink from the neatly arranged packets and cartons. After a while it became dusk.

"Er," began Flora hesitantly, "what facilities do we have? I haven't seen any, and I need to powder my nose." Jack went to the car and returned with a garden trowel in a plastic bag, which she handed to Flora with a grin.

"If you mean you need a leak, this is it." She sat down and carried on eating.

"What?" exclaimed Flora. "What's this?"

Helen explained, trying to look serious. "You dig a hole, put into it whatever you need to put, then fill up the hole." Flora looked aghast.

"But, but, people might see me! It's so undignified."

"Have you seen anyone else?" asked Helen, gesticulating expansively. "There's noone around but us."

"But you three might see me."

"Well do it behind a decent-sized bush. For goodness' sake, Flora, we've all got the same parts, and we have no desire to watch you peeing, anyway." Flora strode off, embarrassed. She returned a few minutes later and sheepishly handed the trowel back to Jack.

"Don't worry, I've cleaned it," she said, and burst into tears. Rachel moved over to sit next to her and put her arm

217

around Flora's shaking shoulders. "I'm sorry," Flora continued, "but I'm not used to this sort of life. I'm not sure this holiday is the best thing for me."

"I wish you'd mentioned it," said Helen, trying to sound sympathetic. "Jack and I did have doubts, and we agreed that if you didn't want to come, we would go somewhere else with more creature comforts. So that we could all holiday together."

"Yes, I had my own doubts, but I thought something different might put the Phong business out of my mind, and I couldn't let you down. You are my very dearest friends, and if Phong gets her claws into Daddy and takes him away from me, well, you three will be all I have left, now that Mummy's, well, no longer with us." Helen and Jack exchanged puzzled glances.

Rachel took charge. "Helen, can you make some tea? Then we can sit and have a chat about Phong. It might help Flora if she can get it off her chest." Helen and Jack set up the camping stove and made tea and opened a packet of biscuits, then they sat down to listen.

"Sorry, Flora, it's a mug," said Jack, and Flora smiled weakly. "Tell us all about Phong. What's all this about her being a witch?"

"You must think me silly," Flora began. "I know Rachel does." Rachel shook her head. "It's just that things happen every time someone upsets Phong. When Daddy's friend first told him about Phong, he said he was happy with what Mrs Henderson was doing, and the very next day poor Mrs Henderson fell and broke her leg. She was a dear old soul and I miss her. If I got home early from work we could sit and have a girly chat over coffee until Daddy got home. And the boys from along the street were out on their bikes one day and one of them accidentally ran over the corner of our lawn while Phong was putting some edging plants in, and she shouted at him, in her language of course, so we don't know if she was just shouting, or swearing, or if she was cursing him, but about an hour later the ambulance rolled into the street and took him away. He had fallen off his bike and broken his arm. And then Mrs Morrison called to ask if we could contribute to the women's refuge Easter party. I know she can be a bit abrupt, but Phong took offence at the way she asked, for some reason or other which I haven't fathomed out yet, and they had a stand-up row in the street, and a week later poor Mrs Morrison had a heart attack. And then there was the poor binman. A few weeks ago he spilt some rubbish while he was emptying our bin. It was our fault - we had put too much in, but Phong was at the door and she yelled at him before he had a chance to pick it up, and he said something like 'Keep your hair on, darlin', I'll get it in a minute'. Well, she screamed at him, 'Don't you call me darling – I pay your wages', which she doesn't, actually, but anyway, later that day he got his arm caught in the lorry's mechanism and now the poor man is going to be off work for six months. Mrs Andrews next door saw all these things and told me later in graphic detail. So in the six months she's been in our house the binman and two neighbours have ended up in hospital; three if you include Mrs Henderson. And I've heard her threatening other neighbours. 'You'll be next' she shouts while she shakes her fist at them. I've tried asking them what it's all about, but they go all quiet and don't want to say anything in case they trigger the curse. I tried to speak to her about it, but she laughs and tells me I am just the useless daughter and

219

Daddy is the boss. Anyway, I think she is getting her claws into Daddy. He daren't contradict her. I've seen him looking very worried at some of the things she says and does. And she gets everything she asks for."

"I don't wish to sound heartless," said Helen cautiously while Flora paused to sip her tea, "but she is just the maid, isn't she?"

"Yes, she is, and I wish Daddy would sack her, but I don't think he dare do it."

"No, that's not what I meant, Flora. I mean, is she *just* the maid, or is there a love interest? How old is she? Is she pretty? Is she single?" Flora was momentarily speechless and her eyes opened wide in amazement. She burst into tears.

"Helen, how can you say such things about my Daddy? Yes, she is pretty and she is single but she is just a year or two older than us. She is far too young to be my stepmummy."

"I wasn't thinking about marriage, but if they are having a roll in the hay every now and then, well, it could be very difficult for Dougie to get rid of her."

"Yes, and Dougie is a looker," chimed in Jack, "he can give me one any time of the day or night."

Rachel gave Jack a prod with her foot. "Not the right moment, Jack," she hissed through clenched teeth, "not very helpful."

"I was just trying to make the point that ..." Jack began but Rachel cut her off with a glare.

"Well, don't," Rachel snapped. Flora howled and burst into more tears.

"Oh, no, Jacqueline. You're younger than me. You couldn't possibly be my stepmummy."

"Forget it, Flora," said Rachel, "Jack was just being silly."

"I wasn't," said Jack, before Helen dug her sharply in the ribs with her elbow. Jack winced and stopped talking.

"Flora, darling," Rachel began, embracing Flora in a bearhug, "I understand that Phong appears to be behind everything that has gone wrong recently, and I understand that you are feeling a bit raw after your mum's passing, I know, I've been through that too, but these things are all coincidences. Try and put Phong to the back of your mind for now. We are here for you. We are your best friends and have been for quite some time, and your dad will be there when you get home to greet you with open arms and it will all work itself out. I pray for you every day, and for Helen and Jack too, and your dad. Try not to worry."

"Rachel," Flora squeaked.

"Yes, dear?" Rachel replied.

"Can you let me go now please? You're almost crushing me to death." The others burst into fits of laughter while Rachel blushed.

"I'm sorry, darling, I was just giving you a meaningful hug." Flora twisted free and gave Rachel a peck on the cheek.

"Look, Flora," said Helen, "forget about the witch and let's think about getting some shut-eye. Poor Jack must be exhausted after all that driving."

"Actually no, I'm not." Jack began but didn't continue because Helen prodded her quite sharply in the ribs again. "Yes, I suppose I am."

"Good idea," said Flora, "I'm going to get ready." and off she trotted into the green tent. About fifteen minutes later she emerged wearing pink cotton pyjamas with little white teddy bear motifs on the top, and holding a little teddy bear under her arm. The others looked at each other aghast. Flora did a twirl so they could see her attire. Jack was struggling not to laugh; Rachel suppressed a giggle. Helen looked stern.

"Flora, what are you wearing?"

"Do you like it?" Flora asked. "I bought these especially for the holiday. Daddy gave me the money for them. I didn't need it, but he likes to buy me presents and I didn't want to upset him. At this time of year I would normally wear a short nightdress, but I thought that might be a bit difficult to manage getting in and out of the sleeping bag, and I might accidentally show too much bare flesh, so these seemed ideal." She gave a huge smile and sat down, cuddling the teddy bear.

"Flora," Helen began slowly, "you've never been camping in a tent before, have you?"

"No," she shook her head, looking puzzled, "this is my first time. Why?"

"You'll freeze if that's all you are wearing," answered Helen, "you need to wear ordinary day clothes." Flora looked despondent.

"Daddy will be disappointed if I don't wear my new pyjamas he bought me," she replied sulkily, "and it sounds a bit unhygienic sleeping in what I've had on all day."

"You can wear the pyjamas, but put trousers and a jumper on top. And wear some thick socks."

"Oh, good idea, but I don't have any thick socks."

"You can borrow a pair of mine," said Jack, "we'll be about the same size." Jack went to the car and returned with a pair of thick grey woolly socks that looked as though they belonged in the armed forces. Not the most elegant socks in the entire universe. Flora accepted the offer, but she obviously wasn't enthusiastic.

"Thankyou, Jacqueline, I'll wash them before I give you them back."

"Oh, don't worry about that, old girl, pleased to be able to help out." Flora returned to the tent and later emerged dressed in trousers and a jumper, including Jack's socks, still clutching the little teddy bear. One by one the others went off with the garden trowel, and then they climbed into their sleeping bags. They called 'good night' to each other in a style reminiscent of *The Waltons* and settled down for the night. In the brown tent Helen and Rachel lay staring up at the roof for a while, then Helen spoke.

"Poor old Flora, all this upset, then having to share with Jack. It's funny, but it isn't."

"That's good for you," answered Rachel.

"Thankyou." Then after a pause, "What do you mean, good for me?" half sitting up.

"Thinking of other people's problems; it isn't something you're quick to do."

"Isn't it? I always thought of myself as being benevolent. Can you explain what you mean?"

"Don't take it the wrong way, dear, you always go out of your way to help people, but you don't often think about people's feelings."

"Do I not? Oh. I wasn't aware of that." Pause. "Yes, I suppose you could be right. I can be a bit crap sometimes, I suppose. Anyway, I was feeling sorry for Flora. She's in that tent with Jack, and she'll hear all about Jack's new car and new computer and she'll be bored silly because she doesn't understand either, and isn't interested in stuff like that."

"New computer?" queried Rachel. "I knew about the new car. What's so special about the new computer?"

"It's her latest project; she's so bloody clever she's scary. She has built a robot thing and it's controlled by this stupidly powerful computer. It can make tea and coffee, toast, microwave ready meals, and deliver them to you no matter where you are in the flat. She has a few problems to iron out. It's fine on her laminate floor in the kitchen and lounge, but it struggles on carpet, and it is so slow your coffee is stone cold by the time you get it. If she speeds it up it spills half of it. Then she wants to make it recognise the food. At present the microwave meals all have to be in certain places in the fridge. She wants it to find them no matter where they are."

"Is this work or is she doing it for some sort of project?"

"Neither. It's for her dad. His mind's totally sharp but his body's giving out, and her mum's showing signs of dementia, so she's making this for the day mum has to go into a home so dad can maintain a bit of independence. Eventually it's going to be voice controlled. I honestly wouldn't know where to start with something like that. She wants to get it all working by instructing the computer from her mobile phone before she starts on the voice thing. Rather her than me."

"Wow! I knew she was clever, but, well, this is a different level to normal humans."

"Yes, last time I stayed over I was woken up by the robot delivering a cold cup of coffee to me in bed. I nearly shit myself because we had got back late and she hadn't told me about it. It's a bit scary when you are half asleep

224

and you hear Stephen Hawking saying 'Coffee, Helen' in your room."

"Yes, I'm not surprised." They lay in silence for a while, then Rachel said quietly, "Flora's changed, hasn't she."

"Yes, she has," Helen replied. "Even I noticed that. She tries to be her old bouncy self, but it isn't working."

"It's not just that," Rachel answered, "she lost her bounce when her mum died. I visited shortly after, at Dougie's request, and she wasn't her old self. I understand; I went through all that a few years earlier, but I think I recovered pretty well. You never get over it, but you do get used to it. Flora isn't showing any signs of getting used to it. No, what I meant was she has a different outlook. She is negative about so many things. She never used to be negative at all. I think this Phong business is really getting to her."

"Yes, but what can we do about it? Can we do anything?"

"I'm not sure we can. But I'll have a think and we'll see how things develop over the holiday. Being away from Phong for a while might be all she needs."

"I hope you're right. You usually are on such things. Anyway, let's get some sleep. Good night."

"Yes, good night. Tomorrow is another day, as they say in the movies."

Chapter 3

Next morning Helen and Rachel were up bright and early. There wasn't a cloud in the sky, and as soon as the sun came up the campsite became quite warm. Birds fluttered from tree to tree, singing as they went. Rachel got the kettle going and made coffee while Helen started making breakfast. Fried eggs and beans on toast for Rachel, and bacon, eggs, sausages and black pudding for herself. They had almost finished when Jack emerged looking tired.

"You look tired, Jack, didn't you sleep well?" asked Helen with a grin.

"Sleep? What is sleep? She spent about half an hour telling me the roof of the tent was the wrong colour for the floor and our sleeping bags didn't match. The woman is impossible. She talked to that damned teddy bear all night too, even when she was asleep. I couldn't work out what she was saying, but she promised to protect it. I came close to throwing it out more than once. Why does the colour of the tent matter? It is for sleeping in. It isn't a fashion accessory. I'm not sure I can face another night like that. You'll have to come up with a better plan."

Helen and Rachel were laughing at Jack when Flora emerged, looking equally tired. Jack wolfed down some breakfast before running off with the trowel. As soon as Jack was out of earshot Flora spoke while she ate her breakfast.

"There's something wrong with that girl," she said with a scowl. "All she talked about were the new car and the new computer. Don't all cars do nought to sixty? I'm sure even my little one does that. And as for the computer, dear me, the poor thing's having problems with the vector

226

interrupts conflicting, whatever that means, but she should know I know nothing about such matters. She should realise she's wasting her breath asking me. I'm sorry, but we'll have to have a different sleeping arrangement tonight or I'll go mad. Poor Teddy didn't get a wink of sleep either." At that point Jack returned, so Flora stopped talking. Helen and Rachel exchanged furtive glances, trying not to laugh. Helen poured coffee while Rachel looked at the map.

"I say, Helen," said Rachel, trying to lighten the mood. "Is this blue thing a lake? Will it be big enough to swim in?"

"Oh, yes," replied Helen, pleased at having something positive to talk about. "I think it will be big enough for swimming, if it's deep enough. And if the water is clean it will be our drinking and washing water for the week. Jack has a testing kit. We'll go there this morning. If it isn't clean we'll have to go to the little town to fill our water containers, but when we've finished breakfast, get your towels together and we'll give it a go."

Rachel was still studying the map. "What's this here? PW in brackets – what does that mean?"

"Thought you of all people would know that," Helen answered with a grin. "Place of Worship."

"Yes, I know that, but why in brackets?"

"That means it isn't in use any more, probably a ruin."

"Okay. I would like to go there one day, if noone minds." She looked around at the others for approval.

"No, that's okay with us," said Flora. "It's your holiday as well as ours."

"That's settled then," said Helen. "We can go there later today, if we get back in time from the lake, and if we don't, we'll go there tomorrow."

They washed the breakfast pots and packed them away, and with towels under their arms they set off. Flora was carrying a little purple bag, and Jack was carrying the water container and her water-testing kit. The sun shone down on the little group as they tramped across the heather, chatting amiably, and soon the problems of the previous day were pushed to the backs of their minds. About half an hour later they arrived at the lake. Flora found a suitably sized bush to get changed behind, and the others stripped off and were in the lake, splashing about, before she emerged. She was wearing a purple swimsuit with matching bathing cap, and gingerly dipped a toe into the water.

"It's a bit on the cool side," she commented, "but not too bad." So saying she joined the others in the water. Swimming across only took a few minutes, so they were soon bored with that, and after splashing about a bit they made for the bank and hauled themselves out.

"By, that was a bit fresh," remarked Helen.

"Yes, my nipples are like organ stops," replied Jack.

"Well, mine are like chapel coat pegs," answered Helen.

"Mine could put somebody's eye out." Jack didn't want to be outdone.

"Mine could cut glass." This from Helen.

"Mine could cut diamonds," Jack retorted.

"Oh, stop it, stop it, stop it!" shouted Flora, crossly running towards them. "Why does everything have to be about your rude bits?" then, turning her back when she realised they were naked, she ran off and hid behind the bush. Rachel butted in angrily.

"You're doing it again. What is wrong with you two? I know it's meant to be harmless fun, but I thought after yesterday you could show a bit of restraint. She's all upset again now, and she had been so happy on the way here. I'm really cross with you two. Why can't you grow up?" She stormed off towards Flora, who was crouching behind the bush, in tears. She held out her arms to Flora, who backed away.

"No, Rachel, you can't touch me. You aren't wearing anything."

"For goodness sake, Flora, I'm trying to comfort you. I think you need to grow up a bit as well as those two. Now come here and let me hug you." Flora was still reluctant. "In a nonsexual way," Rachel added after a pause. She wrapped her arms round the sulking Flora.

"I'm sorry, Rachel," said Flora. "Perhaps you're right, perhaps I do need to grow up, but I've never been used to nakedness. It's something we never did in our house."

"We never did in our house, but we did have showers after PE lessons at school."

"So did we, but we had cubicles to shower in, for privacy."

"We didn't, but my school didn't cost a million pounds a term. You had to be naked in the shower to get all the sweat off. I don't understand why it is such an issue. It would be different if there were men around, but there aren't, it's just us, your closest friends."

"I'm sorry, Rachel, I'll try not to be offended in future."

"Are you ready to go back?"

"Yes, but I'll get dried and changed first." Rachel returned to Helen and Jack, who had been laughing, but were now looking sheepish. They were now dried and fully dressed. Jack was testing the water with her chemical kit.

"I'm sorry, Rachel," began Helen, but Rachel held up her hand.

"Don't apologise, just don't do it again. Do you think you can go a whole week without making fun of body parts?"

"We'll try to, won't we, Jack?" she replied. Jack nodded in agreement, returning from the lakeside.

"Yes, we will. Fortunately the water here is cleaner than what comes out of the tap back home, so no chance of an upset tum. I'll fill the bottle for drinking." At this point Flora emerged from behind the bush, fully dressed, and drying her hair as she walked. She smiled weakly and apologised to Helen and Jack.

"I'm sorry, you two, I'm just not used to such things. I will try to be a bit less straight-laced." Helen and Jack graciously accepted this, and the four set off back to the campsite. Rachel and Flora trailed behind a little, and Rachel tried to engage Flora in the countryside, pointing out flowers, trees and birds along the way. When they arrived back Jack made some coffee while Flora arranged what was left of her father's food parcel neatly on the grass. They selected sandwiches and cakes, and when they had finished eating it had almost all gone. They packed the remnants away into the car while Rachel and Helen studied the map. "That's almost all of Daddy's food gone, but we haven't started on yours. Will there be enough for today?" Flora asked.

"Yes," Jack replied. "Helen and I got quite a lot, and it's all stuff that won't go off. The only thing we'll have to do is visit the lake to top up the water bottle, but we shouldn't need to do that more than once a day." So saying she locked the car and they set off in the other direction towards the 'Place of Worship'. Helen's orienteering skills were good, and they arrived there after half an hour's walk. There was a dip in the ground, and they could see the outline of the church in the grass. It consisted of what had been stone walls, now only about a foot high. It had obviously been a small church, but there were no signs of seats. There was a doorway at one end and what might have been an altar towards the other. The four women walked down the grassy bank into the dip and Rachel made her way into the church. Helen and Flora followed, but Jack stopped. Inside the stone outline they turned to see Jack rooted to the spot some distance away.

"What's up, Jack?" asked Helen. "Aren't you coming in?" Jack shook her head but didn't speak.

"Jack, are you alright?" asked Rachel. She went over to Jack.

"No, I can't come any further," Jack answered, with a quiver in her voice. "This is a bad place. There's something wrong." Flora came over.

"Look, Jacqueline, even I have been in, and you know what I'm like for doing new things."

"No, Flora, it isn't because it is a 'new thing'. It's because it is a bad place." Jack took a few steps back and sat down on the bank. She suddenly seemed more relaxed. Rachel went back into the church.

"I'm sorry, Jack," she said. "I don't see what the problem is. I feel totally at home here."

231

"So do I," chimed in Flora.

"You are used to such places, but I'm not," Jack answered. "And it isn't because it's a church; it's because there is something wrong about it."

Helen had been going in and out of the doorway, pausing to feel the atmosphere. "Sorry, mate," she said. "I can't feel any difference inside or out. But if you're not happy, perhaps we should go back." She came over and sat on the bank beside Jack.

"No," objected Jack. "If I'm the only one to feel anything, it wouldn't be fair on you - Rachel, in particular - to go back now. I'm alright here with Helen. We'll sit and wait until you have finished what you want to do."

"If you don't mind, Jack, I would like to pray here for a few moments, then we'll go back." Rachel went back in and knelt before the remains of the altar and bowed her head. Flora followed and knelt beside Rachel, more in companionship rather than prayer. As they were getting to their feet Flora called out.

"Oh! Look! Over there!" She pointed into the trees on the other side of the dip. "Did you see him?" The others followed her outstretched arm but shook their heads.

"No, Flora," Helen answered. "I didn't see anyone."

"Nor me," added Rachel. Jack remained silent.

"You must have seen him!" Flora complained. "He wasn't hidden in the trees at all. He was dressed like a monk in a black habit. He was looking straight at us. How could you not see him?"

Helen walked quickly over to where Flora had been pointing. "Is this where he was?"

"No, about a yard to your left, and a yard or two further away."

"Here?"

"Yes, exactly."

Helen looked around on the ground for a few moments, then shook her head. She returned to the others. "Sorry, Flora, but there's no sign of anyone being there. No disturbed grass or twigs or anything."

Flora wasn't happy. She stamped her foot. "I suppose you don't believe me, because it's me," she said, sulkily. "If it had been Jacqueline you would have believed her, because she's the stable one, not given to flights of fantasy."

Rachel tried to put her arm round Flora's shoulders, but Flora shook it off and took a couple of steps away and stood with her back to them. "No, Flora, we're not saying we disbelieve you, we're just saying we didn't see anyone."

"Well that's not what Helen's saying," she replied, glaring at Helen.

"No, I'm not," retorted Helen. "I'm saying there wasn't any evidence of the man being there. But if you want to twist my words, well, I'll say no more, but I won't listen any more either."

Rachel put a hand on a shoulder of each one. "Look, you two, let's not fall out over this. I didn't see the man, but that doesn't mean there wasn't a man. Did you see him, Jack?"

"No," replied Jack, "but I wasn't looking that way."

"Look, perhaps we should head back. We can take a gentle stroll and go the long way round to appreciate nature, and have a quiet meal and turn in," said Rachel, trying to defuse the tension.

"Yes," said Helen. "It will be a bit of an early night, but it won't do us any harm. I brought a couple of books along. Might make a start on one of them." Jack got up rather shakily, but after a few steps was back to normal. Rachel walked alongside her on the way back.

"What exactly did you feel back there?" she asked.

"Don't know, exactly," Jack replied hesitantly. "Just that there was something wrong. I don't generally believe in good and evil, but if I did it would definitely have been evil. Like something really bad was going to happen. But I'd rather not talk about it."

Back at the campsite they had beans on toast and mugs of tea and finished off the cake from Dougie's food parcel then sat around for a while, Helen reading, Rachel knitting, Jack studying an electronics manual and Flora sketching some dress designs. When it was bedtime Rachel offered to share the smaller tent with Flora, to great relief from Flora and Jack, even though the bottom of her sleeping bag stuck out the end of the tent.

Chapter 4

The next morning Helen emerged from her tent. Jack was still asleep and there was no sign of life from the other tent. In fact, Rachel's sleeping bag wasn't sticking out of the flap, where it had been last night.

"Perhaps it got too cold and she tucked her feet in," Helen said quietly to herself. Closer inspection showed that Rachel wasn't there. Helen woke Flora and asked about Rachel.

"Oh, I hadn't noticed she was gone," Flora said, sleepily. "Perhaps she's powdering her nose." At that Rachel returned.

"Hello, you two. Where's Jack?"

"Jack's still asleep. Where have you been?" demanded Helen.

"Just been down to the little church. It's really tranquil at this time of day, the dew on the grass, the birds chirping, the sound of distant lambs bleating. Might go there again tomorrow if I get up in time."

"You could have told us," remonstrated Helen.

"I don't need your permission for one thing, and for another you were all sound asleep."

"Yes, but if you'd fallen and hurt yourself and we didn't know where you were, what then?"

"I'm sure you would have guessed eventually." Rachel smiled and set about preparing breakfast. Helen sat down heavily and folded her arms. She obviously wasn't pleased, but Rachel was right. "Anyway," Rachel continued. "What are we doing today? Any plans for somewhere to visit?"

"Yes," replied Helen. "I was thinking we might visit Farmer White to pay our rent, then perhaps a walk through the woods."

"Sounds good to me," said Rachel. Flora had been for a little walk with the trowel, and as she returned Jack was climbing out of the tent. They sat round chatting about inconsequential matters while they ate breakfast. After they had cleared away Helen picked up her rucksack.

"Come on then," she said. "This way. If we go cross-country instead of by road it should take us about an hour to get there, perhaps more if the terrain is a bit rough." It actually took more than two hours, partly because of the rough ground, but also because Rachel and Flora kept stopping to look at unusual flowers.

"I'm sorry to slow you down," Rachel apologised. "But where I live there are very few wild flowers. These aren't out of the ordinary, but I rarely see them in real life – only in books."

"Don't worry," said Jack. "We don't mind. It's your holiday too. As long as you don't mind if we stop to look at some machine or other when I want to."

"Jacqueline, we're in the countryside. Where are we going to see machines?" Flora asked.

"There might be some really ancient old farm vehicles around here. I haven't seen anything modern since we left the cafe. It's amazing how they survived with such old technology." Eventually they arrived at White's Farm. It had a sign advertising farmhouse lunches, and they had a good look at the menu before Helen knocked on the door. It was opened by a cheerful, plump, middle-aged woman, with rosy cheeks and a big smile.

"Hello, Mrs White," said Helen. "I'm Helen Underwood. We're camping on your land and we've come to pay the fee."

"Oh, yes. I remember," said Mrs White. "Come on in, dears, have a seat while I find my glasses." They went in and sat down at a large wooden table. "Now, where have I put them? Arthur, have you seen my glasses?" she called to the other room.

"On the dresser," came the reply.

"Oh, yes. So they are. Miss Underwood's here to pay the camping fee." Mr White came through from the other room and smiled benignly. He was a muscular man with gnarled hands and a weather-beaten face, well over six feet tall and without an ounce of surplus fat.

"Hope everything's okay," he said. "You're the only ones here this week. Last week we had about six or seven families. Sorry about the lack of amenities, last year we tried putting a chemical toilet on the site, but in the hot weather it stank to high heaven. The campers said they'd rather just use a hole in the ground, so this year we didn't bother with it." He grinned. "The way nature intended." They all laughed, except Flora.

"Oh, yes, it's fine," Helen answered before Flora had a chance to speak. "We went for a swim in the lake too. Hope that's okay. Is the lake yours?"

"Oh, yes. When you're up there everything as far as the eye can see is ours. It's been in our family for generations."

"I say, whatever you're cooking smells rather good," butted in Jack, as it was about lunchtime and they hadn't eaten since breakfast. The other three laughed.

237

"Food is Jack's number one priority," laughed Rachel. "I'm surprised she has lasted this long. Shall we have lunch here?"

"Seems like a good idea to me," said Helen. The others nodded in agreement. "What's on the menu today, Mrs White?"

"Well, the schools went back last week, so I don't do a full menu, but there's Lancashire Hotpot and a Ploughman's Lunch. I suppose they calls it a 'Plough-Person's Lunch' these days." She chuckled and Jack and Rachel joined in.

"Yes, 'Plough-Person's Lunch' will be fine for me, as long as there's no meat in it," said Rachel.

"Of course there's no meat in it," said Mrs White. "What sort of a cook do you take me for?"

"Sorry, no intention to offend," Rachel answered. "But I've been to restaurants where they put pate on too. I'm a vegetarian, you see."

"Pate? No such thing on my Ploughman's Lunch. We knows how to do proper food in these parts. Disgraceful." The other three settled for Lancashire Hotpot, and Mrs White disappeared through the kitchen door. Mr White sat down at the table.

"I know it weren't deliberate, but don't you go upsetting my Betty. She's very proud of her cooking; she's won awards, you know." He pointed at a framed certificate on the wall. "County Show, 1997. First Prize." He beamed with pride.

"And did you win awards too, Mr White?" asked Rachel. He looked puzzled. She pointed at a picture of him with a large pig with a rosette.

"Oh, no!" he replied with a broad grin. "That's Grandpa Large with Esmerelda. 1949. Best in Show."

"Sorry," Rachel apologised. "I thought it was you. The similarity is quite striking."

"Yes, I've heard folk say that, but I never met him. Died a week before I was born."

"Grandpa Large?" queried Jack. "That's an unusual name for such a small chap."

"He weren't very big, about the same size as me." The four looked at each other in amazement. "No, 'Large' was what his pals down the pub called him, on account of him being a pig farmer." They looked puzzled. "Him being Farmer White, they called him 'Large' after his pigs." He could tell by their faces he obviously hadn't explained adequately. He pointed at the picture, frustrated. "That there pig is a Large White. Large White, Farmer White who breeds Large Whites. What else could they call him? Large White. They even put it on his gravestone. His real name was Arthur; that's why I am called Arthur, what with him dying just before I was born. You must be city ladies, if you don't know a Large White when you see one. It's called that because it's large, and it's white, you know. Ancient breed, I think. Plenty of meat on it. Good value for money. I don't breed them any more. Vet's bills were too high. They see an ancient breed and their prices goes up before they does anything."

"So what do you farm, then, if you gave up on the pigs?" asked Rachel.

"I have a few sheep, and Betty has a few chickens. Fresh eggs if you want some."

"Oh, yes, we'll have a dozen, please," said Helen. He went outside and returned five minutes later with two boxes of eggs. Helen paid him, settled their camping bill and paid for the meals all at the same time.

"We're getting a bit older and slower now, so the sheep and chickens are just right. Our mornings are taken up with them, and the meals and the campsite, then we can take it easy for an hour or so in the afternoon, before I go up to check on the sheep before it gets dark." At that Mrs White came in with the meals. They tucked in while Mr White disappeared through the door and returned with six mugs of tea. After the meal Mrs White cleared the plates away while Mr White told them about the farm. "This farm has been in my family for four or five generations. When I get too old our son will take it on. He has the farm next door. He inherited that from Betty's family, him being the only Grandchild. It's much bigger than ours, but it's right next door so it will be easy for him to make one big farm out of the two. And he has workers, farm hands, you know, so it won't be a problem." Mrs White returned from the kitchen and sat down at the table with her mug of tea.

"Mr White," began Rachel, "is the little ruined church yours too? Can you tell us anything about it?" Mr and Mrs White glanced at each other. His expression changed from genial to stern in an instant and she looked concerned. He got to his feet.

"I have to go," he said abruptly. "A farm doesn't run itself." He picked up his stick and left hurriedly. Mrs White buried her face in her hands.

"Sorry," apologised Rachel, putting her hand on Mrs White's forearm. "I didn't realise it was a sore point." Mrs White pulled away and got to her feet.

"It'll take me six weeks to calm him down. He's just got over the last time. Perhaps you'd better go." The four glanced at each other and picked up their rucksacks and made for the door.

"Sorry," said Rachel. "I hope he is okay. The meals were lovely." They left and Mrs White slammed the door after them. They were slowly making their way out along the path under something of a cloud when the farmhouse door opened and Mrs White took a few steps along the path.

"You'll not go near the church, if you know what's good for you. Didn't mean to be rude, but it's upsetting." She slammed the door before they had a chance to answer. The girls stopped and looked at each other without speaking for a while.

Jack shook her head. "I agree with her," she said. "There's something not right about that place. I knew it as soon as we got near it. But you all thought I was being silly." Flora and Rachel gazed at the ground. Helen shook her head.

"No, Jack, I didn't think you were being silly. I went to investigate but I didn't feel anything strange. Like Flora's man, just because I didn't see him it doesn't mean he wasn't there." They walked on, slowly, and in silence for a while. Helen stopped and took some little books and pencils from her rucksack. "Come on, let's put that behind us for now. I need your help with my project." She handed them each a book and pencil and consulted the map.

"Remind me," said Flora slowly. "What's this project all about, and why are we looking for ..." She stopped and looked at the book. "... for birds?"

"Last year I took a few Girl Guides away camping, just overnight, but this year I've been asked to take the

241

Brownies away for a week. Being a lot younger, I need to take some parents away too."

"Yes," butted in Flora, "you told us that earlier, but what are the books for?"

"Well, I want you three to tell me if these little books will keep the parents occupied for a day or two. I know the girls will be fine, but the parents can be a bit of a handful. They're the type that will get withdrawal symptoms if they don't see their favourite rubbish TV progs." The other three laughed heartily at this idea, and forgot the incident at the farmhouse for a while. They inspected their books. Flora had birds, Rachel had flowers, and Jack had insects. Each page had a few related items, with space to put the date and place, and what was happening at the time.

"I used to have these when I was a child. They're good fun," said Rachel with a big smile.

"It's all new to me," said Jack, grumpily, "but I'll give it a go for you, Helen. Couldn't I have one for tractors or something?"

"No," answered Helen, "there wasn't one. I thought you might be happy with insects."

"Well, it's certainly better than birds or flowers." They made their way back to the campsite by a circuitous route through a wood, making notes in their little books. Jack enjoyed it more than she expected, and sometimes crawled on the ground to get a good view of something. She had a small magnifying glass in her pocket (no surprise to the others) and made comprehensive notes. Flora was quite overcome with the beauty of some of the birds, and said she would use some of their designs and colourings next time she made some clothes. Rachel didn't say much, but smiled with obvious happy childhood memories going through her head. When they got back Jack and Helen set about making a meal and boiling the kettle for tea while Rachel took the water bottle to the lake to fill it for tomorrow's breakfast. They ate in silence, tired after the long walk, until Rachel spoke.

"Well? Did you enjoy doing the nature books?"

"I certainly did," answered Jack. "Although I have to admit, I didn't expect to." The others laughed. "But I'd rather have tractors or cars or something."

"So do you think these little books will entertain the parents for a few days?"

"Call me sceptical, but no," said Rachel. "But I could be wrong."

"I think they might work for some of them," said Jack. "I would like to spend another day doing insects, then perhaps something else, but not flowers or birds. I'm not one for colours. Perhaps trees or rocks or weather patterns."

"Oh, Jacqueline," said Flora, "You're utterly soulless. The flowers and birds are lovely."

"No, give me something with a motor any day." They cleared away, visited the 'facilities', and went to bed.

Chapter 5

The next morning Flora heard Rachel getting up early. She waited until Rachel had gone, then got up herself and set off following Rachel at a discreet distance. Rachel headed towards the little church. Flora was in a quandary; should she go back for Helen and Jacqueline and risk losing track of Rachel, or should she carry on following? She decided to continue. Rachel wasn't being at all secretive. She was walking at quite a speed, which she could with her long legs, humming a tune, swinging her arms, as though she didn't have a care in the world. Flora had to hurry along every now and then to try to keep up, but was also trying to avoid making any sound. As they neared the church Flora slowed down, as there were fewer trees and bushes to hide behind. Rachel went straight up to it, went in through the doorway, and knelt at the altar remains. She bowed her head and prayed for about fifteen minutes. During this time Flora was kneeling behind a bush and watching. Suddenly she saw something move in the bushes beyond the church. She almost cried out, but managed to stop herself. It was the man in the dark robe! Flora wished she had brought a camera. Hindsight can be a wonderful thing. Just then Rachel rose to her feet, bowed solemnly, and set off back. Flora ran all the way back so that Rachel didn't catch up. When she got back Helen was preparing breakfast.

"Oh, you as well now," she said, with an air of disapproval. Flora was panting and gasping.

She shook her head. "No, Helen," she said between gasps. "I followed to see where she was going and what she was doing." The noise had brought Jack out of the tent.

"What's going on?" she asked.

"They've been to the little church," said Helen. "Nothing to do with me, or so I was told yesterday."

"I didn't want to go," spluttered Flora. "I just followed Rachel to see where she was going and what she was doing."

"You idiots!" shouted Jack at Flora. Just then Rachel appeared. "This is your fault!" Jack shouted at Rachel, pointing aggressively. "If you hadn't gone Flora wouldn't have followed." Rachel looked puzzled.

"Flora?" she said. "Flora wasn't there. I went by myself. Anyway, as we discussed yesterday, we're all old enough to make our own decisions." Jack turned to Flora.

"I only went to keep an eye on her," Flora sobbed. "I didn't want to go but I thought I needed to look out for her because she's my friend. I didn't want any harm to come to her."

"What harm is there in going to a church to pray?" asked Rachel, starting to get annoyed. Jack was furious.

"What harm is there? I don't know how you can say such a stupid thing after what happened yesterday. That poor old farmer and his wife were beside themselves and warned us against it and all you can say is 'what harm is there?' I knew that place was trouble as soon as I got near it. You should have heeded Betty's advice and kept away. You're always telling me you can pray anywhere and don't need to be in church to do it. Well, stick to your own rules in future." Jack was getting red in the face.

Helen made her sit down. "Let's have a cup of tea and discuss this calmly, perhaps over breakfast," she said.

"There's nothing to discuss," snapped Rachel.

"That's right," Jack snapped back. "There's nothing to discuss."

"Well you two can fall out if you want. I'm going to have something to eat," declared Helen and carried on preparing breakfast.

"Oh, please don't fall out over this," pleaded Flora, in tears. "Let's have some breakfast then we can talk calmly. Actually, when I was down there watching Rachel I saw the man in the dark robe again. He was in exactly the same spot. I don't think he saw me, but I can't be sure." The others stared at her, open mouthed.

Helen was the first to speak. "I don't like this. Whatever it is, it is upsetting poor Flora. I don't think we should go there again."

"Don't use Flora as an excuse, I didn't see the man," said Rachel, "but that doesn't mean he wasn't there." She was quick to follow with this last remark, seeing that Flora was about to complain. "But I can go there to pray if I want to. I'm not making anyone else go or not go. It's my decision."

"Rachel," said Helen, trying to calm the atmosphere. "Jack doesn't want to stop you doing anything, she just doesn't want you to come to any harm. That's right, isn't it, Jack?" Jack nodded in agreement. "She had a bad feeling about the place, and there's obviously been something happened there in the past, or Mr and Mrs White wouldn't have got so upset about it. We don't know what happened, but if you want to go there, please don't go alone. Take one of us with you. Preferably not Jack."

"Look," began Rachel, a bit flustered, which was totally unlike her. "I appreciate you all being concerned, and believe it or not, I don't want any harm to come to me either. But I'm not a child, and I can go where I want, as long as it's legal, which going to the church is. And I've never come to harm in a church anywhere, and I've been in churches all over the country, and quite a few parts of Europe, too. Even in Transylvania. But if you really want me to, I'll ask one of you to come with me tomorrow."

"Okay," said Helen decisively. "Change of subject; what shall we do today? I suggest we go to the little town we came through on the way here, perhaps pick up some souvenirs, replenish the food stocks, have a bite to eat and relax by the river. Spot some nature to tick off in the little books, if you aren't fed up with them yet."

Flora put her hands on her hips and turned to face Helen. "There you go again," she said. "Telling us what to do all the time."

"Okay," replied Helen. "We'll do what you suggest, Flora. Tell us what you think." Flora was shocked at this sudden climb down. She stood gazing at the sky for a moment and fiddled with her hair.

"Well," she began slowly, her face reddening, "we can go to the little town, and buy some souvenirs, have lunch, and stuff like that." They all burst out laughing.

"We can't have lunch until we've had breakfast," piped up Jack. "I'm feeling weak from malnutrition. Let's eat." They set about finishing the breakfast preparations in a much more congenial atmosphere and ate heartily, especially Jack, then they cleared away and picked up their rucksacks.

The walk to the town took about an hour and a half, and they split into the usual pairings on the journey. Jack asked Helen all manner of questions about the insects she had spotted, and Helen's knowledge was tested on more than one occasion. But Jack was like that. When she was interested in something, she was *really* interested and quite

247

intense. She could never have a mild interest. Helen was quite pleased. She had been concerned that her little friend was just into machines and ignorant of the natural world. She smiled to herself as Jack quizzed her on the differences between insects and arachnids, and came up with her own theories about how the two types had evolved. Flora and Rachel were having more picturesque conversations. Rachel was quite knowledgeable about birds and flowers, and pointed them out to Flora along the way, giving Flora ideas for fabric designs. By the time they got to the town Helen and Rachel were both in need of a mental rest. Jack spotted a snack bar and suggested they stop for a bite to eat after the long walk, just to keep them going until lunchtime. The others laughed at this, but decided it wasn't a bad idea, as the walk had taken more out of them than they had expected. Jack had burger and chips, but the others just had a cup of tea and a piece of cake. Flora got her tea in a nice cup with a saucer; luxury of luxuries after what she had had to put up with for the last few days.

"I'm sorry, girls," she said with a big smile, "but it really does taste better out of a china cup." After they left the snack bar Jack spotted an old tractor being repaired in an alleyway and went off to talk to the men working on it. Flora turned her nose up at the 'old-fashioned' clothes in the local boutique, but went in to have a look, anyway. Helen and Rachel wandered along the high street slowly, popping in and out of shops selling postcards and other souvenirs, then while Helen was buying food to take back Rachel spotted the local library. She darted in, leaving Helen wondering where she'd gone. She found the local history section and managed to find some old drawings of the little church, but nothing to tell her anything.

"Excuse me," she approached one of the assistants, "what can you tell me about this little church?" The library had already been quite quiet, but it suddenly became totally silent.

"I'm sorry," said the assistant. "I can't tell you anything." The low level hum in the background resumed.

"Does noone know anything?" Rachel asked in a whisper. The assistant leant forward until their faces were almost touching. She, too, spoke in a whisper.

"What do you want to know?"

"We're camping nearby and wondered about it. It seems to evoke strong feelings."

"I can't tell you anything. That doesn't mean I don't know anything," said the assistant with a wink, and glanced at her watch. "I'm on my break in about five minutes. I'll meet you outside." Rachel nodded and left the library.

"Oh, I wondered where you'd got to," said Helen. I've been shopping so that we don't starve."

"Listen, if you see the others coming back, distract them. I'm meeting someone in a few minutes."

"A bit of local talent? I didn't think they'd be your type!"

"No! I'm getting some info about the little church."

"Oh, I see. Well, Jack was quite engrossed in that old heap of rust so she'll not be back for a while. I'll keep an eye out for Flora, but you know what she's like when she gets among dresses." A few minutes later the assistant emerged and grabbed Rachel's arm and led her away. Helen followed. They went into a little alleyway behind the corner shop and the assistant looked around before speaking.

"There would be hell on if they knew I was telling you anything," she said in a loud whisper.

"They?" asked Rachel.

"Everyone! It's something noone talks about, after what happened."

"So what did happen?" asked Helen. The assistant looked around again before continuing.

"About a hundred and fifty years ago it was still an active church, but without a priest. Two monks did all the services, weddings, funerals, baptisms, everything. One day one of them disappeared and the other was accused of his murder. The people of the village as it was then, much smaller than today, were angry, and a mob went up the hill and caught the other one. They burned him at the stake, then they set fire to the church and knocked it down. The authorities came in but they couldn't pin his death on any one person. The villagers were quite proud of this. 'We all stand together' they said. About six months later they found the supposed murdered monk living with a woman in a village ten miles away. The villagers were understandably ashamed, and for a while in the neighbouring places they were referred to as 'The Monk Murderers'. Noone ever talks about it. Absolutely noone. Just about every family in the town today had an ancestor in the lynch mob. It's a source of great shame. They say the ghost of the wrongly accused monk, the one burnt at the stake, haunts the ruins, wanting justice." Helen and Rachel looked at each other. After a moment of hesitation Helen spoke.

"So why are you telling us this? Don't you share in their shame?"

"No, I'm an outsider, and I think it should be made known. It is, after all, a significant part of the town's history. If they knew I'd told you I'd lose my job and get bricks through the window, you know what I mean, so please, please don't tell anyone I told you this." She glanced at her watch. "I must go now. Not a word. Promise?"

"You're safe with us," said Helen, and patted her arm as she went back to work. Helen and Rachel looked at each other.

"Well," said Rachel, after a while. "That's quite a turn-up for the books. So Flora really did see a man in a robe. Well, a ghost, anyway."

"Did she? Do you believe in ghosts?"

"Good question. I can't say I believe in them, but I don't not believe in them either. If there isn't a ghost it's a bit of a coincidence, isn't it?"

"Look, not a word to Flora or to Jack, for now, anyway. Flora can be a bit flighty, but I'm surprised at Jack. She usually only believes what she can get from a science lesson. Not a word." They turned to see the other two making their way up the high street towards them.

"Are you two hungry yet?" called Jack. "It's well past lunchtime. There's a pub along here does some excellent-looking food. I think we should give it a try." Helen and Rachel smiled at each other and made their way along the street to join the other two. They read the menu sign outside the pub.

"Yes, let's give it a go," said Helen, and they went in. The food on offer was all good old-fashioned stuff, and Helen, Flora and, above all, Jack were quite happy. Rachel, on the other hand, was dismayed. There wasn't anything remotely like a vegetarian option, but she asked at the bar and the landlord offered a cheese salad, so they ordered food and drinks and settled into a table by the window. A short middle-aged man with a dour expression came over to them. He didn't introduce himself or apologise for interrupting their conversation. His demeanour was quite aggressive.

"I saw you talking to Carol in the library, and outside, too," he said abruptly. "What was she telling you?"

Helen wasn't pleased. "It's none of your business, thankyou," she said with an aggressive tone in her voice.

"There's things we don't tell strangers around here," he went on. "So she'd better not be telling our secrets or there'll be trouble."

"She didn't tell us anything we shouldn't know," said Rachel. He glared at Helen and Rachel, then turned and left the pub, almost knocking some people over.

"What a rude man!" said Flora.

"If I hadn't been stuck in the corner I'd have sorted him out," said Jack.

"No, Jack," said Rachel. "Violence isn't the answer." Just then the landlord brought their food. He saw what had happened and looked a bit embarrassed.

"Sorry about Mr Miller," he said. "He means well but has a strange way of going about it."

"Means well?" said Jack. "He was lucky not to get a bloody nose. What was he on about, anyway?" The landlord looked around to make sure noone was listening. He leant forward to speak to them.

"The town has a dark past but they don't talk about it," he whispered. "And I can't tell you or I'd be in big trouble. Best not ask. He was looking after the interest of the townsfolk." He went away and, turned putting his finger to his lips, as he left the room.

"What on earth was all that about?" asked Flora, looking from Rachel to Helen and back.

"I popped into the library, found some drawings of the church, and asked the assistant about it, but she couldn't tell me anything," said Rachel in a hushed voice. Helen smiled her approval when the other two weren't watching. They enjoyed the food, and by the time they left the pub it was mid-afternoon. They stood in the high street wondering what to do next, when Jack spoke.

"I say, can we do some more nature spotting?" she said, to everyone's amazement.

"Good idea, Jack," said Rachel quickly before anyone could come up with a better idea.

Helen got the map out of her rucksack. "If we go back along the river," she said slowly, "it brings us back near the lake where we went swimming the other day. Pity we haven't got the water bottle with us; we could have filled up."

"But we have our individual bottles," said Jack. "We can fill them up, then what we've got back at the camp will last us well into tomorrow." And so they set off along the river bank, nature books in hand. "I'm getting into this," Jack said, surprising them all. "Are there many more of these books in the set?"

"Yes," answered Helen. "There's about twenty or thirty, all covering things you might see on holiday. I'll get you some next time I put an order in." Getting back to the campsite took an age as they had to keep stopping to wait for Jack to inspect insects and other bugs, and to be totally sure she had the right one. When they did eventually arrive back it was starting to get dark, but they'd already had a hearty meal, so they just had cakes and biscuits before turning in.

Chapter 6

Rachel was the first to wake. She roused Helen.

"I'm off to the church. Are you coming with me?" she asked.

"No, I'm not awake yet. Can't Flora go?" Helen answered. "On second thoughts, don't disturb her. I'll come." She had decided that refusing the request was playing into Rachel's hands a bit, and Flora might not be the right person to go anyway, especially if the ghostly monk was about. She hauled herself out of the sleeping bag, made a quick visit with the trowel, and trudged off with Rachel towards the church.

"It's very good of you," said Rachel.

"What?" replied Helen, obviously not fully awake.

"It's good of you to come along with me, seeing as you don't do church or anything."

"Oh, I see." Pause. "But as Flora said, we don't want any harm to come to you." Rachel punched Helen's arm, gently.

"Thanks, mate." They reached the church quite quickly, as they weren't being distracted by the countryside. When they arrived Rachel invited Helen to come in with her. Helen thought about this for a moment, then agreed.

"But don't expect any praying from me!"

"That's okay. I understand." Rachel knelt down near the altar. Helen stood to one side and about a yard behind, not knowing what to do or where to go. After about five minutes she heard a rustle and looked ahead to see leafy branches moving; branches in exactly the place Flora claimed she saw the monk. She strained her eyes but couldn't see anything else. Rachel raised her head, then stood up.

"What's up?" she said, following Helen's stare. "Did you see something?"

"Good question. I'm not sure. I thought I saw the branches move, and there isn't any wind today, so I don't know what caused it." She stepped over the little wall and strode purposefully across to the place where the branches were, and examined the ground carefully. She looked around then shook her head. "No, nothing." She came back to where Rachel was standing. She let out a long sigh, then looked around again, this time with her hands on her hips. "I don't know, Rachel," she said. "I'm not sure if I saw the branches move or not. Let's get out of here before I begin to wonder if I'm losing my marbles."

Rachel shook her head. "No, if there's something here, we need to find out what it is, or Jack and Flora, and you, now, too, won't get a decent night's sleep. Let's look for it." She strode away to the bushes, but instead of looking at the ground she stood perfectly upright, closed her eyes, and slowly turned around. "No, nothing here. Are you sure this was the place?"

"Yes, I am, but just what are you doing?" asked Helen, standing with her arms folded.

"Feeling the atmosphere." She moved a few yards away, and slowly turned again.

"Feeling the atmosphere? You didn't do this when Flora saw the ghost when we first came here."

"No." She shook her head. "That's because I didn't believe she'd really seen anything. Now I know that there might be something here."

Helen was exasperated. "Just a minute, you didn't believe Flora, and now you do? If I'd said that you would have dropped on me like a ton of bricks, but because you do it it's okay?"

"What did I say the other night? You don't think about people's feelings. I do. I said Flora might have seen something because I didn't want to upset her. Turns out she might have been right all along; and Jack, too." Helen turned away. After a few minutes she turned back to discover Rachel had moved again and was turning slowly.

"So the long and the short of it is you believe me over the others? I'm surprised at that. I thought you and Flora were bosom buddies."

"Oh, we are. That's why I didn't want to upset her. Anyway, I can't actually feel anything here at the moment. It's a technique I learned from a holy man from the Far East – Buddhist, I think, but I'm not sure."

"Didn't know you'd been to the Far East."

"No, I haven't."

"But you said ..."

"No, *he* was from the Far East. I met him in Wolverhampton."

"So what do we do next?"

"Do? What do you think we do? We go back and have breakfast."

"Then what?"

"Don't ask me. You're usually the one telling everyone what to do. I didn't see any churches in the town, although there probably is at least one somewhere, and going back there might be a mistake. I wouldn't mind having a word with a priest, preferably Roman Catholic."

"Roman Catholic? I thought you were a Methodist."

257

"I am, but Methodists aren't keen on this sort of thing. Roman Catholics are easier to persuade on the subject of evil spirits. But I have a feeling it wouldn't be a good idea to enquire in the town. How far to the next nearest habitation?"

"Haven't a clue. Need to consult the map, but that's back at the camp."

"Let's go back and eat. I'm beginning to understand Jack's point of view. Then we'll go to the next town and you distract those two while I find the Holy Father." Helen went back to the spot where she saw the bushes move, but there was still no sign of the ground being disturbed.

"Okay. Let's do it."

When they got back Jack was already boiling the kettle for tea and Flora was arranging the food in neat, orderly rows and columns on the grass. Helen set to and cooked breakfast while Rachel looked at the map. Flora turned to Helen.

"What are we doing today, then?" she asked.

"Rachel's got the map. She wants to go to another town."

"Well, I hope the people are a bit friendlier. The two old boys didn't want to talk about the tractor; probably because I'm a woman. And that bloke in the pub would have got a bunch of fives if I hadn't been stuck in the corner," said Jack.

"The next nearest, which is about the same distance but in the opposite direction, is called Upper Dale," said Rachel while they ate breakfast.

"Upper Dale, Middle Dale, they've got imagination," laughed Helen through a mouthful of bacon.

"Don't talk with your mouth full," complained Flora. "You're getting as bad as Jacqueline. Where's Middle Dale, anyway?"

"That's where we went yesterday," replied Jack. "Do you go about with your eyes shut?"

"I didn't see any signs saying 'Welcome to Middle Dale'," said Flora.

"That's because we weren't welcome!" said Jack, and they all had a giggle. "But didn't you see Middle Dale Library, Middle Dale Garments, and The Middle Dale Arms?"

"Oh, I see now," said Flora, a bit embarrassed. "I didn't think of that. You can be clever at times, Jacqueline." They all giggled again. With breakfast over they cleared away and set off to Upper Dale. The journey passed without event, and they all ticked boxes in their nature books. Upper Dale looked quite a bit smaller than Middle Dale. The first thing they saw was an old church on the right. 'St Michael and All Angels' it said on the faded noticeboard. There was a small general dealer's shop next to it, with a seat next to it, and what had once been a water trough for the animals, now a very beautiful flower display, quite a contrast to the buildings which were all grey and dull and in need of repair. Flora and Jack flung themselves onto the seat.

"Oh, my poor legs!" exclaimed Flora. "That hill was quite steep for us little ones with short legs, don't you think, Jacqueline?" Jack nodded her agreement.

"It wasn't much better for us!" remarked Helen as she squeezed in between them. Jack hauled herself to her feet.

"Well, I know what I'm going to do," she said, eyeing the shop. "It's been a while since breakfast – I'm sure my legs will recover better with something to eat." The others laughed as Rachel dropped into Jack's empty seat.

"So why are we here, Rachel?" asked Flora. "There doesn't seem much to see or do. I can see the other end of the village from here. But these flowers are truly beautiful." She beamed at the flower display. "I wish I had my camera." At that Jack emerged from the shop carrying a half-eaten pork pie and a can of fizzy orange drink. Rachel got up and Jack resumed her seat.

"I want to visit the church," she said decisively. "You three can come in or stay here or go down into the village." The others agreed to rest their legs for a while then investigate the centre of the village, Jack thinking about finding somewhere for lunch.

"It seems a long way to see such a small place with nothing going on," remarked Flora after Rachel had gone inside.

"Yes," agreed Helen, "but I think she has something specific in mind." They were just about to get up when they heard the roar of an engine. A large motorbike came up the hill and parked outside the church. The rider, clad in black leather and a black helmet, got off and waved a greeting at them, as though they were expected. He took a small briefcase and a carrier bag from the pannier, and disappeared into the church.

"Wow!" said Jack. "I'm in love!"

"Jacqueline, you haven't even seen his face. How can you be in love?"

"Not with him – with the bike!" She got up and had a good look at it. After about fifteen minutes she sat down, her eyes never leaving it. Helen and Flora glanced at each other and giggled.

Meanwhile, in the church, Rachel had made her way to the front pew and sat down for a short prayer. As she looked up the biker was walking past. He had removed his helmet, and was a man in his late twenties, with short dark hair and a short well-kept beard. He greeted her as he went by.

"Good morning. Are you here for the funeral?" he asked.

Rachel shook her head. "No, father, I was hoping for five minutes of your time."

"Don't call me 'father'. I'm nobody's father. Not that I'm aware of," he replied with a smile and a wink. "Call me 'Alan'. That's my name. So how can I be of help?"

"Sorry, I'm Rachel," she said, holding out her hand which he shook. "I hope you can tell me something about the ruined church near White's Farm." His expression changed to one of recognition. He glanced at his watch.

"I have a funeral soon, but I can give you twenty minutes. Follow me." He led her into the vestry and waved towards a chair. He put his briefcase and carrier bag on the table, took some food out, and began to eat. "Hope you don't mind me eating while we talk," he said. "So. You are the ladies who have been upsetting my flock," he said with another grin. Rachel looked embarrassed.

"We didn't know we'd upset them, and we didn't mean to."

"Oh, it doesn't take much. Now tell me what Carol has told you about the church." Rachel looked flustered.

"I didn't mention Carol. I hope I haven't got her into trouble."

"Didn't need to, and no, Carol is made of quite stern stuff. In this village, and the others around here, if you

261

change your mind too suddenly someone three villages away will know in less than half an hour. You'd be scared at what I know about you. A sergeant-major, a tomboy, a mystic and a lunatic. Do you recognise yourselves? And which one are you?" Rachel was cross at this description.

"That's a bit much, considering I don't even know you," she said. "I suppose I am the mystic, but you're being a bit unfair on poor Flora."

He held a hand up in apology. "Their words, not mine. In fact, not even their words. Their words were a lot less polite. And poor Flora has been touched by something dark; we can come back to that, if there's time, if you want to. Tell me what you know and I'll try to fill in the gaps." Rachel recounted her conversation with Carol. Alan sat back in his chair, having finished eating.

"She didn't tell you about Father Edward's exploits, then?" Rachel shook her head. "Dear old Father Edward. He's what you would call an Anglo-Catholic. They loved him. Keen on saying Hail Mary and rosaries and stuff like that. Seemed to forget that we turned our backs on Rome five hundred years ago. Anyway," he paused for a drink. "One day a while ago, about 2015, I think, a few locals and a couple of tourists decided something must be done about Brother Bernard."

"Brother Bernard?"

"The ghostly monk – the one murdered by the villagers in about 1842. So old Eddie decided to do an exorcism up at the old church. Well, that isn't allowed. In the good old Church of England we don't generally believe in exorcisms. And in the RC Church they have a cardinal whose permission must be sought, but he would never give it to an Anglican, and even to Roman Catholics it takes years to come through after a great deal of essay writing and visits to Rome. But let's not spoil a popular venture by sticking to the rules. Apparently -"

Rachel interrupted. "So this happened before you arrived?"

"Oh, yes. I'm here mainly because of it. Apparently a group of about a dozen townsfolk and three or four tourists went up there with Eddie, and he performed an exorcism. Nothing happened, of course. I say nothing happened - what I mean is nothing happened immediately. Over the next few weeks several of those present started to have nightmares. One or two had physical symptoms, such as vomiting and headaches. Old Eddie himself started to go a bit off the rails, to the extent that the church wardens reluctantly called the bishop. Eddie was temporarily suspended, and I was brought in to look after the place." He looked at his watch and started dressing in cassock and surplice from a wardrobe in the corner of the room.

"Do you believe in ghosts, Alan?" Rachel asked while he was dressing. He sat down again, and stared straight into Rachel's eyes. She thought she detected a tear developing.

"No, Rachel, I don't." He banged his fist on the table. "Dammit, I don't believe in ghosts, but I have seen Brother Bernard. I have seen him with my own eyes." Pause. "But no, I don't believe in ghosts. I would like to talk more, but I have to prepare for the funeral." He gave Rachel a business card and ushered her out of the vestry. Rachel stood still for a moment, not knowing what to think, until she noticed people coming in for the funeral. She quickly made her way out and saw a group of people waiting by the church door. She made her way to the seat where the others were waiting for her. Flora got up and was the first to greet her.

263

"Oh, Rachel, what has happened?" she asked. Helen and Jack rose to their feet too.

"You look like you've seen a ghost," said Jack. Rachel was a bit shaky, and Helen led her to the seat and made her sit down. Helen stepped back to give her some fresh air, when a man pushed through. It was Mr Miller, the rude man from the pub.

"Get thee behind me, Satan!" he shouted, pointing at Rachel, with an angry expression on his face. Jack lunged at him but Helen was too quick, and grabbed her by both arms, holding her completely still. "We don't want the likes of you around here!" he said. At that Alan came over.

"Jacob!" he said sharply, and shook his head. "We are here to honour our departed brother. This is neither the time nor the place for that sort of behaviour." He turned to a middle-aged couple. "George, Enid, can you see to Jacob? I'll speak to him later." Then turning to Rachel, "I'm sorry about that. Are you okay?" Rachel nodded. He touched Helen's arm. "You're good," he said with a grin. "I needed someone like you at a baptism last week." He returned to the funeral and led the coffin into the church followed by the mourners. Two or three mourners came over to Rachel and apologised for Jacob's behaviour. Then they were alone. Rachel burst into tears. Helen and Flora hugged her. Jack suggested they find somewhere to have a cup of tea, and went twenty yards or so into the village, then returned announcing there was a snack bar in the main street. They led Rachel into it and sat at a table in the furthest corner from the door. Jack ordered tea and cakes and they remained quiet until they had been served. Helen was the first to speak.

"Rachel, do you want us to go back to the campsite?"
Rachel shook her head.

"No, I'll be alright when I've had my cup of tea." She
smiled weakly. "It's just I've had a bit of a shock."

"Do you want to tell us about it?" asked Flora. "Was it
that horrible man?"

"No," Rachel answered. "I'll tell you later. Let's have a
look around the village then go for a walk through the
woods." The other three looked at each other, ate their cake
and drank their tea, then they all left. They walked down
into the village, but they saw everything there was to see in
less than half an hour. Helen consulted the map and led the
way back towards the campsite.

"If we go back by a different route we can take in more
nature spotting," she said. This cheered them up, and within
fifteen minutes Rachel was back to normal and all four
were chatting cheerfully. As they emerged from a little
wood Helen looked puzzled. She referred to the map and
declared they were lost. Jack took the map, and after ten
minutes agreed. They sat down on the grass and Jack
brought out a compass.

"No wonder we're lost," she said. "I think this map is
wrong. Never mind." She looked into the distance in
several directions. "Okay, we'll go this way. I think it will
bring us back onto the road, but we're about an hour out of
our way." Helen and Rachel glanced at each other.

"How can the map be wrong?" asked Helen in a
whisper.

"I don't think it can," replied Rachel, also whispering.
"But Jack doesn't normally make mistakes with maps, nor
do you."

"Jack seems to know where we're going, so let's not worry about that for now." The little group trudged along, spotting their nature objects, and occasionally stopping to look at something in detail. Eventually the wooded area opened into a clearing.

"Oh, no!" exclaimed Jack. "This is the last place I wanted to be!" There in front of them was the ruined church. They looked at one another in disbelief. They sat down on the grassy bank and Jack took some biscuits from her rucksack and passed them round. "Sorry, girls, I didn't mean to do this. Shall we just go back to the campsite? I'm not comfortable here." They were just getting to their feet when they heard the sound of an engine. Alan appeared, from between two bushes, on his motorbike. He got off and removed his crashhelmet.

"Good afternoon, ladies," he said. "Thought I might find you here. Sorry about old Jacob. I gave him a bit of a lecture on how to treat people, especially visitors." Rachel introduced him to the others. "I already know what you've been up to. The bush telegraph is scarily efficient in these parts. Has Rachel told you about Brother Bernard?" Rachel shook her head.

"No, that was going to wait for when we got back to the campsite. But you might as well tell them now that you're here. What are you doing here, anyway?"

"Sorry, I thought you deserved an apology and a better explanation than I had time to give at the church." He told them what he had already told Rachel, but didn't mention the bit about Flora. "So you see, you really did see a monk. Ever since the exorcism he's been frequenting the place more and more often. Some of the locals refuse to talk about him, some are scared, and some complain to the

266

bishop because I won't do another exorcism. Which I'm actually not allowed to do, and the bishop supports me fully."

"Well, I'm surprised to find a vicar believing in ghosts," said Helen, arms folded.

"That's just it," replied Alan, looking concerned but trying to be casual about it. "I don't believe in ghosts, but I've seen him, and so has Flora, and you've heard him, Helen, and Jack's felt his presence." They all turned to look at Rachel. "Have you seen or felt or heard anything?" Rachel shook her head. "What's different about you?"

"Well, I'm the only practicing Christian of the four of us," she said. "I carry a Bible with me everywhere I go. I have it in my rucksack now." She produced it to show Alan. "Could that make a difference?"

"So do I, but I had mine with me when I saw him. My advice is to go back to your camp and enjoy the rest of your holiday, but don't come back here." They thanked him and he got back onto the motorbike.

"Can I just say," commented Jack, "what a beautiful bike this is. You've looked after it really well. It is all black and chrome and gleaming and not a speck of grime anywhere." He smiled and winked.

"This is my darling. I'm married to my job, and the bike is my secret lover." He grinned and winked, then put his helmet on, started the engine and drove away. They didn't move until the bike was out of earshot.

"Well," said Helen after a moment of silence. "That's that. He's explained what we didn't understand, but I still don't believe in ghosts, even though I heard it the other day."

"I'm pleased to follow his advice," said Jack. "Perhaps we should find somewhere else to camp for the rest of the week." Helen and Rachel nodded their agreement as they got up and set off back to the campsite. "What do you think, Flora?"

Flora seemed distracted, and kept looking behind at the church. "Oh, what? Yes, whatever you say." She tagged along behind but kept looking back. The others were chatting and didn't notice. When they got back they realised they'd missed their evening meal, so Jack jumped into the car and went back to Middle Dale and returned with fish and chips, and a cheese and onion fritter and chips for Rachel. After enjoying the meal they settled down to their pastimes for a while then turned in.

After the usual 'goodnights' Flora lay still for ten minutes or so, then she spoke to Rachel very quietly, too quiet for the others in the other tent to hear.

"Rachel, are you awake?"

"Yes, why?"

"I have something to tell you. Something important, but please, don't think I'm being silly."

"Of course I won't. What is it?" Rachel reached for Flora's hand to reassure her.

"Earlier when we were at the ruined church, well, I didn't say anything at the time because the vicar was there, and because the other two might think I was stupid, or making it up, or something, but honestly, I'm not. Well, are you ready for this?"

"Of course, Flora, you know I am always here for you. Now what is it?"

268

"Well, when the vicar was talking to us, I heard a voice. Not his voice, I heard that too, but, oh Rachel, please don't be cross with me, but I heard Mummy's voice."

Rachel squeezed Flora's hand. "Oh, Flora!" said Rachel, forgetting for a moment to whisper. "Are you sure? What did she say?"

"Yes, I'm sure. She said, 'Flora darling, Flora sweetie, can you hear me? Flora, let me know you can hear me.' Whenever she was trying to comfort me she always called me 'darling' and 'sweetie'. Then as we walked away from the church her voice got quieter and quieter until it faded away. I wanted to go back but I thought noone else would want to." She burst into tears. Rachel reached over, half out of her sleeping bag, and gave her a hug. She stroked Flora's hair and spoke gently.

"Oh, Flora, normally I would say you were being, well, silly isn't the appropriate word, but you know what I mean. When I lost my folks I kept hearing their voices, but that was only for a few days. But after what's gone on in the last few days, I'm not so sure any more. Perhaps your mind is playing tricks with all the upset we've had, and I know you are wound up about Phong."

"Oh, Rachel, don't remind me about that wicked woman trying to take Mummy's place in Daddy's life. What am I going to do if she succeeds? I hate her and I'm scared of her."

"I don't know, Flora. Let's try to get some sleep, and we can have a chat about it tomorrow."

"Yes, okay. Sorry."

"No need to apologise." Rachel fell asleep still holding Flora's hand.

Chapter 7

Rachel woke up after a night of fitful sleep and strange dreams. She turned to Flora. Flora wasn't there. She clambered out of the sleeping bag and poked her head out of the tent. Flora was nowhere to be seen. She quickly roused the other two then disappeared with the trowel. When she came back Helen and Jack were moving about slowly, still half asleep.

"Come on," she urged them. "We've got to find her."

"What?" said Jack. "Flora's missing?"

This galvanised Helen into action. "Give me that trowel here," she said. "I bet I know where she is. We've got to get there before she does something silly." She ran off behind the bushes and returned a few moments later, handing the trowel to Jack. Rachel spoke to Helen while Jack was away.

"Yesterday when we were at the ruined church she thought she heard her mum's voice, and you know how close they were. I bet she's gone to look for her."

"Yes, you're right. Hurry up, Jack!" Jack returned and they set off with their rucksacks. Helen and Rachel's long legs covered the ground in no time, but Jack was struggling to keep up.

"You two go on ahead. I'll catch you up."

When Helen and Rachel arrived there was no sign of Flora. They looked around the church, especially where she had seen the monk, but couldn't find her. Helen cupped her hands to her mouth and called out, "Flora! Where are you?" but she got no reply. They looked at each other. By now Jack had caught up.

"Perhaps she isn't here," said Jack, sounding very unconvincing. The other two shook their heads. "No, I didn't think so either. And if she isn't here, where is she?" Jack took a few steps down the grassy bank towards the church then stopped suddenly. "I can't come any closer," she said, half holding her breath. "You two will have to look over there. I'll look around the edge." She stepped backwards and started to breathe normally again. Helen and Rachel glanced at each other and nodded their agreement, and they left the central area and looked in the bushes around the church. After a few minutes they returned, Helen and Rachel to the church and Jack to the grassy bank. There, in the church doorway, stood Flora, perfectly still, staring straight ahead. They didn't know what to say; noone wanted to be the first to speak in case it startled her. Eventually, after a bit of hand signalling, Rachel spoke, very gently.

"Flora? Flora, it's me, Rachel. Can you hear me?" Flora didn't move. Rachel slowly walked over towards her. As she got closer walking became difficult, like wading through treacle. When she was close enough she slowly reached out and touched Flora's arm. Flora didn't move. From the other side of the church Helen was waving her arms but didn't want to speak in case she alarmed Flora. Or was that what she needed to do? Rachel looked up to where Helen was pointing, but she saw nothing. Helen spoke in a loud whisper.

"Rachel! Get away! The monk – he's there!"

"Where? I can't see him!"

"You must be able to see him," shouted Jack from the bank, not bothered about whether Flora was alarmed or not. "He's almost touching you!" Rachel looked around but saw

272

noone. She stood directly in front of Flora and looked into her eyes.

"Flora, can you see the monk?"

Flora shook her head. "There's noone here but me and my Mummy," she said dreamily.

"Can you see me?" asked Rachel.

Flora shook her head gently. "No, you're not here either. Just me and my lovely dear Mummy."

"But you can hear me?"

"Yes, Rachel. Dear Rachel, my very best friend, I can hear you but you're not here." Rachel looked across at Helen, wondering what to do next.

"Rachel!" called Helen, with urgency in her voice. "Look out! He's going to grab you!"

Rachel looked around but still couldn't see the monk. She wrapped her arms tightly around Flora. "I still can't see him, but I won't let him hurt Flora."

Flora looked up into Rachel's face and smiled. "Best friends forever," she said calmly. "My Mummy always liked you. Now we're going to be together for ever and ever and ever. You and me and my Mummy. My Daddy always liked you too. But not Phong. Nasty Phong. She hated you because you tried to come between me and her. She thinks you tried to come between her and my daddy too. Lovely Daddy. He misses Mummy. Phong doesn't like that. Nasty Phong." She grimaced. Helen tried to step forward, but her legs wouldn't move.

She called to Jack. "Jack, can you move?" Jack tried to stand up but fell back immediately. "No, I'm stuck, but look!"

Helen looked around but couldn't see anything else. "What? I can't see anything. What am I supposed to see?"

Jack pointed, getting agitated. "Look at the church!"

"What? What do you mean? What's happening? I can see the little walls, so what?" Jack tried to get to her feet again, but just fell back.

"The walls are growing!" she shouted. "Soon I won't be able to see Rachel and Flora!" Suddenly they heard the roar of Alan's motorbike. He appeared through the bushes at a speed too fast for safely weaving in and out of the tree stumps. He pulled up sharply beside Jack and she pointed at the church. By now it was almost completely reformed. Helen and Rachel still couldn't see it. Alan removed his crash helmet and threw it to the ground. He looked at the church and nodded.

"What brings you here? How did you know?" Jack asked.

"A strange dream last night and a voice inside my head this morning," he answered grimly, revving up the bike. He knocked it into gear and drove at speed straight at the door of the church, which by now was an old wooden oak door, the type popular on old churches. Helen couldn't see the church, so to her it looked as though he was driving straight at Flora and Rachel. She covered her eyes. As he hit the door there was a mighty crashing noise and a blinding flash. Helen was knocked over backwards and Jack, already on the floor, was knocked unconscious. There were no signs of the others. Helen crawled over to Jack and slapped her face to bring her round. They wrapped their arms round each other and wept. After a while Helen pulled herself away and spoke.

"Are you okay, Jack?"

"Yes, I think I am. But what about Rachel and Flora? What about Alan?" Helen looked back at the church. There was no sign of it ever being there. Even the low ruined walls and the remains of the altar had gone.

"I don't know, Jack. I think they're gone. Gone to, well, I don't know that either. Perhaps to a better place? I hope they're together, but I doubt we'll see them again. Not in this life."

"Oh, shit!" said Jack. "How are we going to explain this to Dougie?"

"You know, I wouldn't be surprised if Dougie already knows." They sat quietly, just staring for quite a long time.

"Do you think Phong was a witch? Do you think she caused all this?" Jack asked, half in disbelief at her own question.

"Don't know, Jack," Helen answered with a big sigh. "Not knowing much at the moment. No evidence one way or the other. It's not like me, not knowing stuff, is it?" Helen nudged Jack.

"Come on, mate. Let's go back to the camp. I wonder how we're going to report this to the police." They got to their feet and had a good look around where the church had been, just in case, but they didn't really expect to find anything. They trudged wearily back to the camp. Except they didn't. When they got back the tents had gone, the car had gone, and there wasn't even any sign of the scorched grass where they had set up the camping stove. They looked at each other in disbelief.

"Let's go back to the town. There might be a police station, and perhaps a bus to somewhere civilised," said Jack. They made their way toward White's Farm where they could join the road and go down into the town. But when they got to where the farm should have been, it wasn't there, and neither was the road. They pressed on a few hundred yards more to the top of the rise. From here they should be able to see the town. It wasn't there. No signs of habitation; no buildings; no farms; no road. Jack turned to Helen and put her arm round Helen's waist and her head on Helen's shoulder. "Oh, shit!" she said.

PW (in brackets)

Part two

Chapter 8

"Shit!" said Jack, as she sat down heavily on a fallen tree. "Shit! Shit, shit, shit, shit, shit."

"Oh, do be quiet!" said Helen as she sat down beside her. "Shouting 'shit' isn't going to help!"

"No, but it makes me feel better."

"I don't see how. It winds me up when I'm trying to think."

"Think all you like. We're stuck, aren't we?"

"If all you can do is shout 'shit', then yes, we are. We need to decide what to do next."

"Okay, as Flora said, you're always telling everyone what to do. Tell me what to do, if you're so bloody clever."

Helen turned to face Jack. "Flora was a lovely girl, and so was Rachel, but they're not here now. It's just us, and at the moment we don't know what's what, so we have to think and make some important decisions. You are welcome to suggest something. What do you think would be a good thing to do?"

"I don't bloody know. You tell me!" Helen took a notebook and pencil out of her rucksack and started writing.

"At the moment, we aren't sure where, or perhaps when, we are. We have no shelter, so we need to find somewhere to spend the night in case we end up here for a while. We have very little food or water. I have my water bottle, and I'm assuming you have yours. I have a few cereal bars in my bag. On the subject of water, we know where we can find drinking water, if it's still there, and if it's still safe to drink. Do you have your water testing kit?"

"Of course. All my toolkit is always in my rucksack."

"Good. What else have you got in there?" Jack took a box and a leather roll out of her rucksack and laid them on the tree between them. She opened them carefully and spread the items out. "Dear me! Have you got a kitchen sink in there? My dad told me to always carry a few essential items, especially when I became a guide leader, but I'm not in the same league as you."

"So where's yours, then?"

"In the tent."

"Fat lot of good that'll do us."

"Quite. What have you got there?"

"Three different-sized knives, two small adjustable wrenches, several pieces of string, a small candle, a flint and striker, a compass, a magnifying glass, a pair of tweezers, a pair of scissors, two files of different roughness, a rubber balloon, three small screwdrivers, and, of course, the water testing kit." She grinned.

"What, no partridge in a pear tree?" Helen smiled back at her. "Look, mate, I'm sorry for shouting, but I needed a bit of hush to think. Let's start from our one position of strength. Let's go up to the lake and see if it's still safe to drink."

Jack packed her toolkit away and looked quizzically at Helen. "Still safe to drink? And you said earlier you weren't sure *when* we are. What do you mean by that?"

"Yes, the things we know were here a few hours ago aren't here any more, so there are three possibilities; we've been thrown into the future, or into the past, or into a parallel universe. If you believe in such things, which I'm not sure I do, so for me the past or the future is more likely, and just because the water is safe in our time it doesn't mean it was two thousand years ago, or will be two thousand years from now. I mean, from then." Jack stopped what she was doing.

"Helen, I'm not sure I can get my head round that. And how come you came up with that theory so quickly?"

"When you were wasting time and energy shouting 'shit' I was weighing up the possibilities. Can you think of anything else that might have happened to us?" Jack thought a while, then shook her head. "No, I couldn't think of anything else either," said Helen with a smile. "Unless we've been kidnapped by aliens from outer space and taken to another world, of course." They both laughed at this idea.

"Or Cuba, or North Korea, or Syria," laughed Jack. "But to be honest, Helen, this isn't a laughing matter, whichever one it is. You're right. We need to find shelter for the night. Let's make our way back to the lake for now. I'll keep quiet so you can think a bit more." They retraced their steps towards where the campsite had been, then veered off to the left to find the lake. It was still there, and Jack's kit revealed it was still safe to drink. They both had a drink and filled their water bottles.

"Last time we were here I don't remember seeing anything like a cave, but we didn't look on the other side of the lake. Let's go see."

The raven fluttered down beside the wolf, who was watching from a clump of bushes.

"You have travelled more than I have, Raven, tell me what creatures these are."

"Yes, Wolf, I have travelled far and wide, but have never seen these before. In the far south across the great divide where the water used to be there are creatures who stand and move like these, but they have dark hair instead of coloured fur. Apes. They stand on two legs, and are quite intelligent. Not as intelligent as me, of course; not as intelligent as you. But they can make and use tools in ways that we cannot. I don't think they are rivals to us, but I am not certain."

"They look a bit unsure about what they are doing. I think I will keep an eye on them."

"Where did they come from, Wolf?"

"I don't know. I followed them here from the depression in the ground near the next wood. They came to the track and went to the brow of the hill, then they sat and talked for a while, before turning back and coming here."

"Which way did they come to the depression, Wolf?"

"That I cannot answer. They did not come on foot."

"But they could not swim there. Did they fly? They have no wings!"

"No, they did not fly. They appeared. They were not there, then they were there. As though they had appeared out of the dark, but it wasn't dark – it was mid-morning."

"This is strange, Wolf. You do right to watch them. I will help keep watch."

"They are not accustomed to this land. We might have to help them."

"That's a dangerous decision to make today. Tomorrow, or the day after, if they need help, we should give it, if they are friendly."

"A good idea, Raven. You are wise. Let us watch without revealing ourselves. Their hearing and sight aren't good; it shouldn't be difficult."

On the other side of the lake the land fell away quite sharply, but there was nothing resembling a cave. They went to the bottom of the slope to a point where the land rose opposite them and to one side.

"Look, Jack, I think this will do if we can't find anything better. If we can make a couple of little fences we can form a shelter to keep the wind out. There's plenty of long thin branches here. We can weave them into a sort of hurdle, and we can set a little fire to keep the wildlife at bay."

"Okay, I see what you mean. How many branches do you want, and what length?"

"Good question. I imagine about ten quite firm and straight, and twenty or thirty soft and springy."

"See what I can do. There's plenty of foliage so our beds won't be too hard." Jack and Helen went off in different directions and returned half an hour later with branches of the required type. Helen built a small hurdle in no time, but Jack struggled.

"Give me that here. I'll finish it off. See if you can find four or five big rocks to help hold them in place." Jack scurried away, relieved that Helen had taken on the weaving. She returned with a rock about the size of a basketball, and Helen approved, so off she went again. She gathered six in total and collapsed beside Helen. "Well done, mate. That's exactly what we need." By now Helen had finished the second hurdle and positioned them in the 'V' of the slope and jammed the rocks in to hold them in place. She looked up. "Do you think it will rain tonight?" she asked.

"Dunno. Back in a mo," said Jack, disappearing to the top of the slope. She returned a few minutes later, shaking her head. "No, I doubt we'll get rain, but tell you what I did notice. The stars are starting to come out, but some of them are in the wrong place."

"In the wrong place? I'm not sure what you mean."

"Come and have a look." Jack scurried to the top of the slope again, with Helen following. Jack pointed to the sky. "See that? That's Orion, the hunter, do you recognise it?" Helen nodded. "But look, three of the stars have moved from their usual positions. The top left, bottom right, and the right-hand end of his belt, they are all slightly off." Helen studied it and nodded.

"Yes, see what you mean."

"And over there, the Plough, it's the same. It's all okay bar three stars out of place." Helen nodded again.

"So what does it mean, Jack?"

"It proves your theory is right, mate. We're either in the past or the future. Couldn't say which, but by quite a long time. Not just a few hundred years. More like thousands." Helen let out a whistle. They returned to the camp and Jack lit a small fire.

"Don't make it too big, Jack, we don't want to set the hurdles alight after all that work. We just want it to be enough to scare off the wildlife." Jack cleared the ground around it and built it up with small stones so that it gave off an orange glow. They shared a cereal bar and settled down for the night.

Early the next morning, before the girls were awake, the raven fluttered down to greet the wolf in the copse where he had spent the night hiding.

"Good morning, Wolf. How are the apes?"

"Good morning, Raven. They built a shelter. As you said, they can make and use tools in ways that we cannot. But they have also made fire."

"Fire! They are obviously not stupid. How did they do that?"

"The little one rubbed stones together and caused sparks. It lit some dry leaves and twigs."

"Very interesting. I once saw apes trying to do that, a long time ago, and a long way from here, but without success. What else have you observed?"

"The big one is the leader. It makes the little one do the hard work. But the leader does work too; clever work with the front paws which is too difficult for the little one. I don't know if they are male or female. If, indeed, their species has male and female."

"Oh, I think there will be. They are too advanced to be neither. Do you want me to watch while you get some rest?"

"Thankyou, Raven. I am not used to being awake for the whole of the daytime." He went further into the wood, curled up and went to sleep. The raven perched in a tree overlooking the campsite.

Helen woke first and looked around. Nothing had been disturbed through the night. The fire was still glowing, but only just. She got up and stretched her aching limbs and had a drink of water. About half an hour later Jack awoke.

"It wasn't just a bad dream, then," she said.

Helen shook her head. "No, unfortunately not. We've got to grips with water and shelter. Today we need to concentrate on food. Did you see any berries when you were collecting wood and stones?"

"Wasn't looking for them, to be honest. But yes, I'm starting to get a bit peckish. I suppose we don't want to use up our last bars and things until we are desperate."

"That's right. We need to find berries or currants or other fruit for a start, then we need to think about meat. Squirrels or rabbits would do, or we can go down to where the town used to be and see if there are fish in the river."

"Good idea. Never thought of the river. Let's go there first while we have the energy."

Chapter 9

Rachel woke up with a thumping headache. She looked around and didn't know where she was. She was holding Flora's hand, and Alan was about ten yards away. Everything was green. They were surrounded by tall trees with green barks, laid on soft green undergrowth, and creepers were trailing from one tree to the next. The little bit of sky she could see was blue, but the canopy was so dense she could hardly see it. Flora lay next to her, and she couldn't really tell if she was asleep or unconscious. Or dead. There was a hum of insects in the air, but she couldn't see any. She tried to get up and realised every joint in her body was aching as though she had just done a marathon gym workout. She got to her feet very gingerly and slowly stretched every joint and muscle until she had a semblance of normality. Kneeling by Flora, she tapped her face gently until her eyes fluttered open.

"Oh, Flora, thank God you're still alive!" Flora looked dazed, but when she saw Rachel's face she smiled. She tried to move but suffered the same stiffness that had inflicted Rachel. Eventually, with Rachel's help, she got to her feet and stretched life back into her aching limbs.

"Oh, Rachel, where are we?" Rachel looked blank. Flora wasn't used to this. Rachel always knew what was what.

"I'm sorry, Flora, I haven't a clue. Are you okay on your own? I want to see to Alan." Flora nodded, and followed Rachel across to Alan, who lay totally immobile. Rachel knelt beside him and stroked his face; Flora knelt on the other side and stroked his hand. His eyes opened, but he struggled to focus at first. He tried to move, so Rachel helped him bring life to one limb at a time until he was able to sit up unaided.

"Wow!" He sat up and looked around. "Where are we?" He saw Rachel and Flora and smiled at them. "Are you two okay? And where are the other two?"

"I don't know, to both questions. As far as I can tell, there's just us. I hope they are okay," Rachel said disconsolately. "Wherever we are, I think we're a long way from home. And we need to sort out some sort of food and drink. I have a bottle of water in my rucksack, and a couple of cereal bars, but that's all."

"Well, I've got some water and snacks in the panniers on my bike. Where is it?" They looked around, but couldn't find it anywhere. Alan was distraught. "My bike! My lovely bike! It's got to be here somewhere." He ran into the nearest clump of trees searching for it. About five minutes later he returned, empty handed, and sat down looking glum. "I'll look for it again later. Finding food and drink are more important at the moment. How long have we been here, Rachel?"

"Don't really know. I woke up about five or ten minutes before you and Flora. What do you think happened to Helen and Jack?"

Alan shook his head. "We've obviously been thrown quite some distance. You don't get vegetation like this near Upper Dale. Either they've been thrown somewhere else, or they've been left behind. Haven't a clue. Anyway, that fruit over there - " he pointed at a green fruit the size of a large pear hanging from a tree branch - "that, if it's what I think it is, is a good source of moisture. It isn't water, but it's the next best thing." He got up and plucked the fruit from the branch, and bit into it. A broad grin spread across his face.

"Yep, this is excellent. We have food and drink for a day or two." He plucked another two and they sat down and ate.

"This is lovely, thankyou, Alan," said Flora.

"Yes," said Rachel. "How did you know about this fruit?"

"My dad was in the diplomatic service when I was young, and we lived in India for a few years. My older brothers would take me for walks in the edge of the jungle. 'Adventuring' we called it. Dad used to go mad when he found out. Said it wasn't safe. Mum didn't mind; she would secretly send one of the native servants to keep an eye on us, but we didn't know about that until we were grown up. We thought it was great fun." Rachel and Flora looked at each other and smiled.

"I didn't know you came from such an illustrious family," said Rachel. "I'm not sure that's the right word, but you know what I mean."

"You don't know much about me at all, either of you. But that's a minor issue. We can only eat these for two days, then we need something else."

"I could eat these for ever and ever. They're delicious," said Flora with a big smile.

"No, after the third day they would give you the runs, and in a big way," he smiled. Flora stopped eating for a moment to think about that.

"I'll just finish this one, then have another in a few days' time." Rachel and Alan laughed.

"No, but seriously, until we find out where we are we need to find food and water and shelter. When it gets dark in the jungle it gets dangerous. If we can't find a cave, or somewhere we can block the entrance, we might need to spend the night up a tree." Flora's face fell.

"Oh dear, I've never been up a tree. What if we fall out?"

"We'll just have to get along," said Alan with a mischievous wink to Rachel. Flora thought about that for a while, then she laughed.

"No, silly, I mean fall out of the tree."

"Sorry, Flora, I knew what you meant. Just winding you up. But we need to find somewhere for the night. These fruit are packed with energy, so what we've eaten will keep us going for a while, and we'll put another three in your rucksack, Rachel, if you don't mind, just in case. Now stand perfectly still, don't move, don't speak. Can either of you hear running water?" After a while they all shook their heads. "Okay, let's go that way," he said, pointing to where the gaps between the trees were slightly bigger. "And stick close together." They set off slowly, Alan in the lead, Rachel bringing up the rear, and Flora in the middle.

The tiger had arrived just as Alan and the girls were waking. He was accompanied by a panther and some small birds. "What do you make of this, Panther?" he asked. The panther shook his head.

"These are humans," he said. "But of a different kind to what I've seen before."

"I know they are humans," answered the tiger. "But what are they doing here? Where did they come from? They have left no tracks. How did they get here?"

"Good question, Tiger. They obviously did not walk. The branches overhead show no indication that they fell from the sky. The birds tell me that they were not here, then suddenly they were. It is a mystery to me."

"What should we do about them? Do you think I should tell the Princess? Would she be pleased or would she be cross?"

"You know her better than I do. Either way, I'm sure it would mean extra work for the likes of you and me, so that we couldn't just get on with our normal lives."

"Yes, Panther, that's what I'm worried about. I might follow them, at a distance, and see what they get up to. They might not survive, and that would be the end of our problem."

"Yes, Tiger, but I cannot stay. I have things to do in another part of the jungle."

"Eat?"

"Yes, I have a deer safely up a tree. I haven't eaten for a few days and was just about to start on it when I got the message you needed to see me. Keep watch, and I'll be back in a day or two."

"Enjoy your meal. I'll watch."

They made slow progress but after about an hour Alan signalled to them to be quiet. They stood motionless for about a minute.

"I can hear water!" Alan whispered, with a smile. "Come on, this way." He followed the sound until it brought them into a clearing with a stream running through it. The stream flowed quite quickly through steep rocks, and splashed into a pool about thirty yards away. Alan went to the bank and cupped his hand to collect some water. He tasted it, and smiled. "I don't have the proper stuff to test it, but I think it's okay." He sat on the bank and the others joined him. They drank from the stream and Rachel replenished her water bottle, which was less than half full by now. Alan rose to his feet and looked around. "I can't see anything like a cave. Let's go upstream a bit – the animals will congregate downstream around the pool." He led the way up the hill and Flora struggled to keep up until Rachel called to him to slow down. "Sorry, Flora, I forgot your legs aren't as long as mine." Further up the valley there was a small waterfall cascading down a rock face. It was only about ten feet high, but it was enough for the water to make quite a splash. "Stay here a minute," he said, and walked quickly to the rock face. He came back a few minutes later absolutely drenched, but grinning from ear to ear. "This'll do for tonight, perhaps a bit longer. Follow me." Behind the waterfall was a cave. It wasn't a big cave, but they could get in along a narrow ledge and get far enough back to rest on a dry area.

"I'm absolutely soaked," said Flora, "and I don't have any other clothes to change into." Alan and Rachel stripped to their underwear and spread their clothes out on rocks to dry. Flora looked askance, and wondered what to do. Rachel knew what she was thinking.

"Your clothes won't dry while you're wearing them," she whispered while Alan's back was turned. "Bite the bullet and take your top and jeans off, then when they are dry you can put them on and take your undies off." Flora wasn't comfortable with this, but saw the sense in doing it and followed Rachel's instructions. Alan realised what the problem was, and said, "You two stay here and get dry. I'll see if there's anything to eat nearby." He picked up Rachel's rucksack, emptied its contents into the corner at the back of the cave, and went out. The girls picked up their wet clothes and wrung them out at the mouth of the cave, as best they could, then spread them out to dry.

"I'm scared, Rachel," said Flora, almost in tears. "We don't know where we are, do we?" Rachel shook her head. "Are we going to die?" Rachel sighed and put her arm round Flora's shoulders.

"Alan seems to know what he's doing, if this is his sort of jungle. Let's trust in his knowledge and skills for now." Just then Alan returned with a smile on his face.

"Hello, you two. There's plenty of fruit not far away. This'll keep us going for a few days." He emptied the rucksack onto the floor of the cave. There were berries of several different colours, and seven or eight larger fruits.

"Are you sure they're safe to eat?" asked Flora.

"Yes, I've seen most of them before. I picked some mushrooms, too; some are definitely safe, one or two I'm not sure about, but they don't look like those I know to be poisonous." They sat down and ate some of the fruit.

"Alan," said Flora. "Do you know where we are?"

"Not at the moment, Flora, but I'll make a guess tomorrow. I think we've missed noon today, and that's one of the easiest times to get your bearings. I'll have a look at the stars tonight, see if they give any clues."

"Gosh, you're clever," Flora answered in admiration. "I wouldn't know where to start with things like that."

"Oh, it's not that difficult. When I was a teenager I used to go sailing with my uncle on his yacht. He taught me how to navigate by the sun and the stars."

Rachel laughed. "You're right. There *is* a lot about you we don't know."

The tiger had followed them to the cave, and watched Alan's excursion from a distance. Now he had gone back into the cave the tiger lay down and went to sleep. The next day the panther returned.

"How are they coping?" he asked.

"I haven't seen much of them, but I followed them to this cave yesterday," the tiger answered. "The little one is obviously a child. She doesn't do much work, and what she does she doesn't do very well. The two big ones look after her all the time. The man has been out seeking food. He seems to know what he is doing."

"When are you going to tell the Princess?"

"Not yet. I want to know more about them before I tell her anything."

"I just came back out of curiosity. I still have other things to do. I'll return in a day or so."

"Okay. Enjoy the rest of your meal."

Chapter 10

Helen and Jack made their way down the hill, looking for berries on the way. They found a few that looked like brambles, and picked them. They were good to eat, but there weren't many. When they got to the river Jack cautiously dipped a foot in. It only came just above her knees, so she stepped in with both feet and waded out into the stream. It was flowing gently so she wasn't in danger of falling over. She stood with her back to the sun and peered into her shadow.

"There's a few tiddlers here, but I don't know if they're edible," she called to Helen, who took off her shoes and socks and joined Jack. "Every now and then a bigger fish swims by. How do we catch them? I've only ever used a rod and line, and we have neither." Helen looked around. She pointed to the opposite bank.

"You see those plants over there? They look quite firm. Do you think you could make a spear out of them?" Jack followed her outstretched arm and nodded. She set off wading across towards them. "Take care," Helen called after her. "It might be deeper in the middle." Jack raised a thumb in acknowledgement. At its deepest point it only came up to Jack's waist, and she was soon back with half a dozen firm sticks. She sat down on the bank and after about twenty minutes was the proud owner of six spears.

"Right. I've done my bit. I've never caught fish with spears before, so I'm in your hands." Helen hadn't done it before either, but she had watched others do it, so she had a fair idea. The task took patience, but after a while they had four decent-sized fish which Helen put into her rucksack.

"Let's go back along the stream, see if there are any more fruit," suggested Helen.

"Good idea, mate," answered Jack, and they set off. They found a few berries, again, good to eat but not plentiful, then in a sheltered part of the wood they came across some mushrooms which they picked and put into Jack's rucksack. An hour later they were back at their makeshift camp. The fire had almost gone out, but Jack brought it back to life while Helen prepared the fish on skewers. They sat and ate and cooked a few mushrooms on the skewers. After the meal they sat back and rested. It had been quite an energetic morning, but the food had filled a hole.

"What do we do next?" asked Helen. "I mean, do we try to live here, or do we try to find other people, or what?" Jack grimaced.

"I was wondering the exact same thing, mate. We can live here for while providing we can find a more varied diet, but do we stay here until we die of old age, or do we try to find Rachel and Flora, or some other people, or what?"

"We've already established that Middle Dale doesn't exist. We could try Upper Dale, but I don't think we'll have any luck. It's a waste of time going back to the site of our original camp, or the church, or White's Farm, because we already know there's nothing at any of them. I don't honestly know what to do next," said Helen.

"Well," said Jack, after some thought. "We more or less know the way to the nearest coast, so if we are in the past, people will most probably come from the east, so if we head that way we might meet someone. I know it's not much of an idea, but it's the best alternative to becoming the old maids of the woods." Helen laughed.

"Yes, I know what you mean. Let's stock up on fish and berries and mushrooms and set off first thing tomorrow." Jack nodded agreement and they made their way back to the stream.

The wolf waited until Jack and Helen were out of earshot, then came out of the wood to greet the raven.

"Have you had an interesting time, Raven?"

"Yes, they are clever animals. I followed them down the hill to the stream. You are right, their sight and hearing are poor, compared to ours. But they are clever. They made tools and caught fish, and they gathered berries and mushrooms, and when they returned they put them on the fire. I don't know what that does. Do you think it changes them to make them easier to eat?"

"I don't know, Raven, but when you think about the work involved, it must do something."

"Yes, quite. I have been trying to learn their language, but without success. They are going back to the stream. Perhaps they want more fish. I couldn't live on such a diet."

"Nor could I. Should we help them?"

Raven thought about this for a moment. "Yes, I think we should, but not too much. It would mean showing ourselves, and we don't know if they are friendly."

"You stay hidden for now. When they return I will help them. I will catch a hare or a squirrel for them and see what they do with it. You stay alert in case they try to attack me."

Helen and Jack returned from their expedition with their rucksacks bursting with fish, berries, mushrooms, and a few beech nuts and pine cones they had found by coming back a different way. Helen was striding ahead with her longer legs, with Jack trotting along three or four yards behind. Jack froze.

"Helen," she called in a loud whisper. "Stay perfectly still. Don't move a muscle. Don't make a sound. There's a wolf behind that tree in front of you." Helen stopped. She slowly moved her head so she could see the tree, and she could see the wolf's head. It had something in its mouth, and was walking slowly towards her.

"Jack!" she whispered as loudly as she dare. "What do I do? Do I stay still, or do I run, or do I try to fight it?" Before Jack had a chance to answer, the wolf was about two yards away from Helen. It sat down and dropped whatever it was carrying and pawed at it, pushing it towards Helen. It looked up at Helen, then down at the object, then up at Helen again, then it got up and took a few steps back. "Oh, Jack, I think it's bringing us a present. It's giving us food." Helen slowly walked to the object, which she then realised was a hare. She picked it up, bowed solemnly to the wolf, never taking her eyes off it, then in a quiet voice, but not a whisper, she said "Thankyou, Mr Wolf." She bowed again and took two steps back. The wolf ran off and disappeared in an instant, so suddenly that they didn't see where it went. They remained still and silent for a while, to make sure it had gone, than Jack burst out laughing.

"'Thankyou, Mr Wolf'? What's all that about? I don't believe what you just said." Helen looked embarrassed.

"I was just being polite. He brought us food." She looked down at the hare. "It's trying to help us, somehow. But I don't know why. I imagine either of us would make a decent meal for a wolf family, but it didn't try to attack us." She sat down suddenly and burst into tears. Jack came over and put her arm round Helen's shoulders.

"Cheer up, mate. We're both still alive and we have supper."

"Sorry, Jack, it's just the thought of how close I came to *being* supper."

"Yes," said Jack with a big grin. "You'd make a better meal than I would. You've got a lot more meat on you." They both laughed and cautiously made their way to the camp. Helen set about preparing the hare while Jack got the fire going. "I say," said Jack, while they were waiting for the hare to cook. "As we're setting off tomorrow morning, perhaps we should have a wash in the lake tonight. We don't know when we'll next find enough water to wash properly."

"Good idea," agreed Helen. "We could do that now while supper's cooking. And thinking of having enough water, I think we should follow the stream. That way we'll have drinking water, and I imagine it will lead us to the coast."

"Or another lake, but it's a good idea anyway." They walked the short distance to the lake, undressed, and jumped into the water. They carried their clothes back, as they didn't have any towels, and were dry by the time they got back to the camp. They dressed and tucked in to the hare, which they both enjoyed.

"What do you think, Raven?"

300

"I think it was trying to express gratitude. They were alarmed at first, but they didn't panic and run away. These apes are interesting. I shall enjoy watching them. I'll stay here until it gets dark. You get some rest, then take over at dusk." The wolf found a quiet place among the trees and went to sleep. The raven watched the girls, and followed them to the lake and back. At dusk the wolf returned. The raven flew down from her perch and settled on the ground beside him.

"You missed something strange," she said.

"Oh? What happened? What did they do?"

"They went to the lake and washed."

"Why is that strange? I do it. You do it, though generally not in the lake." The raven looked him squarely in the face.

"They removed their fur and washed, then put the fur back on." Both animals stood in silence for a moment.

"Removed their fur?" the wolf said in disbelief. The raven nodded. "And put it back on?" The raven nodded again.

"Look at them," she said. "They have their fur." Wolf moved a little so he could see them.

"What are they like without fur? What colour are they?"

"The fur must be even, because they looked very much as they do now, but they were pink, like baby pigs. And I think they might both be female, because they have udders, which we can't see under the fur." The wolf sat down, picking his spot so he could watch the girls without being seen.

"That is very strange. I've seen birds lose their feathers, but they take a while to grow back, and I've seen animals change colour in winter, but the fur doesn't come off completely. This is very strange."

"Strange indeed. But it will soon be night, and they will sleep, so I'll get some rest while you watch. I'll be back at morning." She flew away and settled in a tree some distance away. The wolf had a good vantage point, so he stayed where he was.

The next morning the tiger was awake and watchful before the friends stirred. Alan was the first to move about. He had a drink and ate some of the fruit, then he woke Rachel.

"I had a look at the stars last night while you and Flora were asleep. I'm no further forward as to where we are. One thing I did notice, and this is very strange, so don't tell Flora yet, some of the stars are in the wrong place."

"In the wrong place? What do you mean?" said Rachel, looking puzzled.

"They're not where they usually are, and stars change position extremely slowly. This isn't the same time as it was when we left the church." Rachel looked worried.

"Do you mean we are in the past or the future or something?" Alan nodded. "Have we been asleep for a few hundred years, do you think?" Alan shook his head.

"More like a few thousand years." He grinned. "Anyway, we are all okay. I'll go for a scout round while you and Flora have breakfast, then we need to decide what to do next." He left the cave and set off, looking for a hill. He decided to follow the stream, and in about half an hour he was on higher ground with very few trees. He could see for miles, but there was very little to see. The jungle continued all the way to the horizon in all directions but one. Over in the west there was what looked like a clearing which turned into a plain with a few trees. He made his way back to the cave. Flora was awake and enjoying a breakfast of fruit and water. She smiled as he came in.

"Good morning, Alan," she said. "Did you have a good night?" He nodded.

"Yes, thanks. You?" She nodded. "I've been out having a look around and over to the west there's what looks like a plain. I think we need to go that way to find people. If they turn out to be hostile we can come back here and try to come up with a different plan."

"Good idea," said Rachel. "Better than any other ideas at the moment. We can pick berries on the way, and we still have some of those big green fruits left from yesterday." They finished eating and packed up the remaining food and set off following the stream uphill. It was slow going, as Flora was neither strong nor nimble, but they were patient with her, as she was obviously doing her best. When they got to the top of the hill they sat down. Flora was exhausted, so they rested for a while. Alan took the opportunity to have a good look at the horizon. He pointed to the west.

"See over there? There's a plain, and everywhere else is thick jungle. I know it means leaving the stream, but if we're going to find people, that's the way to go. Going any other way just puts us in among the wild animals." They got to their feet and set off.

The tiger had been following them. What are they up to? What are they looking for? How do they know they're going to the village? Have they been here before? He looked around and saw some small birds following him.

"Birds, what can you tell me about these people? Do you know where they came from? Have you seen any others like them?" The birds flapped about.

"No, Tiger, we haven't seen anything like them here. They are like the people in the village, but they are different. The male seems to know what he is doing. He knows how to find food and drink. But that's all we know. We don't know where they come from or how they came. They were not here, then suddenly they were. They lay on the ground for a long time. We thought they were dead. Then they moved."

"Thankyou, birds, I will follow them. If you see Panther, tell him where I am." The tiger followed the three, staying far enough back to remain unseen. He thought they were heading towards the village, and wondered whether to stop them or not. He followed until he could remain hidden no longer, then he ran ahead under cover, and emerged from the bushes in front of them. Flora screamed until Rachel put her hand over Flora's mouth. Alan stood in front of them and made himself look as big as possible, but showed no aggression. The tiger stood perfectly still, and stared at Alan. Who was going to blink first?

Chapter 11

Helen and Jack packed their few belongings into the rucksacks and put the remaining food on top. Jack made sure the fire was out, then they made their way to the stream and followed it down the hill. The raven followed at a distance. After a few hours they found a place to rest. Jack made a fire while Helen prepared the fish and mushrooms.

"I wonder where this will take us," said Helen, gazing into the cloudless sky.

"The thing is," said Jack, "if we stayed where we were we might be there until we died. At least by moving on we have a chance of finding Rachel and Flora, and Alan, or perhaps some other people." Helen nodded.

"Yes, I think it's the right move. I wonder if we'll see the wolf again."

"He might be following us, seeing as you were so polite to him. I hope he comes along. That hare wasn't brilliant, but if we have to eat fish every day for a week I'll go bananas. I'm not sure how Rachel coped with being a vegetarian."

"Yes, not even fish, but back in civilisation there's plenty of variety. Some of those vegetarian dishes can be quite nice, if you know what you're doing and have the right herbs and spices."

"That's something I haven't seen yet," said Jack through a mouthful of fish.

"What's that?"

"Herbs and spices."

"Oh, there's probably some around, but we don't necessarily recognise them in their raw state. Some have to be roasted and ground up before we can use them."

"Yes, s'pose so." They finished eating and put the fire out and moved on along the bank of the stream. The raven waited until they were out of earshot then flew down and examined the remains of the fish meal. She devoured the guts which Helen had removed before cooking but was a bit hesitant about the cooked leftovers. A few hours later Helen sat down.

"I need to rest my legs a bit," she said, rubbing her calf. "And we need to think about somewhere to spend the night." Jack nodded her agreement.

"Yes, my legs have just about had enough for today. I can keep going for ever on flat ground, but this is a bit rough to go on too long. I haven't seen anything suitable, no caves or anything, so we might need to spend the night up a tree."

"I did actually think about bringing the hurdles along, but decided they would be too cumbersome."

"Yes, we did right to leave them behind. I'm not tall enough to carry them any distance. Let's have some berries then we can scout around and see what there is here. It's starting to get dark."

"Good idea." Helen emptied her rucksack onto the ground and they shared out the berries. After a drink from their water bottles they felt quite refreshed, apart from their aching legs, and Helen went off to see if there was any shelter nearby. She returned about half an hour later, shaking her head. "No, it looks like a tree tonight. There's a decent-sized tree up ahead. That'll do, if it isn't too difficult to climb with rucksacks on." She indicated a stout tree in a clearing about a hundred yards away. They picked up their rucksacks and set off for it. They had covered half the distance when a wolf sprang out in front of them. They stopped dead in their tracks. Without moving her head Jack spoke to Helen in a loud whisper.

"Is it our wolf?" she asked.

"Don't know," replied Helen. She cleared her throat and addressed it firmly but calmly. "Hello, Mr Wolf." The wolf sat down in front of her, about ten yards away. It made a gentle growling sound, which didn't seem aggressive. Helen sat down too. After a while Jack nervously sat down beside Helen and slightly behind. Helen continued. "Are you the same wolf we saw yesterday?" The wolf made a sound like a cat miaowing, but much deeper. Helen glanced at Jack. "Do you think that is yes or no?" Jack shrugged her shoulders. Helen turned back to the wolf. She got up onto her knees and stretched out her arm, keeping her hand closed in a fist. The wolf crept forward and touched it with its nose. Helen smiled. "Yes, you are. We are looking for somewhere safe to spend the night." Jack butted in.

"I think you're expecting too much there. Suppose English isn't its first language." The wolf seemed agitated at this and whined a little.

"Look, you've upset him now. Do be quiet." She turned to the wolf again, and gestured sleep by putting her hands together and resting her head on them to the side. The wolf got up and walked away a few yards, then turned round to see if they were following. It didn't resume until they had got to their feet and picked up the rucksacks. It led them through some trees to a large clump of bushes, and through the bushes into a cave. Helen bowed politely, said, "Thankyou, Mr Wolf," and bowed again. The wolf turned

307

and disappeared in a flurry of grey fur. Jack's mouth hung open in disbelief. She sat down in the corner.

"Well, I've seen everything now. I'm not sure I believe that, but I saw it with my own eyes."

"Yes, know what you mean, but it worked. Do you think he actually understands me?"

"I don't know if he understands the words, but he definitely understands you. Anyway, let's make ourselves comfy for the night and see where we go tomorrow. Shall I make a fire in the mouth of the cave?"

"Good idea." Jack got some twigs and branches together and made a little fire, and they settled down and went to sleep.

The raven flew down and settled beside the wolf. "You've got a new friend," she said. "Have you been learning her language?"

"No, Raven. I can't understand a word, but I seem to know what she wants, and she seems to understand me."

"I have some information about these apes. Owl talks to the travelling birds, those that come from distant places, those that fly over the sea, and she says there are apes like this and they can be reached by going into an endless cave, and it isn't far from here. She told me, and I think I know where the entrance is. Shall we take them there tomorrow?"

"I assume they want to find more of their kind, so yes, perhaps we should. I'll find them something to eat in the morning, then see what we can do to lead them to it. How far is it?"

"For you or me it would be less than half a day; for them almost the whole of daylight. I might need to make myself known to them, but they seem friendly – they haven't threatened you. Yet."

"Noone threatens me, Raven. But you can always fly out of danger if they become hostile. They can't fly and I haven't seen them jump yet, either. But that's for tomorrow. Let's get some rest; I'll stand guard here, and we'll meet again at first light." The raven flew off and the wolf settled down, out of sight among some bushes near the cave.

Alan stood motionless, staring at the tiger. He couldn't remember whether he should avoid the gaze, or stare him out. The tiger, which had been sitting for quite a while, suddenly lay down. Alan dropped his gaze and motioned to the others to sit. He too sat, and looked at the tiger, but without making eye contact. The tiger growled, gently. Alan thought it might be trying to talk to him, but he couldn't understand the sound, and didn't know what to do. He sat patiently, waiting for the tiger to make the next move. After a while he decided the tiger might be waiting for *him* to make the next move, so he slowly got to his feet. The tiger got up. Alan took two steps forward. The tiger came forward and sat immediately in front of him. Alan gingerly took five steps back. The tiger lay down. After experimenting with this for a while, Alan decided the tiger didn't want him to go that way. He went back to Rachel and Flora and explained this to them. They set off back to the hill, and when Rachel glanced over her shoulder, the tiger had disappeared. After a brief discussion, they set off back across the plain, and the tiger immediately appeared in front of them.

"I don't know what this is about," Rachel said quietly, "but this tiger doesn't want us to go that way." Alan nodded. They made their way back to the top of the hill while they were discussing the situation.

"Yes, I think you're right. So which way should we go? In all the other directions it's just jungle as far as the eye can see," he said.

"Is there any way," Rachel asked, slowly, "where the jungle isn't quite as thick? I don't really want to be lunch for a tiger."

"Well," Alan began looking around, "that way," he pointed, "the trees aren't quite as tall. But I can't really tell from up here. Let's give it a go; we've nothing to lose by trying." They set off at a gentle pace.

When the tiger realised they had abandoned the route to the village he turned and trotted away across the plain. As he reached the village some of the younger children fled, but he was well known to the adults, and they simply moved out of his way. The village consisted of about twenty huts made from wood and reeds. Some had a small fire by the door, where they were cooking food. The ground on the main paths between them was hard with use, but in other places it was soft and dusty. He went to the princess's house, which was of similar design, but bigger. As he approached, the men standing by the door moved out of his way. The princess was sitting on a large comfortable chair, with two young women sitting at her feet. She was in her early twenties, with a pretty face and smooth skin. She was dressed in the same style as the other women, but her clothes were obviously of higher quality.

"Welcome, Tiger. What brings you here today?" she said. He sat down in front of her.

"I have news from the jungle, Princess," he growled. "There are new people. They are like you, but they are not like you."

"Oh, I haven't heard this from anyone else. How are they different?"

"Their skin is a different colour, their clothes are different, and they don't understand when I speak to them. But they are not stupid. They know how to find food and drink and shelter, and they know how to make fire. They find their way by the sun and the stars, but they do not know where they are going." The princess thought for a moment, then she addressed the tiger.

"Bring them here. I want to see them. Do you think they are a treat to me? If they are, I will have them killed." The tiger looked angry.

"I will bring them, but you will not harm them. If they are hostile I will protect you, but you will not harm them." The princess began to look angry.

"I will decide that. You are just a tiger. If I want them dead, they will be killed." The tiger let out a loud roar. Everyone shuddered, and the guards readied their spears.

"No, I am the tiger and you are just the princess. Your father, the king, decides. He will take counsel from me and the other senior animals. I will bring them, but you will not harm them." He turned and left. The princess called after him.

"Come back! I haven't finished speaking!"

"Yes, you have," the tiger called over his shoulder without breaking step. The princess rose to her feet and pretended to kick one of her maidservants before sitting down and demanding food and drink.

The wolf was up and about as soon as first light showed through the branches. Helen and Jack woke some time later, and found a dead squirrel at the mouth of the cave. It was still warm. Helen stood up and called, "Thankyou, Mr Wolf," and proceeded to prepare it for cooking. Jack laughed.

"You really have a connection with that wolf, don't you," she said with a smile.

"I don't remember you complaining when you ate the hare, and I don't think you will when you eat this squirrel," Helen said with an even bigger smile. "I prefer him bringing us food rather than eating us."

"Good point. So when we've eaten are we setting off along the river again?"

"Can't think of a better plan at the moment." Jack ventured out and returned with berries in her rucksack. They enjoyed their meal, then Jack made sure the fire was out before they set off. They had only gone about ten yards when the wolf appeared in front of them. He stood motionless until they got near, then he turned to face them and was obviously deliberately blocking their path. Jack was a bit nervous, but Helen remained calm. They stopped, and she smiled at him.

"Hello, Mr Wolf. We want to go that way. We want to follow the river downstream." The wolf threw back his head and howled briefly. The raven appeared and flew down to settle beside him. They all looked at each other in silence for a little while, then the raven flew about ten yards to the left. The wolf followed her, but stopped about half way.

"Are they trying to tell us something?" Jack whispered.

"Yes, I think they want us to go that way," Helen replied quietly. They followed the wolf slowly, and as they caught up the wolf and the raven moved forward another ten yards. This continued for a few hours, the little party of travellers picking up speed as their confidence grew. The terrain was largely flat, so it wasn't too tiring. As lunchtime approached Jack became uneasy.

"I'm starting to get hungry," she whispered to Helen. "How do we tell them to stop for food?" Helen shrugged her shoulders.

"Haven't a clue, mate. I speak neither wolf nor raven. Flora's the linguist, but she isn't here."

"No, I wonder where they are. Hope they're okay."

"Yes, so do I. Here's an idea; let's just stop and sit down and get some food out of the bags. They'll take the hint, surely." Jack nodded, and they both stopped walking. The wolf noticed immediately, and turned back. Helen and Jack sat down and opened the bags and took out some berries. The wolf called to the raven, who also turned back. They came to where the friends were sitting and rested, but not too close. After a drink from their water bottles they packed their bags and got up. "Well, that seems to have worked. We're going to need water sooner or later. There's plenty of berries in the bushes, but we've turned away from the river."

"Yes," agreed Jack. "I was thinking that. But surely they will need water too, so they will take us to water eventually."

"Good thinking." The raven led the way again, with the wolf a yard or so behind. Helen and Jack followed, chatting quietly about berries and water.

Chapter 12

Rachel, Flora and Alan reached the bottom of the hill and set off in the new direction. The terrain was a bit more uneven, but it didn't slow them down too much. After a while the bushes around them reached waist height, but they kept going. They picked at the berries along the way, which were plentiful, and at midday they stopped for a rest and each had one of the big green fruit Alan had found in the clearing. While they sat they were out of sight of anything nearby, but they couldn't see anything either, so it came as a shock when the grasses to one side parted and the tiger appeared. Flora let out a little scream but Rachel was quick to stifle her. The tiger made some growling noises then turned and walked away. They didn't move. The tiger came back and repeated the noises.

"I think he wants us to follow him," said Alan, getting to his feet. They packed what remaining berries they had into the rucksack. The tiger turned away again, and they followed it. They took a meandering route through the grass, which by now was almost at head height, the tiger occasionally looking back. Alan wasn't sure if it was checking they were still there, or if it was trying to encourage them. The tiger made no sound, but kept an even pace which wasn't too hard to keep up with, not even for Flora with her little legs. A few hours later the grass had reduced to knee height, and then opened up into a plain with very short grass, and they could see the village up ahead.

"Oh, look!" said Flora. "There's a village. There must be people, and we'll get something to eat and drink." Rachel smiled.

"I hope they're friendly," she said. "I hope we won't be 'dinner', if you know what I mean." Alan shook his head.

"No, if we're where I think we might be there aren't cannibals around here. Not many, anyway." He smiled as Flora looked shocked. "Only joking, Flora. I very much doubt they'll eat us, but that doesn't mean we'll be made welcome either. Try to look friendly, but be on your guard. Try to stay together." Flora and Rachel looked at each other, wondering what to expect. As they neared the village Flora took Rachel's hand. The people moved out of the way as the tiger approached, then came to greet the three friends. Alan waved his arm in a friendly way and spoke in several languages, but noone seemed to understand. He gestured eating and drinking, and two men and two women came and led them away into one of the houses. They brought in some fruit, followed by vegetables which had been cooking on the fire at the entrance. Then some children came in bearing wooden bowls containing fruit juice. During the meal Alan talked to their hosts in several languages, and while he managed to convey meaning, there was no lingual understanding.

"Come on, Flora," said Rachel. "Have a go – you're fluent in several languages." This attracted Alan's attention. Flora was uneasy but Alan made encouraging gestures.

"Yes," she said, "but not from this part of the world. The only eastern language I speak is Arabic, which isn't spoken in South-East Asia; all the others are European languages."

"That's worth a try," said Alan. "I doubt it'll work, but there's no harm trying." Flora said a few basic words and sentences in Arabic, but there were no signs of recognition.

316

She tried her European languages, but with the same result. "Don't worry," said Alan. "Just make the occasional sound, and above all, keep smiling." After the meal they sat around on cushions which were quite comfortable, trying to converse but without success. At one point Rachel told them a joke, but no-one laughed.

"Never mind," she said. "*I* enjoyed it." They sat trying to chat until dusk, when they were shown into another little house with three beds made from wooden frames and canes to provide support. Each had a pillow made from a cotton-like material and stuffed with feathers, and a cotton-like sheet for cover. They fell asleep quickly.

Helen and Jack followed the raven through meadows and woods. The wolf had dropped back to take up the rear, as though he were ready to defend the party. Suddenly the raven veered off to the right and Helen and Jack followed. A few minutes later they came upon a pond, where the wolf sprang ahead to drink. Helen and Jack tasted the water, and it seemed okay, so they filled their water bottles and had a good drink. The wolf approached the raven and they appeared to be talking.

"We will soon be at the endless cave, Wolf. It is a long cave so we will need to eat soon."

"I'll get some food for the apes, and we can eat just before we go in. I'll call when I return, then I'll follow your calls to find you." So saying, he ran off.

"Look, Helen," said Jack, pointing at the wolf. "He's running away. Should we follow him?"

"Yes," replied Helen, getting to her feet. "We don't want to be left here in the middle of nowhere." As Jack got up the raven flew in front of them and flapped agitatedly.

As soon as she settled they set off again, following the wolf, but the raven flapped at them again. They stopped.

"I think the raven doesn't want us to follow him," said Jack. "Let's follow the bird instead." They let the raven get a few yards ahead, then followed. The raven seemed quite calm, and led them away from the pond towards a wood, but went around it instead of through it. On the other side of the wood was a cave entrance behind some bushes. The raven came to rest on the ground just behind the bushes and remained motionless. Jack and Helen glanced at each other, and sat down just a few feet away. "It'll be dark soon. Do you think it's telling us to rest?" Helen nodded.

"Yes, almost certainly. I wonder where the wolf is?" She turned to the raven. "Mr Raven, or are you Mrs Raven? Do you want us to rest here?" She gestured sleep with her hands. The raven made some gentle cawing noises. "Yes, I think it does. How do you tell the gender of ravens? Any idea?" Jack shook her head. "No, me neither. Let's have a drink and a few berries." As they were getting the water bottles out the raven suddenly flew straight up and cawed loudly for a few seconds, then returned to the ground. They were startled by this, but realised what was happening when the wolf appeared through the bushes, carrying a dead squirrel. He approached the pair and placed it in front of them then took a few paces backwards. Helen stood up and picked it up. "Thankyou, Mr Wolf," she said solemnly. "Jack, can you make a fire here?" Jack looked around.

"There's plenty of wood," she said, "but none of it is dry. But I'll have a go. I don't fancy raw squirrel." She got up and selected some branches that were not quite as new as the others, and made a little fire. The wolf and raven backed off suddenly, alarmed.

318

"Oh, dear," said Helen while she was preparing the squirrel. "They're not used to fire." She turned to address the wolf and the raven. "Don't worry, we won't harm you with the fire." She put the entrails three or four yards away from the fire, and the wolf and raven devoured them quickly. When the squirrel was cooked they ate it, and put the bones and leftovers where they had put the entrails. Again, the wolf and the raven devoured them quickly. They settled down and went to sleep. When they awoke Jack put the fire out and the wolf and raven looked a bit more relaxed. Helen and Jack ate the remaining berries and had a drink from their water bottles, and made ready to set off. The raven fluttered up into the air and set off. Helen and Jack followed, and the wolf brought up the rear. The raven flew into the cave. They followed her, and even though there was no light, they could see where they were going. It was like walking through a wood at dusk; they couldn't see anything clearly, but they could see sufficient to avoid walking into the walls, or stumbling over uneven ground. The cave seemed to go on for ever. They walked for what must have been two days, but they didn't need to rest, and they didn't need food or drink. It was an unreal experience, but they were able to keep going, and never doubted the raven's guidance. Eventually they saw light ahead. It opened up into a clearing, and they blinked in the bright sunlight until their eyes became accustomed. The raven settled on the ground, so they took this to signify rest, and sat down. Looking round they saw some grassland to one side and jungle to the other.

"I don't think we're in England any more," said Helen.

"No, perhaps we're over the rainbow," laughed Jack. Helen smiled.

"Nice try, Jack, but I haven't got the energy for that sort of thing." They hadn't noticed, but the raven had disappeared, and she returned carrying a large green fruit, about the size of a small melon, which she dropped in front of them. Jack picked it up and cut it into four pieces.

"Thankyou, Raven," she said.

Helen smiled. "See, you're doing it too." Jack smiled an embarrassed smile, and offered the pieces to the raven and the wolf, and each took a piece. Helen took the third. They ate in silence, enjoying the flavour and the moisture. They retreated to the mouth of the cave and lay down to sleep, the wolf outermost to protect the others. After a short sleep the wolf woke them and they set off across the grassy plain.

"Look, Jack!" said Helen excitedly. "There's a village up ahead!" Jack couldn't see it at first, being much shorter than Helen, but eventually she saw it, and they both quickened the pace. The raven flew in front to slow them down, while the wolf ran ahead.

Alan woke up, being shaken gently by a man from the village. He smiled and spoke to the man, but the words didn't mean anything. The man gestured to him to come outside, which he did, while a woman woke Rachel and Flora. There was fruit in a wooden bowl, and something cooking on the little fire by the door to the house. He expressed his thanks, and sat down to eat and drink. Rachel and Flora joined him after visiting the toilet, which was a hole in the ground behind the house, but with a reed screen to provide a bit of privacy. After breakfast the couple indicated it was time to go, so they stood up, but instead of going further into the village, they were led away, back the

320

way they had come. The man suddenly stopped and pointed ahead. A wolf was running towards them at speed. Alan wondered what to do. Should he prepare to defend them? Or would the tiger come to their aid? Or was it a tame animal, perhaps a pet? Rachel and Flora were partly hidden behind Alan, then the wolf stopped and sat down. Rachel could see beyond it.

"Look!" she pointed excitedly. "There are some people behind it!" They followed her outstretched arm.

"It's them!" shouted Flora. "It's Helen and Jacqueline!" They set off at a trot to greet their friends, when the tiger raced past at speed. It came to a halt by the wolf. The friends stopped behind the tiger, still unsure about the wolf.

"Greetings, Wolf," said the tiger.

"Greetings," said the wolf. "What animal are you? You know me, but I have never seen your type before."

"I am Tiger. I have seen your type, but never as big as you. Are you a wolf?"

"Yes, I am a wolf, but from a distant land. We have never been here before. This is my friend, Raven."

"Greetings, Raven. You are both welcome here, and so are your human friends, if they come in peace."

"Greetings, Tiger. Human, you say? To us they are apes. They are strangers in our land, but Owl told us to bring them here. Owl is very wise, so we did as she suggested." The tiger shook his head.

"No, apes are different, although they have similarities. These are humans. We have many humans here, but we have three new humans. They just appeared a few days ago."

"These two did the same. They were not here, then they were. They did not walk or fly or swim to us. They were not here, then they were. A few days ago."

By now Helen and Jack had caught up. They were alarmed at the sight of the tiger, so they stayed close to the wolf. Realising the cause of their hesitancy, the wolf, raven and tiger moved from between the groups of people. Helen and Jack rushed forward to greet the others. There was a great deal of hugging and kissing, and they greeted the couple from the village warmly, not realising there was a language difficulty. The tiger led the way back to the village, with the wolf and raven bringing up the rear. The villagers came out to greet them, and marvelled at the size of the wolf, and had never seen a raven before. The group sat down by the little house and food and drink were brought, but the tiger wandered off further into the village. He went into the princess's house.

"Princess, I have brought the humans to the village," he said. "They are friendly. Do not harm them."

"Tiger, you are forgetting your place," the princess sneered. "I will decide if they are to be killed or enslaved or freed. I am the princess."

"That is not your decision to make. Your father, the king, is he here or is he away? If he is away, the decision is mine. If he is here, the decision is his."

"He is away, but I am the princess. When he dies I will be the queen, and all power will be mine."

"When he dies, perhaps, but at the moment, remember, you are just the useless daughter. You have no power, and you certainly have no wisdom."

"We'll see about that! Guards! Kill the tiger!" The three guards looked at one another but did not move. The tiger looked at them.

"The guards answer to the king. They know what to do. I will bring the strangers in to see you, but you will not harm them." He turned and slowly walked back to the house where the visitors were resting. He spoke to the couple, who got them to their feet. They followed the tiger, with the couple and the wolf and the raven at the rear. They followed into the princess's house. Flora froze and grabbed Rachel's hand. Rachel felt the blood drain from her face.

"No!" said Flora, with a tremor in her voice. "It's her! It's Phong!" Rachel put her arm round Flora's shoulders while the room suddenly became silent. The princess glared at Flora.

"Who is she?" she asked angrily, pointing at Flora. "She knows my name. How does she know my name? How does she know my name? She isn't one of us. She doesn't look like us, she doesn't dress like us, she doesn't talk like us and I can't understand what she says, she can't be one of us, but she knows my name. She must be evil. Kill her!" The guards look at each other, then they looked at the tiger. They didn't know what to do. "Kill her!" shouted the princess. The friends didn't understand a word, but they could tell it wasn't good. The tiger and the wolf moved forward to stand in front of them, and the raven perched on the wolf's head.

"You have no reason to kill her," said the tiger quietly. "They come in peace. I haven't learned their language yet, have you, Wolf? Have you, Raven?" They both shook their heads. "But I believe they have come from another time and another place, and simply wish to return. I will help

323

them to return. They have no profit from staying here, with such an inhospitable welcome from you. I am taking them away from you before you do something utterly stupid." The tiger turned away and left, with the friends, the wolf and the raven following him.

"Stop! Come back with my prisoners!" the princess screamed.

As they left the tiger spoke to some of the small birds. "Find my brothers and sisters. Tell them to meet me at the enchanted pool. Tell the panther and the bear to come here to keep watch over this useless daughter of the good king while I am away."

Chapter 13

The tiger led them across the plain to a small lake sheltered by trees. He gently pushed the five friends to a rock face by the pool. He walked slowly to the opposite side of the pool and five other tigers emerged from the bushes and stood beside him. He spoke to the wolf and the raven.

"This is something you will probably never see again. We tigers are solitary creatures; we only come together when our special powers are needed. This is one of those times." The tigers all faced the friends, and all gave out a mighty roar, as though they were one. The roar was so mighty it lifted the friends off their feet; an opening appeared in the rock face, and they were flung into it, tumbling head over heels time and time again, in a turbulence such that they did not know which way was up, did not know which way they were travelling, did not know how they got to their journey's end.

The tiger spoke to the raven and the wolf. "Brother Wolf, Sister Raven, you have done well to protect these humans and bring them to me. I am grateful, and I hope one day our paths will cross again. But for now, farewell. We have sent them home. They are safe. Go with the blessing of the animals of the jungle." He stepped back, and the wolf and the raven faded away.

The blue people carrier pulled into the car park of a roadside restaurant. The four friends got out and stretched their limbs. They walked slowly across the car park, stopping to let a black clad rider on a black and chrome motorbike leave and roar off down the road. They could still hear the roar long after he had disappeared from view.

In the restaurant they took a table by the window with views across the rolling hills and groups of trees. They ordered food, Rachel having difficulty making the waitress understand that she was a vegetarian and didn't eat meat, but eventually succeeded by ordering several side dishes.

"I hope Dougie's food parcel has some vegetarian stuff for Rachel," said Jack.

"Yes, it will," said Flora. "He sent Phong to Waitrose with strict instructions."

"Phong," said Jack dreamily. "I know that name from somewhere, but I can't think where."

Printed in Poland
by Amazon Fulfillment
Poland Sp. z o.o., Wrocław